DEVIL SMOKE

CJ LYONS

Also By CJ Lyons:

Lucy Guardino Thrillers:
SNAKE SKIN
BLOOD STAINED
KILL ZONE
AFTER SHOCK
HARD FALL
BAD BREAK
LAST LIGHT

Hart and Drake Medical Suspense:
NERVES OF STEEL
SLEIGHT OF HAND
FACE TO FACE
EYE OF THE STORM

Shadow Ops Covert Thrillers:
CHASING SHADOWS
LOST IN SHADOWS
EDGE OF SHADOWS

Fatal Insomnia Medical Thrillers:
FAREWELL TO DREAMS
A RAGING DAWN
THE SLEEPLESS STARS

Angels of Mercy Medical Suspense:
LIFELINES
WARNING SIGNS
URGENT CARE
CRITICAL CONDITION

Caitlyn Tierney FBI Thrillers:
BLIND FAITH
BLACK SHEEP
HOLLOW BONES

PRAISE FOR NEW YORK TIMES AND USA TODAY BESTSELLER CJ LYONS:

"Everything a great thriller should be—action packed, authentic, and intense." ~#1 *New York Times* bestselling author Lee Child

"A compelling new voice in thriller writing…I love how the characters come alive on every page." ~*New York Times* bestselling author Jeffery Deaver

"Top Pick! A fascinating and intense thriller." ~ 4 1/2 stars, *RT Book Reviews*

"An intense, emotional thriller…(that) climbs to the edge of intensity." ~*National Examiner*

"A perfect blend of romance and suspense. My kind of read." ~*#1 New York Times* Bestselling author Sandra Brown

"Highly engaging characters, heart-stopping scenes…one great rollercoaster ride that will not be stopping anytime soon." ~Bookreporter.com

"Adrenalin pumping." ~*The Mystery Gazette*

"Riveting." ~*Publishers Weekly Beyond Her Book*

Lyons "is a master within the genre." ~*Pittsburgh Magazine*

"Will leave you breathless and begging for more." ~Romance Novel TV

"A great fast-paced read….Not to be missed." ~4 ½ Stars, Book Addict

"Breathtakingly fast-paced." ~*Publishers Weekly*

"Simply superb…riveting drama…a perfect ten." ~Romance Reviews Today

"Characters with beating hearts and three dimensions." ~*Newsday*

This book is a work of fiction. Any references to historical events, real people, or real locales are used fictitiously. Other names, characters, places, and incidents are the product of the author's imagination, and any resemblance to actual events or locales or persons, living or dead, is entirely coincidental and not intended by the author.

Edgy Reads

Cover art: Toni McGee Causey, stock photo: lassedesignen/Dollar Photo Club

Library of Congress Case # 1-3352756051

DEVIL SMOKE

CJ LYONS

PROLOGUE

FIDDLER'S KNOB, SCOTIA COUNTY, PENNSYLVANIA

363 DAYS AGO...

CHARLOTTE BIT DOWN on her clenched fist and swallowed back a cry of pain as jagged stones sliced her bare feet. Quiet. The night was too quiet. The silence unforgiving.

She winced as each step snapped twigs, slipped across dead leaves, jostled loose rocks. The soles of her feet were slicked with blood—her blood, leaving a trail, but in the dark and the fog, no one would see it. She hoped.

Faster. She careened into a sapling, its branches lashing without mercy. Keep going down, the road will find you, just keep going down.

Without the steep slope of the mountain to guide her she wouldn't have had a hope. Not in this fog, so thick it felt like cold fingers curling around her body, brushing her face, grasping her hand to tease her away from the path that would save her. Cunning, sly, deceitful fog, beckoning to her, coaxing her deeper into the woods.

Devil smoke, Granny Callabrese called fog thick like this. The kind of fog where the dead walked in hopes of luring you into the grave.

Bare feet, no coat, only jeans and a torn shirt. What day was today? Had she missed Tommy's game?

Her mind was as murky as the night surrounding her. She'd hit her head, that much she knew from the blood making her hair sticky. What else? She felt bruised head to toe, wasn't at all sure how she'd gotten to the top of the mountain. All she knew was waking to darkness, the smell of fresh moss and ancient smoke smothering her, rocks piled up all around her, trapping her until she dug her way out. Had she been hiking and slipped? Was there a rockslide? Or something else?

Images, too terrifying to be memories, wisped past her vision. A woman's face…her own? Tears, screams, shouts for help. A man, fist raised…no, no, she couldn't look. She shoved the—memories? nightmares?—aside, burying them deep. Focus. She needed to focus. On what was real, what was important. Tommy. Nellie. Bright lights in her blood haze, they kept her running even after she'd pushed far past exhaustion. Her family. Home.

The terrain abruptly flattened as if someone had gouged a notch through the mountainside. Dead leaves and twigs gave way to gravel that dug into the ruined flesh of her feet. Gasping for air, she hobbled across the narrow strip of cleared earth. Relief surged through her when she stepped onto rough asphalt. The road. Help. Home. She was almost there, almost free.

Fog cloaked the road, caught between the mountaintop overhead and the steep decline to the valley below. It was thicker down here, left her skin clammy even as she shivered in the May night. Cars—where were the cars? He'd be back soon, maybe already was, maybe he was coming for her right now.

He? He who? Had she been with someone? If so, why hadn't he helped her?

Why was she so frightened at the thought of him finding her?

She spun, trying to remember which direction to take back to the main highway. The fog circled around her, a ghastly embrace. Willowy figures danced at the edges of her vision, beckoning with outstretched arms and faces that could be familiar.

No. I'm not going with you, she screamed inside her head, both hands covering her mouth to muffle her cries of pain as she limped down the road. *Go away!*

Home. She just wanted to be home. Curled up beside Tommy. Nellie stretched out on the floor at their feet, coloring, her legs kicking in the air because as a four-year-old, perpetual motion was her natural state of being. Their faces hung in her vision, framed by tears.

Charlotte kept going despite the pain. One foot. The other. *Go, go, go,* chanted her invisible companions, the wraiths conjured by the devil smoke, urging her on.

Headlights pierced the fog. Blinded, she stood, shielding her eyes with her hands.

"Stop!" she shouted, remembering too late that *he* could

be near, that he might hear as well. But she had to get the driver to stop. She stepped farther into the lane and waved her hands. Could he see her in the fog?

"Stop." This time it was an anguished cry, her strength too far gone to scream. "Please..."

Brakes screeched. She felt the rush of the car hurtling toward her, felt it straining to stop. But it kept coming, closer and closer. Instinct had her ducking her head, arms up, as if that could stop a three-thousand-pound vehicle.

But somehow it did. The car lurched to a halt. Only a few feet away from turning her into road kill.

She straightened, her adrenaline long since drained past empty—which was exactly how she felt: empty. Home. If she could just go home...

The fog swirled black and blue against the headlights' glow, the light bruising.

"Help me, please." She limped toward the driver's side, squinting. The car looked familiar, so familiar. She stepped closer. It *was* familiar—it was her car. Her gaze snapped up to the driver, now opening the door and emerging, a featureless silhouette against the harsh glare of the lights.

Why didn't the fog try to smother him? she wondered even as she realized the thought was born of hysterical relief. She was saved. She was going home.

With no strength left, she fell to her knees, sobbing as the man approached. "Tommy? Take me home. Please, I want to go home."

CHAPTER 1

363 DAYS LATER...

"I WANT SUGAR LOOPS!" Nellie screamed.

Who knew a five-year-old's voice could blister paint? Tommy Worth tried to ignore his daughter's outburst, reminding himself of the principles of good parenting. Set clear boundaries. Catch them being good. Never negotiate with terrorists.

Right now Nellie's siege of the Worth kitchen was about to come to a messy and triumphant conclusion as she banged her chair against the table hard enough to rattle the plate of low-fat sausage and scrambled egg whites. She not only refused to eat, she threatened to crash her wholesome and nutritious breakfast straight onto the floor.

"Glinda's mom lets her eat Sugar Loops anytime she wants," she said with a huff as he continued to ignore her. "She can even have Sugar Loops for dinner if she wants. Her mom *loves* her."

Tommy bit back a retort about Glinda's mom being a ditz and her daughter being destined for childhood obesity. Instead, he concentrated on the chicken salad he had prepared last night. This time he'd gotten it right, re-creating Charlotte's recipe to the letter. Last year Nellie had begged for chicken salad every school day. Charlotte had mixed it each night before bed, her last "mommy-job" before it was "grown-up" time, Tommy's favorite time of day, even if all they did was sit side by side on the sofa and read.

He spread a healthy dollop of chicken salad onto a slice of whole grain bread before tasting a tidbit that clung to the knife. Delicious. Just the right amount of salt and pepper, a dash of mayo, and a loving touch of Charlotte's secret ingredient: honey mustard. The best chicken salad ever.

Nellie's lunch box wasn't going to come home with this sandwich uneaten today—not like it had every other day. No way.

Tommy added a pear, carrot sticks, and some whole grain pretzels to the lunch box, then dared a glance at Nellie, who sat glaring at her uneaten breakfast, arms crossed over her chest, face pinched into a scowl. Great, the silent routine. This could last for hours.

Sighing, he grabbed another piece of bread and slapped together a PB and J. Just in case.

He added the sandwich and snapped the lid shut. Blinking hard against the glare from the early morning sun, he knew without a doubt that when he cleaned out the lunch box that evening, there would be an uneaten chicken salad sandwich left abandoned and neglected.

"Time to go," he announced in a too-chipper voice.

"I'm hungry," she whined.

The sound danced along his nerve endings, producing a fight-or-flight tug-of-war.

He was a pediatrician. He couldn't send his daughter to school without breakfast. It was cruel; it was unhealthy. But he also didn't dare give in to her whining. Do that once and he was doomed.

He swore he felt Charlotte's fingers brush against the back of his arm, felt her standing beside him. How many mornings, how many evenings had she stood right here, her feet where his were now, her hands dancing over the countertop, hips swaying in time with the music that was her constant companion?

"If you're hungry, you can take some sausage to eat in the car. I've packed you an extra sandwich with your lunch," he said, keeping his tone bright and cheerful, refusing to surrender to misery or despair. He scooped the eggs into the trash and turned back to get the sausages. Nellie snatched them away, munching on one greasy link as if it were finger food.

"It's too hot, I don't want to wear a coat." She trudged behind him out to the car. He kept her jacket over his arm. "My backpack is too heavy. You carry it."

"It's your backpack. You need to take responsibility for it." He opened the garage door.

She took a bite of sausage, a hawk snapping off the head of a field mouse, eyeing him with the same ferocity.

He circled around the rear of his ancient Volvo station wagon and opened the back passenger side door for her. "Hurry up, we're late."

She dragged her backpack carelessly along the pavement—the Hello Kitty backpack, the one she had saved up her allowance to buy special, which should have been a warning of just how much of a snit she was in—to the rear of the car, stomped her feet, then dropped it with a thud. "I told you. It's too heavy."

"Eleanor Rose Worth," he snapped. "You pick up that bag and get into this car right now."

Her feet remained planted, her arms across her chest, her glare as incandescent as a lit match. "No."

His temper flared, temper mixed with grief, churned with disappointment and fear. If he, with his training, couldn't handle a five-year-old's tantrum… He grabbed her arm, pulled it down to the backpack, forced the strap over her elbow, and tugged her toward the car.

She didn't cry, didn't say anything, just scrunched up her face in the fiercest, most meanest look a five-year-old could possibly conjure. A look designed to banish monsters under the bed, to fell bullies in their tracks. A look that screamed: *You don't love me!*

Tommy didn't even remember getting her into the car, fastening her into the booster seat, or backing down the driveway. His hands gripped the steering wheel like it was the last bit of flotsam in a churning monsoon.

"Daddy, are you mad at me?" Nellie asked from the back seat, her voice as shaky as Tommy's grip on his own emotions.

Unshed tears burned his throat. He swallowed before answering. "No, sweetie. I'm not mad at you. It's just, sometimes the things you do, well, they make Daddy sad. Very sad." Don't dump it all on her. "It's okay, though. You also make Daddy very happy, and I need that. We'll get through this, Nellie. I promise."

But her five-year-old mind seemed headed in another, more mysterious, five-year-old direction. "Were you mad at Mommy? Is that why she went away?"

He almost ran the car into the curb, but instead slowed and pulled over. To hell with school and staff meetings and cases waiting. He climbed out of the driver's seat, went back to the rear, and slid into the empty space beside her.

"Mommy didn't want to go away," he said, taking her hand in his.

He blinked back the sudden rush of fear that he might someday lose her as well. Despite the warm May morning, his hands and feet were numb, frozen as if his heart couldn't spare the blood necessary to keep them alive.

"I wasn't mad at her. Even if I was—even if you were—that's okay. Mommy didn't want to leave us. You had nothing to do with it, Nellie."

"I know that." She looked away, out her window at the parade of azaleas lining the sidewalk leading up to an anonymous brick colonial, then looked back, directly into his eyes.

Charlotte's eyes were that same hazel, with tiny flecks of gold that changed with her mood. Just like Nellie's. Now the gold had vanished. Buried under a somber green the color of inscrutable jade.

"But why don't you bring Mommy back?"

He rocked backward, banging his head against the window. "Bring Mommy back?"

His voice didn't sound like his own; it sounded like a stranger's. A stranger who hadn't spent days being scrutinized by the police, press, and Charlotte's parents, being accused of killing the woman he loved.

A stranger who hadn't faced lurid insinuations that things must have been terrible behind the walls of the Worth home if Charlotte had vanished of her own accord.

What had brought him almost to violence were the "helpful" strangers placing calls to ChildLine asking, How could a social worker like Charlotte who worked abuse cases leave her daughter behind in the same house with a monster like Tommy? If the home was so intolerable that the mother ran away without a trace—or worse, the father killed her—shouldn't someone step in and take the child away? For her own good, of course.

Thankfully, Charlotte's parents had put an end to that. They'd moved into Tommy's house for almost a month—not just to keep an eye on their beloved granddaughter, but also as a quasi-suicide watch over Tommy, who'd driven himself about mad searching for Charlotte, for clues, for a way to go on living without answers...

That was a year ago. A year ago this week, in fact. He'd spent the last few weeks reliving the horror for the parade of obligatory anniversary stories—including a segment on a national TV show that specialized in unsolved crimes. But if it helped find Charlotte, helped bring her home...

Now, facing a daughter he'd tried so very hard to protect from the circus-freak-show atmosphere created by Charlotte's disappearance, he dragged in a breath. "Sweetie, everyone's trying the best they can to find Mommy and bring her home. You know that."

The adults in Nellie's life, including a pediatric trauma counselor, had tried to explain what being "missing" meant. But how do you make a five-year-old understand the limbo between being here and being nowhere?

They'd even talked about death—just in case. Tommy and Charlotte's family refused to believe she was dead, but they needed Nellie to be prepared. Of course, the detectives and most of the world thought that was absolutely the answer to the mystery. So much easier to make a corpse vanish than a thirty-three-year-old woman.

"But—" Nellie chewed on the corner of her collar. A few months ago it would have been her hair, but she'd finally let him take her for a haircut, even though it wasn't the same as the way Mommy cut it. "Yesterday, Matthew said his grandfather died but the doctors shocked him and brought him back and now he's fine, and you're a doctor so how come you didn't do something like that for Mommy, why didn't you save her, why'd you let her go away and never come back?" The words emerged in one rushed breath. "Why, Daddy?"

Tears chased down her cheeks. A tourniquet tightened around Tommy's chest.

Christ, he didn't know how much longer he could take

this, this feeling so raw. Helpless, powerless, angry, sad—there just were no words to describe it.

How the hell was he supposed to heal his daughter if he couldn't heal himself?

Chapter 2

Lucy had only been working at Beacon Falls for two weeks, but every morning when she climbed the steps to her office situated in the rounded turret of the century-old Queen Anne, she couldn't help but smile. As much as she'd loved being Lucy Guardino, FBI Supervisory Special Agent, there was something to be said about working in the private sector.

She opened the door to her office. Sunlight beamed through windows on the curved wall, casting the antique loveseat and chair across from her desk in a glow of soft amber. It was Monday, so she watered her plants—a scant few drops for her bromeliads, an ice cube apiece for the orchids, and a careful dollop for the African violets that she cherished with extra attention because they'd been her mother's favorites.

After her coffee was brewed, she settled behind her desk, with its graceful curves that matched the circular space, and began catching up on the cases she was supervising. A mitochondrial DNA match from a molar recovered in a John

Doe case in Kentucky meant that John Doe not only now had a name, but also a family to reunite with his remains. Valencia Frazier, her boss, would handle taking the news to the family and walking them through the logistics. Also, a new request for assistance in reviewing a cold case from Florida had arrived. She'd just began to skim through it to see which of her team would be best suited when a knock came and she looked up.

Two men appeared in her doorway. Lucy smiled and waved them in. Both of average height, they couldn't be more different. Don Burroughs, a Pittsburgh Bureau of Police detective from the Major Case squad, was in his mid-forties. Brown hair, brown eyes, he appeared totally unassuming…until those eyes latched onto a discrepancy at a crime scene. Then he became an unrelenting wolfhound following a scent.

The other man, Japanese and with a face that was half smooth babyish innocence and half wizened seen-too-much, was Deputy US Marshal Timothy Oshiro. Every time Lucy saw Oshiro, an image of an ancient cypress tree flashed through her mind. Roots sunk so deep it was the original unmovable object…and if it ever came up against Oshiro's unstoppable force, it would be doomed.

The two of them together? She grinned. Things were about to get very, very interesting.

"You guys get lost on the way to Krispy Kreme?"

"Hey, Guardino," Burroughs said, flopping into the antique Queen Anne chair across from her desk as if he was taking ownership of her office. The second thing his gaze landed on was the wedding ring on her left hand—after he'd checked out her bust line. Old habits. Although he was back with his wife, and last she'd heard things were going well, those were still the first two details Burroughs noticed in any woman. Probably had been since he was twelve. "Wow, you came up in the world."

Oshiro didn't rest on such formalities. He barreled around her desk and plucked her from her chair to give her an extremely non-regulation bear hug. "Lucy-Mae," he exclaimed. "How the hell are you?"

"I'm good," she said with a laugh. "Long as you don't crack a rib."

He set her down gently, taking care of her left ankle. Last case she'd worked with him she'd ruined the progress she'd made rehabbing from a previous injury, and now she had permanent nerve damage, forcing her to wear a special brace and live in near-constant pain.

"No cane?" he asked.

"Gave it up for Lent." It was May, and she'd only abandoned the cane a little more than a week ago, but he understood the sentiment and nodded his approval. "I take it you two aren't here to catch up on old times?" She hadn't seen Burroughs in a while, but Oshiro and his not-quite-girlfriend, June, had come to her daughter Megan's birthday party last month.

The two men exchanged glances. Oshiro backed off to balance his bulk against a blank space in the wall near the door, letting Burroughs take the lead.

"Got a case for you," the detective started.

"A city case or a US Marshals case? Or both?"

"It's your own damn fault," he said. "Coming here to Pittsburgh, forming that inter-agency, multi-jurisdiction task force."

"The one the FBI dissolved." That and her permanent disability had led to her joining the Beacon Group, but it still rankled that the Bureau had ended a program that in less than two years had set a national standard for successful prosecutions.

Burroughs shrugged. "What'cha expect? Typical bureau-crackpots. Anyway, a few of us have kind of kept it going. Unofficial like. We get together every month or so, swap case files that are bugging us, keep the ideas flowing, you know?"

"And somehow you got Timmy Oshiro working real cases instead of chasing fugitives?" She arched an eyebrow at the Deputy Marshal, who grinned in return. Oshiro led the multi-agency Western Pennsylvania Fugitive Apprehensive Strike Team, and his FAST squad lived up to its name.

"A few of the locals assigned to me brought open cases with them. You know, to work on during down times," Oshiro answered. Many of the actual man-hours the FAST squad spent tracking fugitives were occupied by the tedium of surveillance. "Seemed the perfect way to kill two birds," he continued. "Work their cases that jump jurisdictions. Brainstorm, make some calls, review all the boring shit, so the guys on the street, can, well, stay on the street, knocking on doors. No biggie. Saved us from OD'ing on caffeine and doughnuts."

"We don't work anything off the books," Burroughs hastened to add, although Lucy knew from experience that the detective didn't mind cutting corners when it came to red tape—as long as his ass and pension were well covered. "It's all legit. Just keeping the lines of communication open, like you did with your squad. And it works. We've helped close some real whodunits."

Lucy leaned back in her chair, squinting at the two men. "I get it. You're Batman and Superman playing Justice League. What have I got to do with it?"

Another look between the two of them. "You know anything about amnesia?" Oshiro asked.

Okay. Wasn't expecting that. From Oshiro's grin, she could see that he was pleased to catch her off guard. "I think you're confusing me with Nick," she said. Her husband, a psychologist who specialized in trauma.

"Actually, tried him first," Oshiro said. "Before we left the hospital this morning. But he was in with a patient."

Burroughs backed things up. "See, two days ago, Saturday, there was this girl, almost hit by a truck when she ran out of the woods. Was hiking the trail at Fiddler's Knob, you know it?"

"Sure. Beautiful rhododendrons and mountain laurel—and there's a pretty waterfall above the old iron furnace. But that's Scotia County, right? Outside Pittsburgh city limits. And definitely not federal jurisdiction—not for an almost hit and run."

"Wasn't a hit and run," Burroughs corrected her. "Trucker stopped. Turns out the lady was covered in mud, had slipped and fallen up on the mountain somewhere. Only she couldn't remember what happened. Couldn't remember anything."

"Your amnesia. What did the doctors say?" She still didn't understand why a simple accident required the efforts of two law enforcement agencies, especially when it happened in neither of their jurisdictions, but she knew better than to rush Burroughs.

"They admitted her for a concussion. Said she had a mild sprained ankle and contusions consistent with a fall. Nothing major. Except for the fact that she has no memory of who she is or anything before Saturday." Burroughs glanced at Oshiro, handing off the conversational baton.

"The hospital kept her for the weekend, ran a bunch of tests, said there's nothing more medically to do. Called social services, who turfed it to the staties. Turns out the vehicles at the trailhead's parking lot were vandalized on Saturday, and there was one car they hadn't matched with an owner yet, so they didn't have to work very hard. She's a Sarah Brown, address in Pittsburgh."

Burroughs took over again. "The lot's isolated, people lock their wallets and stuff in their cars before they hit the trail, so it's not uncommon for thieves to strike there. But definitely inconvenient. Anyway, the staties asked us to join in on the fun."

Made sense. Most rural county sheriff departments in Pennsylvania only served papers; they didn't actually do any law enforcement. Which left the state police stretched extremely thin. Especially their investigators.

"Except we have no evidence at all that she was the victim of a crime other than the smash and grab," Burroughs continued. "Best anyone can make out, she went for a hike in the woods, slipped and fell and hit her head—docs said it probably wasn't even enough to knock her out, just a bruise—and now, poof, lost her entire life." He paused for dramatic effect. "Then I got a look at her apartment."

He stopped, and neither man filled the silence. Damn, they'd gotten her curiosity revved up—exactly what this little soap opera routine of theirs was designed to do. They both knew she was a sucker for a good story, couldn't stand cliffhangers. "And?"

"And nothing," Burroughs answered. "I mean *no-thing*. Literally. No photos, no personal mementoes, not even a freaking Christmas card list. Nothing to rebuild her old life or give us a clue who she is."

Now she knew why Oshiro was so interested. June had a vacant past as well, had had to rebuild her childhood from scratch.

"You said her car was broken into. Maybe that's where she kept her computer or phone or a tablet, and they were stolen?" It amazed Lucy how some people, her husband and daughter included, ran their entire lives from their phones, didn't even bother with computers anymore. She much preferred the safety net of multiple backups and encryption, plus she hated squinting at the tiny screen—or being forced to admit she needed reading glasses. "If the thieves knew where she lived—"

Burroughs shook his head. "No. I get what you're saying, but this is different. Her place wasn't burglarized. It was sterile."

Ahhh. She raised an eyebrow in Oshiro's direction. "As in witness protection sterile? But when the staties ran her through NCIC, wouldn't your brothers in WitSec have heard alarm bells?" It would have been standard procedure for the state police to run Brown's name through the National Crime Information Center after they'd identified her.

"Exactly why Burroughs called me. I put out a few feelers, but she's not one of ours. We swung by her place this morning on our way here. And he's right. Nothing to even start tracing her. A cipher."

"You think she's on the run from someone."

"Neither of us get the vibe that she's involved in anything criminal—" Burroughs hastened to put in. A bit too hastily? Lucy wondered. He didn't usually go the extra mile, especially when there wasn't even an official police case left to investigate. She bet this Sarah Brown was attractive. "Prints were clean."

Which meant no criminal record, but little more. A routine check wouldn't access any of the confidential databases.

"I met her, Lucy." Oshiro's expression turned serious. "If she's running, stirring the wrong pot to put her life back together could put a target on her."

"But she deserves to have her life back," Burroughs argued. Lucy had the feeling this was a re-run of an argument they'd already had more than once. "How's she supposed to know who to watch out for if she can't remember anything?"

"You're certain her slip and fall on the mountain was an

accident?" Lucy asked.

"The staties are. Because of the vehicular smash and grabs they took statements from everyone. One couple was near her when she fell—said they heard her shout, but it happened right before they heard the sound of the glass breaking and all the car alarms going off in the parking lot. And when they looked, she was back on her feet, so they didn't stop. They didn't see anyone near her either. Trucker's statement was that she wasn't scared or running from anyone, just disoriented."

Oshiro took a deep breath. "So… Since we have no crime, we can't really help more. The docs discharged her from the hospital this morning, saying there's nothing more they can do, it will just take time, so..."

"So..." Burroughs said, his voice up ticking hopefully.

"So..." Lucy finally relented, giving in to their obvious plea for help. It was nothing short of emotional blackmail, but she was intrigued. "Given the city's perpetual lack of resources, especially when there's no crime apparent, and given that the Beacon Group specializes in identifying missing persons..." Never mind that they were usually John and Jane Doe corpses, not living unidentified persons. "You came to me."

"See?" Burroughs said with a grin. "Told ya she'd take care of everything. Nothing to worry about, Guardino's on the case."

Oshiro tilted his head, not as certain. "What do you say? You in, Lucy-Mae? I'll owe you one."

Lucy snorted. Oshiro owed her about twenty-three thousand and one favors…starting with saving his life as well as June's and her baby's a few months ago. But when he twisted his face in that earnest little-boy expression he did so well, she couldn't resist. And he damn well knew it.

She stood. "I'm in."

Burroughs hopped to his feet. "Great. Sarah's waiting downstairs."

"She's here?"

"We didn't want to waste any time. She's anxious to get her life back," Oshiro said. "You can understand that."

"Besides, even if you said no, what's she got to lose?" Burroughs added. "So she spends a morning with two handsome law enforcement professionals. Win/win, right?"

Lucy somehow managed to restrain an eye roll as he rocked back on his heels and puffed out his chest. "All right. But first, let me get my team on board."

CHAPTER 3

TOMMY PARKED HIS Volvo wagon beside Lucy's Subaru. He was running late but couldn't resist the temptation to pause before entering the house.

Most people visiting the Beacon Group for the first time were fascinated by the sprawling Queen Anne mansion perched on the bluff overlooking the Monongahela River. The ancestral home of the Frazier clan, whose roots went back long before the American Revolution, it wasn't the first house to stand sentry on this land, and it wouldn't be the last.

Instead of focusing on the curved turrets and numerous gables, Tommy's gaze settled, as it always did, on the eternal flame in its iron tripod guarding the edge of the bluff a hundred feet from the house. The current owner and leader of the Beacon Group, Valencia Frazier, had created the flame as a memorial to her murdered husband, as well as to the generations who'd come before, lighting bonfires each night to warn strangers of the treacherous waterfalls that lurked, invisible, around the sharp bend of the river.

As Tommy stared across the expanse of lawn, the flames barely visible with the sun directly behind them, he regretted never having the chance to bring Charlotte here. She would have loved the view over the river gorge, the wry idiosyncrasies of the house and its not-quite-random architecture, and the tranquil gardens. Sometimes, during the walk from his car to the house, he imagined her with him, her hand warm in his, the breeze fluttering her skirt against both of their legs, they were so closely in step with each other...

He walked up the path, as he did every day, up the porch steps, crossed below the gingerbread adornments and through the front entrance, closing the solid, handcrafted oak door, shutting memories and wistful thoughts behind him. Locking out Charlotte. Locking himself inside a facade of normality.

This morning he was surprised to find a woman standing in the small parlor that served as reception area. For a moment, the way the sun caught her hair, turning it copper-gold, he had the flitting feeling... Then she turned to him. No, he realized in dismay as he fought to cover his reaction. Not Charlotte.

She smiled at him, her expression worry free—unlike the vast majority of people who found their way to Beacon Falls, seeking help in solving old mysteries gone cold, seeking loved ones lost forever. She appeared to be in her late twenties. Her face was round with the slightest sprinkling of freckles, her hair was red—almost the same shade as Charlotte's, which was what had confused his senses, ever on alert for any hint of his wife—and she wore a simple cotton blouse tucked into jeans under a lightweight fleece jacket.

"They told me to wait here," she said. "I hope that's okay?"

"Of course." He should have kept going through the room to the staircase that would take him up to the second floor, where Lucy and the others would be waiting. But he couldn't help himself. "Do you need anything?"

Her smile widened as if she was unaccustomed to small kindnesses. She shrugged, one shoulder rising. "A little prayer, if you're so inclined. Or a bit of luck if you're not." She gave a nervous, self-deprecating laugh. "Sorry. Not sure exactly what the protocol is."

"You're waiting for—"

"Lucy, Lucy Guardino. They said she has a team who could, who might, be able to help."

"I'm Tommy Worth." He extended his hand. "I'm on Lucy's team."

She took his hand without hesitation, but there was a strange pause before she replied. "Sarah Brown."

There was the faintest uptick in her voice, as if she was asking a question. Or maybe she was from California.

As he shook her hand, he was close enough to smell her. Almonds and cherry blossoms. He blinked against the memory that swamped him—it was the same shampoo Charlotte used. He couldn't help himself—he dropped her hand and pulled away. "Nice to meet you, Sarah."

He crossed the room and stumbled up the stairs. Halfway up, out of sight of the reception area, he sagged against the sturdy oak banister. For the first time in his professional career, he actually considered turning around and going home, calling in sick. But he wasn't sick. He was…floundering.

Was it only a year ago when he'd known exactly who and what he was: husband, father, doctor, advocate?

Now who was he? Because he really wasn't a husband anymore, was he? Not after losing Charlotte. A stupid way to put it, as if he'd misplaced his wife like a sock lost in the laundry. If only he could look under the dryer, clean out the lint filter, and find her again.

And single parent? Another stupid term. One parent to do everything, be everything. How could anyone ever hope to fill Charlotte's place in Nellie's life? It was a black hole, too vast to comprehend, sucking him dry.

Doctor? Advocate? Hell, most days lately he came home from work and didn't even remember what he'd done all day. As if he were sleepwalking, needing Charlotte to kick him, nudge him, shake him free from the tendrils of this nightmare. If only…

He doubled over, his chest heaving as if he'd run up the stairs. Red spots danced in his vision as he fought to breathe. Just breathe. One breath in, one breath out. One foot up, then the next. This was his new life.

Days, hours, minutes…all meaningless compared to the Sisyphean task of existence. His heart was broken, but it was a stubborn organ and persisted in carrying on. A metronome he obeyed solely for Nellie's sake.

CHAPTER 4

LUCY SENT OSHIRO and Burroughs to wait while she walked down the hall to the conference room—actually a former bedroom/sitting room suite outfitted to suit their needs—and her team's weekly meeting. Having a squad performing actual live investigations as opposed to back-end research designed to assist law enforcement agencies was a new venture for the Beacon Group. Lucy still had her doubts about using civilians in investigatory roles, but so far things had gone well.

As she entered the conference room, she was surprised to see that their tech analyst, George Washington Gamble, was the only one present. Wash, as he liked to be called, was in his early twenties, the youngest of the team, paralyzed from the waist down, confined to a wheelchair, and had quickly proven himself essential.

"Tommy's on his way," Wash said before she could ask. He sat at the space at the head of the table, manning the computer and communications equipment set up level with his wheelchair. "I saw him drive up a few minutes ago. Don't even ask me about TK, though."

"Sorry I'm late," Tommy said, banging in through the door. He caught his laptop bag on the handle and pulled up short to disentangle himself.

"You're not. We're still waiting for TK," Lucy said.

"Nellie had another tantrum this morning." Tommy sank into a chair with a sigh. "Not sure how much more I can take."

Lucy glanced at the pediatrician. Tommy had worked in the ER at Three Rivers before leaving to join the team at Beacon Falls. He was usually the steadying force, balancing Wash's juvenile humor and TK's rambunctious hyperactivity, but today he seemed frazzled. More than that, exhausted.

"How was your weekend?"

He shook his head. "What weekend? Feel like I spent it in a blur. Never even got a chance to review the Olsenhauser case. Sorry."

Before she could answer—she'd assigned the case review to him a week ago—the door banged open and a blond whirlwind breezed in.

"TK, why is it that you have the shortest commute of anyone here, yet you're always late?" Lucy asked. TK O'Connor lived a few yards across the estate's driveway in the gatehouse. In exchange for free room and board, the former Marine MP coordinated security for the Beacon Group.

TK didn't take the bait. Instead she bounded around the table, beaming. "I've got a damn good reason. It's official. David Ruiz's father received his pardon, and as of today is a free man.

Because of us."

"Woohoo!" Wash gave a whistle and did a wheelie in his chair while Tommy gave TK a high-five. "Surprised Mr. Lovey-Dovey Investigative Reporter didn't come in person to give you the good news."

"He's with his father in Texas, helping him with the transition," TK said primly. "But he's invited me down to Baltimore for the Memorial Day weekend."

"Oh, the Inner Harbor," Tommy said. "You'll love the seafood there."

"If they make it out of the bedroom." Wash waggled his eyebrows suggestively.

"Hush. You're just jealous."

"Hunk like that? Damn right I am."

"Okay," Lucy said, "let's get to work."

Sometimes Lucy hated that at thirty-nine, she was the oldest on the team. Made it hard to feel like one of the guys when she constantly had to play mother hen. She'd never felt that way in the FBI, probably because Walden, her second in command, was not only older than her but had no problem playing the enforcer to her maverick. Here, the tables were turned: she found herself forced to rein in her younger team members.

It didn't help that only TK had any type of law enforcement experience. During her career as a Marine MP, TK had been assigned to a Female Engagement Team, which meant she'd been on the front lines with Special Forces during raids on villages, searching for insurgents. It wasn't a traditional law enforcement background, and TK had never worked investigations, but Lucy had already grown to trust the younger woman—even if she didn't always approve of her methods or attitude. She frowned at TK's scuffed boots and ripped jeans. Or her idea of professional attire.

"We have a new case," Lucy told them. She buzzed the receptionist to signal her to send up Burroughs, Oshiro, and Sarah Brown. "It's a bit of an unusual twist on our usual."

"Cold case?" Wash asked, fingers poised at the ready above his keyboard.

"Not really. Actually, it's only a few days old, so I guess you'd call it a warm case."

All three frowned. The Beacon Group's mission was to help victims' families find answers, and hopefully justice, for unsolved cold cases. The only time they were called in on a current investigation was to help with critical missing persons; those cases often overwhelmed law enforcement resources, so the Beacon Group assisted by providing support in the form of research, data entry, logistical coordination, ancillary administrative and organizational personnel, and of course the use of former law enforcement officers such as Lucy.

"Did I miss a report of a missing person?" TK asked.

"Not missing," Burroughs said as he barreled through the door, holding it open for the woman who followed. "Found. Miss Sarah Brown, meet the team who's going to help—" He stopped short, his gaze fixed on Tommy. "Dr. Worth. I'm surprised to see you here."

Tommy's glare in return was one of anger and distrust.

Lucy hurried to intervene. "Ms. Brown, nice to meet you. I'm Lucy Guardino. This is Wash, our cyber analyst, and TK, our—" She hesitated, stumbling over how to describe TK's mixed pedigree.

"Girl Friday," TK supplied with a grin. "I sort of fill in wherever."

Sarah beamed and nodded.

"And this is Dr. Tommy Worth, specializing in forensic evaluations," Lucy concluded.

Oshiro had somehow crowded his bulk into the room, nudging past Burroughs, who remained frozen in the doorway, still staring Tommy down as if he were a rabid dog.

Tommy stood. "Nice to meet you, officially. Before we go any further, Detective Burroughs probably wants to tell you how my wife went missing last year, and how, despite the fact that I was working in the ER at the time with dozens of witnesses and video to prove it, I was the main suspect—"

"*Am*, not was," Burroughs corrected.

"Even though they've never determined that she didn't leave voluntarily. In fact, the Pittsburgh police have all but closed her case. Which is why I left the ER to come here, in the hope that the Beacon Group could help me find her."

"Not closed by me." Burroughs' eyes narrowed. "I think I know exactly who's behind your wife's disappearance, Dr. Worth."

The temperature in the room dropped as everyone stared at Tommy. He flushed and pushed his chair back. His lips thinned with anger, but then he glanced at Sarah Brown and his expression softened, as if he'd realized the greater priority. "Happy to excuse myself if it will help."

Lucy didn't know all the details of Charlotte Worth's case—she hadn't been working with the Beacon Group long enough to get involved—but she did know that Valencia Frazier was personally overseeing the ongoing investigation, and that the police, FBI, and Valencia herself had all cleared Tommy.

Well, all of them except Burroughs, obviously.

"Gentlemen." Oshiro broke the silence. "Please. We're here to help Ms. Brown to find her past. She can't remember anything since she was found wandering two days ago with a minor head injury."

"Oshiro's right," Lucy said. "We should focus on the case at hand. And," she turned her glare onto Burroughs, "I'll decide who works any case my team handles."

"It's all right, Lucy," Tommy muttered. "I get it. I'll leave."

"Wait." Sarah Brown stepped away from Burroughs and toward Tommy's side of the table. "Do I have a say? I'd like Dr. Worth to stay, please. I think his insights might be extremely helpful." She turned to face the rest of them. "After all, he's the only one here who really understands what I'm going through."

"Then it's settled." Lucy nodded to Tommy, who sat back down. "Ms. Brown, can you tell us what little you do remember?"

Sarah settled herself into the chair across from Lucy, next to Tommy. "Only if you call me Sarah. Sarah feels right. More than Ms. or Miss. And 'Mrs. Brown' feels like you're talking about my mother—which, I guess, maybe you are. Because I don't feel married. At least, I don't think I am. Hopefully, that's what we'll find out, right?"

CHAPTER 5

TOMMY FOUGHT NOT to squirm as Burroughs continued to stare at him. He'd halfway expected a visit from the detective, what with the anniversary of Charlotte's disappearance coming up, but he'd never thought he'd be confronted with him here at Beacon Falls.

The only thing the detective and Tommy had ever agreed on was that Charlotte hadn't left voluntarily. The rest of the police had lost interest when the trail went cold and evidence suggested that Charlotte might have left of her own accord—something Tommy would never, ever accept. Not that he and Charlotte didn't have the occasional argument—difficult to avoid since they both worked in the same hospital and their cases often overlapped—but *they* were solid. What they had together, that was real.

Even if Charlotte *had* left him, she'd never, not in a million lifetimes, leave Nellie. Which was the core of Burroughs' case against Tommy. He had questioned Tommy for hours, driving home the point that there must have been something god-awful terrible going on inside the Worth house, something so horrific that the only way Tommy could protect himself and keep custody of his daughter was to kill Charlotte and silence her permanently.

Typical cop, always jumping to the worst-case scenario. And once the story was solidified in Burroughs' mind, he simply would not let go. Last time Tommy had seen the man, he'd told Tommy, "You might have the rest of the world fooled with your 'aw shucks, I'm just a doctor who loves kids' act, but you don't fool me. Not one bit. I'll be watching. Nothing better happen to that little girl of yours, or I'll be all over you faster than a bum on a chipped ham sandwich."

Now, seated only a few feet away from the detective, Tommy fought to meet the man's gaze. Not because he felt guilty, but rather because, despite leaving the ER to focus on finding Charlotte, Tommy had failed to bring his wife home. He didn't give a damn about failing in Burroughs' eyes. But...Nellie. He'd failed *her*.

Someday soon, she'd know that. Understand it. And he'd have to face her. He'd no longer be her hero, the daddy with the superpower to fix all ouchies and scare away any boogiemen. He'd be the man who'd lost her mother, the one left behind with no answers.

The sudden sound of laughter cut through his thoughts. He glanced up, realized Sarah was relating the story of how she'd been found. "So then I say to the trucker, 'Who you calling ma'am?' And he turns beet red, starts apologizing, but I say, 'No, really. I have no freakin' clue who I am or how I got here.' Then the you-know-what hit the fan."

She turned to smile directly at Tommy, as if realizing he was only just now tuning in and forgiving him for his lapse. "He runs me to the nearest hospital—guess I'm lucky the guy was so nice, I mean, he could have gotten away with anything and I wouldn't have known any better. The ER docs say everything looks good except my ankle is a little sprained and my brain is a little bruised. They kept me overnight while the state police came, took my fingerprints and all. Good thing I'm not a wanted criminal, right?" She leaned forward. "Know who cracked the case? PennDOT!"

"PennDOT?" Wash asked. "They're the ones who found out who you were?"

"The staties ran her face through the DMV facial recognition software," Oshiro said. "Found a match to the registered owner of one of the vehicles at the scene."

"Just like they do on all those TV shows," Sarah added. "Kinda feels like I'm in one—like this isn't even real."

"What about the car?" Tommy put in, daring Burroughs' wrath. "Or her driver's license? Wouldn't the DMV have access to former addresses? Might be a starting point."

Burroughs rolled his eyes. Thankfully, it was Oshiro who answered. "Yeah, we thought of that. Her previous address was to a vacant lot in Altoona."

TK looked up at that, but Burroughs quickly added, "Vacant because it was an old bottling plant that was used for Penn State-Altoona student housing before the owner sold it and tore it down to make way for a strip mall. We're waiting for him to dig out the housing records and for the folks at Penn

State to check their enrollment records."

"Your car was broken into?" TK asked. "Was it the only one? Targeted?"

Burroughs answered. "There were seven cars at the trailhead left unattended."

"He means parked," Sarah interjected.

Both Oshiro and Burroughs smiled at her comment. "Anyway, they were all broken into," Burroughs continued. "Isolated area like that, great opportunity for a smash and grab."

"At least Sarah's was locked," Oshiro added.

"Right," she said brightly. "So we've established that I'm not an idiot, leaving my car—vehicle—" she added with a nod to Burroughs, "unlocked. Since the car is a Prius, I'm guessing I'm environmentally conscious as well."

"Cell phone?" Lucy asked.

Sarah shrugged. "Not with me. Maybe I'm forgetful? Or it needed charging?"

"Anything else in the car? Receipts, notes, maps?"

"Only thing left was broken glass, a spare tire, and a jack," Burroughs answered.

"And a repair bill," Sarah added ruefully. "I didn't even know the car was mine. Only thing I recognize, including my face, is this." She reached into her bag and pulled out a slightly battered, professional-looking camera. Despite its size and obvious weight, she hefted it easily in one hand. "Had it with me when they found me. ER nurses said the only time I got hysterical that first night was when they tried to take it from me. Like it's my baby or something."

"Did you run the info from the camera card?" Wash asked.

"All the photos are from Saturday, all taken at Fiddler's Knob," Burroughs said. He slid a data storage card across the table to Wash. "Here's a copy. Maybe you can get more from it than we did."

"But surely there was something at your current address to give us more information?" TK persisted. Tommy noticed that Burroughs gave Lucy a little nod at that.

Sarah smiled. "I guess not. Detective Burroughs went through my apartment while I was in the hospital. I was only there long enough to change clothes before we came here." She gestured to her outfit. "At least I remember how to tie my shoes and button a shirt without help."

As a joke, it fell flat. Sarah tensed the slightest bit, and Tommy realized she was straining to make it seem as if this was a totally normal situation—when it was anything but. He edged closer to her, hoping that knowing they were all on her side would help.

"Nothing on the public appeals?" Lucy asked Burroughs.

"Not yet. We'll keep them going, update you with any progress." Burroughs shifted in his seat, frowning at Tommy—or at Sarah, it was hard to tell. "Honestly, I'm not sure where to go next."

"Which, I'm guessing, is where we come in." TK sounded excited. Tommy had to admit, it was nice not to be digging around cases where all they had to work with were decomposed bodies and ancient trails of clues that led nowhere. "Boots on the ground."

"You mean fingers on the keys," Wash said with enthusiasm.

"Exactly," Oshiro said. "It's not a criminal case, but we'll assist with the public appeal and any court orders you need to access databases."

"Not that that's not going to lead anywhere fast," Burroughs cautioned. "Without a crime or exigent circumstances, cutting through the red tape is going to take forever. Companies and organizations are more concerned about protecting themselves against a violation of privacy lawsuit by releasing the wrong info than they are helping someone who may or may not have a right to that info."

"How can I prove I have a right to anything if I can't find out who I am?" Sarah asked. She spread her arms wide. "It's like I don't even exist."

"So we have a name, social, basic demographic data—"

"I'm not data," Sarah interrupted Lucy. "I'm a person. Please help me. I just want my life back. Do I have a family out there worrying about me? Or maybe not, since they haven't come forward, but maybe they don't even know I've lost them."

She stood, fists balled in frustration. "Maybe I'm some crazy cat lady, living alone, and not one single person in the world would have noticed if I never came home. I don't know. Or maybe..." Her voice dropped and she seemed to focus on Tommy, but that was probably just his imagination since he was fighting with everything he had to hold it together; her questions were a mirror image of the ones he'd been struggling to answer for almost a year. "Maybe there's someone out there who loves me, who's waiting for me…and to him, I'll just disappear. Poof."

She rapped her knuckles against her head. "All because of some stupid slip and fall. My life—my real life, who I was—could vanish forever. And he'd be left waiting, never knowing. I can't take the thought of that. Could you?"

The tear surprised Tommy. Only it wasn't Sarah's tear. It was his. Funny, he could barely feel it. His face felt frozen, numb. But inside—

He pushed back his chair and turned away before the others could see. "Excuse me," he mumbled, not trusting his voice, as he forced himself to walk, not run, from the room.

He lurched down the hall, toward the stairs, needing air, needing space, needing…he wasn't even sure what.

CHAPTER 6

BURROUGHS, CLEARLY ANGRY at Tommy's reaction to Sarah's story, turned to follow him, but before Lucy could intervene, Oshiro placed a palm on the detective's arm, holding him in place.

"You'll help her?" Oshiro's question was for Lucy alone, but she answered for her entire team.

"Yes."

"Okay, then. We'd best get back to work. Right, Burroughs?"

Burroughs narrowed his eyes at Lucy. "Right," he said grudgingly.

He and Oshiro moved to the door.

Lucy followed, intending to check on Tommy. When she drew near Burroughs, he glanced back at Sarah, who'd sat back down, arms folded in a posture of waiting.

As they stepped into the hall, he said to Lucy, "Watch Worth around her. He's trouble. If I'd known he was working here—"

"I can take care of my team," Lucy snapped. "And our

client."

He made a sound in the back of his throat but nodded. "Keep me in the loop."

"Will do."

The two men left, and Lucy turned to the window beside the staircase landing. She could see Tommy pacing along the edge of the bluff, hands balled into fists, shoulders hunched, his entire body twisted into a walking question mark.

Questions, she thought. She had plenty of those. How to get some answers?

Before she could decide on a direction, the door behind her opened and TK emerged, followed by Wash, his chair gliding over the polished oak floorboards with ease.

"Tommy okay?" Wash asked. Despite his frequent joking, Wash was the most empathetic member of the team.

"Are you sure he's the best person for this case?" TK asked. "Maybe he needs a little time. Get his head together."

Lucy frowned. "He handled sexual assaults and child abuse cases all the time when he worked in the ER. This case should be relatively pain free."

Wash and TK both looked away from Lucy. Damn, she hated being the new kid on the block. "Okay, what am I missing? I mean, I know his wife is gone and that's why he came to work here. But this isn't a missing person case. We have the person. It's her past we're trying to find. If anything, that should bring him some relief or hope, right?"

"It's just that Charlotte's case, the anniversary..." Wash stalled out.

"It'll be one year in two days," TK finished for him. "Still no leads. No idea if she went voluntarily, if someone took her, if she had an accident, or…if she did something to herself. Nada. Not a single blessed clue. Every time the cops start looking, every time he tries to chase down a lead, it just breaks his heart all over again."

"You think Sarah's case is too close to home for him?"

Both of them nodded.

Lucy hesitated, watching Tommy out the window. Misery radiated from him as he walked the bluff. She knew from her own experience with trauma that isolation was not the solution. Plus, she wanted to keep an eye on him.

"Benching him is only going to make things worse," she decided. "TK, you and I will work directly with Sarah. Why don't you get started, gauge her baseline?"

"Baseline?" Wash asked. "The girl can't remember anything. How are you going to get any kind of baseline?"

"She remembers more than she realizes," Lucy said.

"She dressed herself, remembered how to tie her shoes," TK added. "Remembers how to use idioms in her speech."

"But that's all like muscle memory." Wash gestured to his legs strapped to his chair. "After I got shot I remembered how to walk, but that didn't mean my legs could do anything about it."

"Which is why we need to see where Sarah's memories start, map them out. Like a minefield," TK said. She glanced at Lucy. "You want a cognitive interview, right? Use her sensory impressions as triggers?"

"Right." Lucy added, "Wash, Tommy can work with you

on the leads the detectives couldn't close out."

Which basically meant database diving—Wash's favorite pastime—and dumpster diving, tracking down the origin of anything of Sarah's they could get their hands on. Including her garbage.

And it was past time that Lucy delved into the specifics of Tommy's wife's disappearance. If it was going to impact his work, she needed to know more about Charlotte Worth.

LUCY WAITED FOR the others to clear the hallway before attempting the steps. Going down was always more painful than going up, but she refused to use the house elevator. Every step was rehab, she told herself as she gritted her teeth against the pain and slowly hobbled down the staircase.

She grimaced as her weight settled onto her left leg. Days like today, she regretted abandoning the cane, but it felt like too much of a crutch. Honestly, it didn't even decrease the pain—instead, it alerted other people to hover and try to help, which was, in its own way, just as painful.

Since coming to work at Beacon Falls she'd cut back to only one physical therapy session in the morning, and then Nick helped her with stretches and a massage at night. But the damaged nerves around her ruined ankle had appreciated the neglect even less than they had the extra strain of the rehab sessions. Valencia had offered Lucy use of her pool in the residence wing's solarium; maybe Lucy could start swimming over lunch.

As she reached the bottom of the steps, she let out a wry laugh. Here she was worrying if accepting her boss's offer would be too intrusive, while at the same time they were about to go digging through every private detail of Sarah's past to try to rebuild her life. Talk about intrusive. She hoped Sarah realized what she was asking for.

She waved to Missy, the receptionist, and went out in search of Tommy. She spotted him near the tall wrought iron tripod with its eternal flame, looking out over the river gorge to the rolling hills and farmland east of Beacon Falls. He'd stopped pacing, but the worry hadn't left his posture.

"Burroughs was right," he said without looking at her as she drew near. "I shouldn't be on this case."

Lucy mirrored his posture and simply nodded. Waited.

"Wednesday, it will be a year since Charlotte—" He swallowed. "What good have I done her? Leaving the ER, coming here to work her case after the cops gave up. At least Burroughs agrees with me, that something happened to her. The other cops, the PIs we hired, they all think she left me. That I must be some terrible ogre, must have done something horrific for things to be so desperate that she'd abandon Nellie. They say all the evidence points that way."

Finally he turned to her, despair tightening his face. "No one seems to understand that the so-called evidence is just facts we twist, trying to make sense of it. Evidence isn't truth. I know my wife. I know her truth. She didn't leave. Not because she wanted to."

"Her life was stolen from her," Lucy said. "One way or the

other. From you and your daughter as well." She let her words hang for a moment, the spring breeze scattering them across the gorge. "Just like Sarah Brown's."

His posture straightened and he rocked on his heels. "You want me to stay on the case?"

"I think you can help her. TK and I will work with Sarah directly. But you've got a good eye for details, for evidence that doesn't add up. I suspect that's why you were such a good pediatric ER doctor. After all, most kids can't tell you what's really going on with them, and most parents are too upset, trying to create a story that makes sense of a world where their child could be sick or injured. I know that's how I was when my daughter was sick."

He nodded, still not making eye contact.

"Is the press hounding you about Charlotte's anniversary?" she asked.

"Not just the press. Her folks think it's important to remind the public, keep her story out there in case someone remembers or sees something new."

"It's their way of feeling like they're not powerless."

"But we are. Nellie, this morning, she asked me why I couldn't bring Mommy home. That if I could save lives and make dying kids better, why didn't I want to bring Charlotte back. Like I'm some combination of an uncaring god, neglectful husband, and lousy father all rolled up into one." His lips thinned and the muscle at his jaw clenched. "Maybe she's right."

"She's how old?"

"Five. How do you explain 'missing' to a five-year-old?

She has a grasp on the idea of death, but the idea that her mommy could be gone, not dead, not alive, not home, not anywhere...hell, I can't grasp it. A year now, and I still have no idea if I'm doing more harm by giving her false hope that Charlotte might come back or if it would be better for her to accept that Charlotte's gone for good."

"Maybe that's the problem. She's trying to follow your lead—"

"And I'm going nowhere except spinning in circles." He drew in a breath, raising his shoulders into a shrug. "I think that's why I've been avoiding the whole anniversary thing. A year is too long for Nellie to linger in limbo. It's time to decide how we're going to live."

They stood in comfortable silence. Finally, Lucy said, "Maybe you're right. You shouldn't work this case. Take a few days off, be with your family."

"Nellie's in school today, and the empty house..." He gave a shake of his head. "Besides, you need someone to go over Sarah's apartment, inventory her personal possessions. It'll keep me busy. Shouldn't take more than a few hours. But I think maybe I will take the rest of the week off. Spend time with Nellie. Figure out the answers to the questions I've been avoiding all year. Like how to say goodbye to Charlotte when it's the last thing I want."

Lucy nodded her agreement, not sure how to help Tommy deal with the turmoil other than to focus on work and the case at hand. "I know the doctors said Sarah was fine to go home, that she only had a mild concussion, but she seems so...unconcerned? I mean, relatively speaking." She'd seen victims in shock, denial, even stunned. But Sarah was smiling, joking about her predicament.

"*La belle indifférence*," he said. "The mask of denial. A kind of psychic defense mechanism for when things are so confusing the brain can't make sense of them, so it defaults to whatever emotion is most socially acceptable. Usually a pleasant smile—best way to gain strangers' trust and get their help. Evolutionarily speaking."

"Okay. But it feels like there's more."

"You think she does remember something?"

"Maybe not consciously. Maybe this is more than a simple concussion. Maybe there's something she wants to forget."

"Psychogenic fugue?" His tone turned musing. "Rare. Very rare. And not something we see in kids, so I don't have much experience with it. Maybe your husband does?"

"I'll ask. But Burroughs and Oshiro both got the same impression after seeing Sarah's apartment: that she'd purposely lived a life with no ties to her past."

"Like she's on the run from someone?" He straightened, his gaze traveling past her to the house behind them as if seeking any potential threat. "Then we need to protect her."

"Hard to do until we know who she is and what, if anything, she's running from."

He nodded grimly. "Right. I'll get her keys and head over, get started on her place. Maybe Burroughs missed something."

Chapter 7

NELLIE RACED THROUGH the empty school courtyard searching for something to hit. Or some*one*. Anyone.

But the recess bell had rung, the playground was empty, and there were only the tall, heavy, mirror-like glass doors reflecting her image in waves, making her look like she'd soon wash away to nothing.

She was late. Not her fault—they'd made her chase the ball after it went over the fence—but Sister Agnes said if you came in late, you had to report to the office. Sign in. Be escorted to class. And no more recess for a whole week.

Nellie scrunched up her face, blinking back tears. Everyone was gone. Everyone always left her behind.

She thought of walking into class, Sister Agnes yanking her by the hand, giving her that "you're wasting my time, young lady" look while she told everyone, including Miss Cortez—who was so nice and who Nellie wanted so much to like her—that Nellie had broken the rules and come in late from morning recess and disrespected her teacher and classmates and needed to apologize and promise not to disrespect again even though it hadn't been Nellie's fault, and why were grownups in charge of what she did, anyway?

They were all stupid, stupid, stupid. They left and didn't say goodbye and they didn't do what they were supposed to do like save people or not leave or not go missing and they were just...

"Stupid, stupid, stupid!"

The sound of her voice startled her. But she felt better. And the girl in the mirror-door looking back at her seemed to approve. Nellie hunched her shoulders hard, tightening up her elbows and fists, stomping around in a circle. "Stupid, stupid, stupid."

The forbidden word filled her with power. No wonder grownups said it was a bad word. "We don't use that word," they said, but they lied—she heard them use it all the time.

"Stu-*pid,* stu-pid, *stu*-pid." Oh, she liked that last way: it felt like she was spitting out something yucky. Another thing "we don't do."

Well, Nellie was going to do what she wanted, go where she wanted, and she was most certainly not going to walk into Sister Agnes's office and say sorry for being late because she was the only one skinny enough to slip between the fence bars and chase after the ball. Her breath whooshed out of her and she reeled against the sandstone wall, dizzy with rebellion.

She glanced across the playground to the building that towered over everything, even Sister Agnes's school. The church. It was older than the school—older than her Papa

Callabrese, even. It had been here forever, built of stones that were slick and cold to touch and as big around as she was tall. Tall and quiet and solid and peaceful. The church wasn't going anywhere. It was here to stay.

Plus, soon, Nellie thought, Miss Cortez would be leading all the K-1 students to morning Mass. Nellie could hide in the church and rejoin them—and no one would ever have to know. Especially Sister Agnes.

It took both hands and all her strength to haul open the towering wooden door to the church. Inside, it was dark, though not like at night when she couldn't see, more like shadows stacked on top of each other. She shivered. Kinda spooky.

The door swung shut behind her with a thud, sealing her in, and she jumped. Then she dragged in a breath, inhaling vaporized beeswax and incense and all sorts of holy stuff that tickled her nose. She strode forward. It was church. Safe haven from evil—that's what Father Stravinsky said.

Dipping her fingers in the holy water and dripping it as she made the sign of the cross, she stepped from the little room in the front past two more massive doors that were always open to the real inside. Here the ceiling went up and up and up until large wooden beams met like Noah's ark turned upside down. Stained glass lined the walls, casting sparkly splashes of color across the gray marble floor and the dark wooden pews.

She stepped forward, feeling bold, ignoring the skittery feeling dancing inside her stomach. She crept past the alcove where the Lady of Sorrows was, making sure not to look at the larger than life statue of the young mother cradling her dead son, a big sword piercing her heart. If she looked at it too long, the Lady looked like Mommy, and she couldn't even think about Mommy with a sword sticking out of her heart.

Where to go? Should she crawl into a pew and hide? Or behind the curtain that led behind the altar? Maybe hide in the back corner?

Glancing around at possibilities, she made the mistake of looking at the form hanging high over the altar, his face glaring right down at her, telling her bad girls went straight to H-E-double hockey sticks.

And she was a very bad girl.

Nellie scampered backward, her sneakers slipping on the marble floor. She hated Jesus-nailed-to-the-cross. The pretty, stained glass Jesus-walking-on-water and Jesus-healing-the-sick she liked. Jesus-nailed-to-the-cross she was angry with. He was supposed to be the shepherd of souls, but he hadn't shepherded her mom back home. She had prayed to him every night to find Mommy, wherever she was lost, but he never answered her.

Jesus-nailed-to-the-cross made her wonder if anyone got to heaven. She shuddered; she didn't want to think about that. Mommy wasn't in heaven, singing with the angels—even though some of the kids said so. Her dad would have told her that if it was true. Her dad sometimes messed things up, like this morning, but he never lied.

Jesus wasn't supposed to lie either, but Nellie didn't really know or trust Jesus. She trusted her dad.

She stood still, scowling up at the bleeding Jesus so high

up in the rafters that she had to crane her neck back to meet his angry, pain-filled gaze.

You'd better find my mommy soon and bring her back home, she shouted in her mind, not daring to give voice to her rage. *You'd just better!*

Chapter 8

Lucy watched as Tommy returned inside the house to retrieve Sarah's apartment keys. She checked the time on her phone: nine fifty. Nick should be between patients. Usually she tried not to call him at work, but she needed his advice.

"What do you know about global amnesia and psychogenic fugues?" she asked when he picked up.

"Hey honey, how's your day going?" he chided, but there was laughter in his tone. Nick was well accustomed to Lucy's over-involvement in her cases. "Does this explain the messages on my machine from Oshiro and Don Burroughs?"

"Same case. Not a police matter, so they came to us." She filled him in on Sarah's predicament. "We're digging into her past—credit check, searching her apartment, all the usual. I thought starting with a cognitive, sensory-based interview might help. But I don't want to make things worse."

"No, I think you're on the right track. With a TBI," traumatic brain injury, Lucy translated, "she might not be able to focus for long. Watch for headaches, vertigo, nausea. She might be confused, emotionally labile."

"She's pretty upbeat. Tommy said it was a defense mechanism."

"*La belle indifférence.*" Nick said it in a fake French accent, which made it sound sexy. Of course, Nick could make anything sound sexy—to Lucy.

She forced herself to focus on the case. "Any other tips for the interview?"

"Patients with retrograde amnesia tend to follow Ribot's Law: they lose more recent memories, the ones closest to the traumatic event, but may retain some sense of their remote past."

"So we should start with trying to access memories from her childhood, then work forward in time?"

"Exactly. And don't pressure her too much. Overwhelming her or adding any stress inhibits recollection. Let her set the pace."

"If we can't get anywhere, what would you recommend? Is it too soon to try hypnosis?"

"When did she hit her head?"

"Two days ago."

He thought about it. "I'd make sure the other symptoms of the concussion clear first. Unless there's an urgent need to intervene."

"Nothing urgent. Just trying to get her life back."

"Good luck. Call me if there's anything I can do to help."

When Lucy returned inside she was surprised when Missy directed her to Valencia's private wing. Valencia met her in the hallway outside the sturdy oak door leading to the kitchen. As always, she was dressed as if she were on her way to have tea with the First Lady. She wore a burgundy silk sheath, and her gray hair was swept up into a deceptively simple twist that Lucy knew was too complicated for her to ever re-create with her own rambunctious curls.

"Tiffany thought the kitchen might be a more relaxing place for a chat," she explained. Valencia was the only person who used TK's given name without fear of repercussions.

"Good idea." Even Lucy, whose culinary skill set began and ended with pressing a button on a microwave, adored Valencia's kitchen. The room somehow radiated all the love and care that had gone into the hundred years' worth of meals prepared there. It was a perfect place to get an anxious interview subject to relax. "So, things are working out? Having TK live here?"

When Lucy had first met TK, the former Marine was camped out in an empty closet at the gym where she'd been teaching parkour and self-defense classes, and all her possessions were able to fit into the rucksack she carried on the old motorcycle she used for transportation. TK had reminded her of a feral cat then—homeless but too proud to ask for help. But now, living on the estate with Valencia, TK had shed her restless, aimless energy and was laser focused on her work.

"I love having her here," Valencia said. "And she's a huge help to Xander." The estate's manager and Valencia's personal assistant, Xander Chen, was in his sixties. Hong Kong born and raised, he had a British accent that always made Lucy think of Batman's butler, Alfred. "But don't blame me for her new attitude—that's all on you."

"Me?" Lucy was surprised. It felt like she and TK argued about everything.

Valencia's smile widened. "The Texas case was a wake-up call for her. Seeing you in action, she realized how much she still has to learn. You're her role model."

Lucy couldn't help but glance down at her injured foot. Not even forty and already forced out of the job she'd loved, facing permanent disability, stripped of all her police powers, and placed in charge of a group of civilians? "Not sure I'm comfortable with that idea."

"Get used to it." Valencia meant more than simply mentoring TK, Lucy knew. It was hard though, seeing Burroughs and Oshiro this morning, being reminded of everything she'd lost when she left the FBI. "You have a lot to offer, Lucy. And I think you'll be surprised at how much working without the constraints of law enforcement's bureaucracy and regulations can offer in return."

"Like interviewing a victim in your kitchen."

"More than that. If Detective Burroughs and Deputy Marshal Oshiro hadn't gone the extra mile in bringing her to us, the police would have had little to offer Sarah once they established her identity and that no crime was involved. Social services can't do much either—they're much too bogged down in cases of abuse and neglect, helping those who can't help themselves. But we don't have those rules to follow, constraints placed by caseloads or a results-driven administrative culture. We can help her, make certain she doesn't fall through the cracks." Valencia glanced at the closed door beside them. "Besides, it's nice to work a case that you already know has a happy ending, isn't it?"

Lucy couldn't disagree. But there was another case that concerned her. "TK and Wash are worried about Tommy working this case. Apparently the anniversary of his wife's disappearance is this week?"

Valencia's expression clouded. "I should have thought to give you a heads-up on that. I apologize. How's he holding up?"

"He's going to document Sarah's apartment for us, then he's taking the rest of the week off to be with his daughter and hopefully escape the press."

"I'd hoped that working Sarah's case would keep his mind off Charlotte." Valencia sighed. "But it's probably better this way. Her case…it's so frustrating, so many false trails."

"Then you think she did leave voluntarily?"

"The evidence points that way. Most of it. But, no, I don't believe that. I just can't find anything to prove otherwise."

"I'd like to take a look. If that's all right with you." Lucy was torn between the desire to find the truth—and help Tommy—and the knowledge that meddling in co-workers' private lives never ended well. But if she was going to continue to work with Tommy, she needed to know everything.

Valencia's nod was slow in coming. "I'd appreciate it. Fresh eyes might be exactly what we need."

CHAPTER 9

WHILE THEY WAITED for Lucy, TK bustled around the kitchen, arranging the chairs at the farm table into an intimate grouping at the end closest to the stone fireplace that filled an entire wall. Sarah sat at the table and watched with the slightest trace of amusement on her face.

"Let's start with the basics," TK said. "Coffee? Tea? Soda?"

The question brought a frown to Sarah as she considered. "I'm not sure." Her mouth twisted as if she was trying to re-create the taste of each option. "I can almost imagine how they smell, taste, but..."

"Smell is the most primal trigger of memories." Ever since she'd begun working with Lucy, TK had been reading everything she could on interviewing techniques to complement what she'd already learned from her Marine training. She poured a cup of black coffee and set it before Sarah, followed by a glass of cola and an iced tea. "Real tea will take a few minutes."

Sarah started with the iced tea. She sniffed it cautiously, then took a sip. "This is good, but needs something. It's kind of tart."

"Sugar coming up." TK spooned and stirred while Sarah tried the cola.

She immediately wrinkled her nose. "No. Bubbles. Ugh."

"And the coffee?"

Sarah tasted it. "Bitter, but feels familiar."

"Try adding sugar and milk," TK suggested. As she watched to see if Sarah completed the coffee-making ritual reflexively or if she had to taste-test her way through it, she distracted Sarah with more questions. "Any sense of where you drink coffee? Does it feel like you're home alone? Just waking up? Or picking it up from a Starbucks?"

Sarah added two teaspoons of sugar and a healthy dollop of milk, stirred, then tasted and nodded in satisfaction. "Good."

"You got it on the first try," TK praised her.

"So the memories must be there, just waiting to come out. Starbucks," Sarah mused. "I can see it, know what it is. They have the mermaid logo, right?"

"Right."

"But it doesn't feel like an everyday thing. When I think of it, it feels like, I can almost hear someone's voice."

"Like maybe you're meeting someone?"

Sarah nodded eagerly, cradling her coffee mug in both hands and inhaling deeply. "This smell, it smells like... Do we know what direction the kitchen in my apartment faces?" she asked excitedly. "I can almost feel the sun coming in at a low angle. Like this is part of my morning. Coffee and sunshine."

"We'll take a look when we take you over to walk

through it. Let's try some more smells." TK selected a few spices from Valencia's well-stocked cabinets. As she was arranging them on a plate and covering them with a tea towel so Sarah wouldn't be able to see the labels, Lucy came in and poured herself a cup of coffee.

"I like coffee with milk and sugar," Sarah announced proudly.

Lucy raised her own mug in a toast. "Good start." She sat down at the far end of the table and nodded to TK to continue.

"Close your eyes," TK told Sarah. "Just tell us whatever comes to mind with each smell. Don't try to identify the smell if it doesn't come right away, instead concentrate on where you were when you smelled it, who you were with, any memories at all."

Sarah nodded and closed her eyes. TK started with vanilla. "Oh. Warm and happy. I feel like I'm being hugged—like I'm a little girl. There are a lot of voices, all women, and we're in a kitchen like this one only not as big. The oven is being opened and closed and my hands are wet—I'm washing dishes!" she exclaimed. "I'm young, not sure how old, but it's a holiday..." Her face creased with concentration. "Thanksgiving? Christmas? It's cold—the window over the sink is cold. I'm standing on a step so I can reach it."

"Who's with you?" TK asked in a gentle voice.

"Women. All older. I can't remember their names, see their faces, but I feel safe. I feel loved." Her eyes popped open, glistening with tears. "My family. I was home. But why can't I remember more?"

"Relax. You're doing great. Let's try another."

Sarah shook her head in frustration, her hair falling around her face. "No. It's so damn hard. I mean, why can I remember stupid things like George Washington and how to make my coffee and that gray is not a color I'd ever wear, but I can't remember my name or face or my own family?"

TK looked to Lucy, who nodded and shifted to the chair beside Sarah. Lucy placed her palm on Sarah's arm. "My husband, he works at the VA, with PTSD patients. A lot of them also have traumatic brain injuries, memory problems. He says there's a pattern to how memories are lost and found again—that usually the older the memory, the more likely it is to remain."

"So we have to go through this over and over until I rebuild my entire life? I know you're trying to help," Sarah said, sounding miserable, "but I just want to go home. Can't we continue this there? Maybe something will trigger things. Bring it all back. I really want to go home now."

Made sense to TK. But Lucy hesitated. "Sarah, when you were in your apartment earlier with Burroughs and Oshiro, what did you feel?"

"Nothing. I mean, it's a small place, was easy enough to figure out where my clothing was, simply because there weren't many options, but nothing looked familiar. But we were only there for a few minutes, just long enough for me to change and get cleaned up after the hospital."

"No sense of belonging?"

"No. Felt like a hotel room or something where it just happened that the clothing they said belonged to me was hanging in the closet. But maybe there's more—a favorite blouse or piece of jewelry, I don't know." She frowned. "Why don't you want me to go home?"

TK wondered that as well. She eased back in her chair to watch both Lucy and Sarah.

"It's not that." Lucy glanced at TK, then Sarah. "It's just that most people, their homes have personal items. Notes scribbled in a calendar, photos on the fridge, mementoes..."

"Right. Exactly. Let's go see." Sarah stood eagerly—then paused and frowned at Lucy. "Wait. If any of that stuff was there, Detective Burroughs would have showed me, wouldn't he? It would have given him a starting place. But he didn't. Which means he didn't find anything." She shook her head. "How could that be?"

TK stood beside Sarah, annoyed at Lucy for upsetting her further. "Don't worry. We'll get to the bottom of it. But you're right. Maybe there's something he missed that you'd recognize. We won't know until we go check it out."

"But…who lives like that? What kind of person am I?"

"I wasn't trying to upset you," Lucy said. "Why don't you wait in the reception area while TK and I clean up here, and then we'll take you home?"

Sarah nodded, her face a blank. But then she glanced up. "Will Dr. Worth be there? I'd feel much more comfortable if he was."

"Why? Do you feel sick? Need a doctor?"

"No. I'm fine. Just, I don't know, he feels…not familiar, that's too strong of a word. Comforting? I feel like I can think better, my mind's not as fuzzy when he's around. Does that make any sense?"

TK smiled. "Tommy's a pediatrician. I think he has that kind of calming influence on us all."

"Okay, then. I'll wait for you out front."

Sarah left, and TK turned to Lucy. "What the hell was that all about?"

"I wish I knew. But Burroughs and Oshiro both felt like there's more going on with Sarah. Like maybe she purposely erased her past."

"No. She's not faking it. No way."

"Not that. More like, maybe she's hiding from someone, keeping a low profile."

TK snapped to attention. "Lucy. The public service announcements—if she really is hiding from someone, we've just broadcast her face to the world."

Chapter 10

TOMMY PULLED HIS Volvo up to the curb and looked out the window at Sarah Brown's apartment building. It was a seven-story yellow brick building directly across from Shadyside Hospital. Anonymous would be how he'd describe it. No wonder the cops hadn't found anyone who knew her here. She could have come and gone for weeks without seeing another resident.

He left the car and trudged up the steps to the building's entrance. At least Sarah had still had her keys with her when she'd been found. He let himself into the lobby, checked her mailbox—empty, not even any junk mail—then took the elevator up to the fifth floor. The walls of the corridor were narrow, the carpet beige, the paint close to the end of its useful lifespan. The architecture had that pre-World War Two feeling, with high ceilings and elaborate molding—facts the otherwise bland decor hadn't been able to obscure.

As he prowled down the hallway searching for 517, the smell of bacon and cabbage wafted from behind one of the doors. It reminded him of summer vacations visiting his grandparents' house. How he'd loved those summers filled with hay bales, barn cats, horses, swimming holes, and ice cream hand churned as fireflies swirled against the twilight sky.

Until last year he'd carried that feeling of carefree contentment with him every day, even all these years later. Being with Charlotte, coming home to her and Nellie, it had felt like that. Every single day.

Until last year.

He reached Sarah's apartment door and inserted her key into the lock. He hesitated, then knocked before turning the key.

A thrill rushed through him as he opened the door onto Sarah Brown's life. It felt weird, trespassing into someone's private space even if it was for her own good. This wasn't part of his usual job—nothing about this case was. Usually he spent his time at Beacon Falls reviewing medical records and on the phone discussing lab protocols and findings that maybe didn't make it into the official record.

The door opened onto a small foyer with a coat stand—empty—then expanded into the living room. The floors were oak, and there was a generic tan area rug in the center of the living room, between a matching modern beige sofa and chair that faced a large screen TV. Light streamed in through a wall of windows opposite the door. The artwork on the walls was as generic as the rug and furniture. No clues there.

He closed the front door behind him and stood listening. The construction was solid—he couldn't hear anything, or at least not now, midday when most of the building's occupants were presumably at work. The apartment faced the rear of the building, so no sounds of traffic either. He stepped farther into the living room, still feeling as if he were a criminal, or worse, a voyeur.

He started by walking through the one-bedroom apartment, recording everything for Wash, zooming in on anything that was personal and that could provide information, like the contents of Sarah's trash cans. The kitchen can was empty, except for a Giant Eagle grocery bag serving as a bin liner, but the one in the bathroom, in addition to an assortment of cotton balls and makeup removal pads, had a receipt from a Sheetz convenience store for gas and a soda. He snapped several close-ups and sent everything to Wash, then slid the receipt into a manila envelope from his messenger bag.

Maybe it was the smell of Sarah's shampoo concentrated here in the tiny bathroom with its vintage hexagonal black and white tiles and lack of ventilation, but suddenly he was swamped with a vision of Charlotte. It wasn't one of his treasured memories, where she was smiling and laughing; this vision was from that last morning, as he pulled out of their driveway and caught sight of her leaving the house, phone to her ear, frown on her face.

Last glimpse he'd ever had of her. He had no idea who she was talking with, where she was going, or why she was upset. According to the police, she'd neither received nor made a phone call that morning—at least not on her regular cell. If she had gotten a call, it must have been on a second, untraceable cell phone, which implied an intent to deceive. Police jargon for: she was hiding something from Tommy.

The fact that they'd traced her route to several ATMs, where she'd withdrawn cash from accounts she'd kept separate from their joint account, had only confirmed their suspicions. The only other location where they'd placed Charlotte before her car was found two days later, abandoned at a secluded scenic overview beside the Youghiogheny River, was the Sheetz where she'd bought two prepaid cell phones.

Tommy startled, emptied the receipt from the envelope back into his palm. Stared at the address. The Sheetz where Charlotte had last been seen was the very same convenience store Sarah had visited Friday, the day before her accident.

He shook his head, tried to deny how rattled the realization that Sarah had crossed paths with Charlotte made him feel. It was as if a chill breeze swept through the room, despite the fact that there were no windows in the bathroom and the door was closed.

Nonsense, he told himself, almost but not quite speaking out loud—that's how real this felt. Two women visit the same convenience store a year apart? Doesn't even rise to the level of coincidence. Was he so far gone that he'd grasp at any will-o'-wisp that might lead him to Charlotte?

He shook his head, put the receipt back into the envelope, and continued his inventory. But it was hard to shake the feeling that someone was watching him. The goose bumps rising on his arms didn't help.

Before he could start in on the scant contents of Sarah's closet, the sound of a knock at the front door made him jump. He jogged through the living room and peered through the security peephole. It was Sarah.

He opened the door. She held a large package wrapped in plain brown paper in her arms.

"You have the only set of keys," she said.

"Of course, sorry. What's that?" he asked as he drew back to let her enter. It was strange to see her do a double-take at the sight of her own apartment. She moved awkwardly as if not knowing where to go.

"I don't know. It was sitting at the mailboxes in the front lobby."

"Wasn't there when I came in. But that was around forty-five minutes ago."

She hefted the package. "It's not very heavy for how big it is."

He ushered her around the corner to the kitchen/dining area, where there was a glass-topped circular table large enough to seat four. No place mats, no centerpiece, just the plain glass reflecting the light from the window beside it.

"It does face the morning sun," she said as she set the package down. It was about three feet by four feet, a little less than a foot in height. No postage or barcodes, just her name and address on a printed label. No return address.

She left the package to rummage through the kitchen. "If I were me, where would I keep the scissors?"

"You didn't come here alone, did you?" he asked, watching her open and close drawers.

"TK brought me. She's downstairs at the rental office getting a copy of my application, since they were closed when

Detective Burroughs stopped there earlier."

"Good thinking."

"Aha. Found them—although, for a junk drawer, there's not a lot of junk, is there?" She brandished a pair of scissors, and Tommy glanced at the open drawer. Scissors, packaging tape, some plain envelopes, an assortment of screwdrivers, and a hammer.

"Maybe let me open it?" he suggested. "In case we need the paper or something?"

She frowned, her features sagging with disappointment for a brief moment, then said, "Why not? You're already treating my home like a crime scene. Although," her smile returned, "given my almost criminal lack of taste in decor, guess I really can't complain."

"You don't like it?"

"No. Too modern, stiff. No personality. And those pictures on the walls? Yuck."

Another knock came on the door. Sarah went to open it, returning with TK, who was holding a sheaf of papers.

"Occupation: freelance photographer," TK read as she walked through the living room. "Employer: self. Hmm, guess that doesn't help us much." She glanced around the room and grimaced at the decor. "Apartment: pre-furnished."

"Thank goodness," Sarah said. "I was beginning to doubt that I possessed any taste whatsoever." She pressed against TK, looking over her shoulder. "Does it mention next of kin? An emergency contact?"

TK rifled through the pages. "No. Sorry. It's blank. And

the only reference was your previous landlord—same Altoona address as your old driver's license." She handed Sarah the papers and looked past her to where Tommy stood at the table with the package. "What's that?"

"It was waiting at the mailboxes." Sarah dropped the rental papers onto the couch. "We were just getting ready to open it."

"Why isn't there a postage mark or delivery label?" TK examined the package from every angle. She shook it. Frowned. "This is weird."

"Trust me," Sarah said, reaching for the scissors again. "You don't know weird. Not until you wake up one morning staring at a stranger in the mirror. It's addressed to me and I'm opening it." Tommy opened his mouth to protest, and she added, "Carefully."

With precise movements she slit the tape without cutting the paper, allowing the wrapping to unfold, revealing a white box. She raised the lid. A card fluttered out, past Sarah's hands. She gasped.

Tommy and TK stared at what lay inside. A wedding gown, carefully folded amid billowing pink tissue paper.

"It's beautiful," Sarah said, dropping the lid to reach a hand to the white silk, but pulling back before she could actually touch it. "Is it for me?" She turned to stare at Tommy and TK in turn. "I'm getting married?"

CHAPTER 11

TK STARED IN horror as Sarah's expression crashed and burned, morphing from wonder and delight to despair. Thankfully, Tommy was standing right beside her, so when she crumpled, tears streaming, hands clutching at air, he caught her. He helped her over to the couch. She fell, sobbing into his arms.

"I'm getting married? I don't even know who I am. I can't remember who he is," Sarah blubbered. "Someone out there loves me and I can't, I can't—"

TK felt bad for Sarah, but was glad to be out of range of the waterworks. Crying wasn't going to help them complete their objective. She spotted the small white card that had flown free when Sarah unwrapped the dress. She crouched down, retrieved it from beneath the table, and without asking permission, despite the fact that the front said "Sarah" in plain block handwriting, she opened it.

An unforgettable dress for an unforgettable woman.

I'll be with you. Soon.

Then we'll be together. Forever.

No signature, just a cloying XOXO. Ugh. TK couldn't

decide if the author was hopelessly sentimental, trying too hard, or controlling and coercive. After all, why would a husband-to-be send the bride her dress? Wasn't that the one thing the bride got to splurge on and decide for herself?

She pulled the dress out, searching for any labels that might trace it back to its origins. Nothing.

On the couch, Tommy had finally calmed Sarah down. The girl—she was only two years younger than TK, according to her driver's license, but somehow she acted much younger, definitely more innocent, whether that naivety came from her memory loss or life experiences, and absolutely more trusting—had curled up against Tommy's side, her head on his shoulder, one of his arms wrapped around her. He glanced up at TK, his expression begging for help.

"Why don't you have a ring?" TK asked. Her words sounded blunt and recriminating, but she didn't mean them that way; she simply hated puzzles. "An engagement ring?"

Sarah startled, sniffed, then disengaged herself from Tommy and sat up, her left arm stretched out, staring at her fingers. "You're right. I didn't have it at the hospital."

"Maybe you lost it when you fell?" Tommy suggested.

"I doubt it. Anyway, if I had one, I couldn't have had it for long." She waggled her fingers in the air. "No tan lines."

"You only rented the apartment two months ago," TK said. "If you were already engaged by then, wouldn't you have listed him as an emergency contact?"

Sarah shrugged. "I don't know. Would I? Is that what people do?" Her sigh rattled through the room with its barren decor.

"People definitely don't go from no ring to a wedding dress in two months," TK said.

"Most people," Tommy cautioned. "Maybe he's in the military and there's limited time before the wedding. Or maybe the dress is something else entirely. You're a photographer—maybe it's a prop for a photo shoot?"

Sarah's eyes widened and she nodded, obviously liking the idea. But TK shook her head and handed her the card. "Not unless whoever sent it has an extremely bizarre sense of humor."

Sarah held the card and read the bold, blunt handwriting. Her hand trembled, her eyes drew together, lips tightened, and her entire body cringed away from the small, plain white card. It slipped from her hand, which was frozen out in front of her as if fear had paralyzed her.

"Do you know who wrote that?" Tommy asked, taking her hand and folding it in his.

Sarah shook her head, over and over, not making eye contact with either of them, her gaze darting around the room, searching for the exit. It was a look TK was extremely accustomed to: primal terror.

"No. No. No." Each syllable emerged in time with her head shaking. She drew her knees up to her chest and hid her face by burrowing into Tommy's side. "I don't know. I can't remember. Nothing. Except. Except." Her breathing grew fast, and TK feared she was hyperventilating.

"It's okay," Tommy said, pulling back so that Sarah was looking directly into his eyes. "We're not going to let anyone hurt you. Breathe. That's it. Slower. In and out. Good." He held both of Sarah's still shaking hands in his. "Now. Don't worry if it makes sense or not. Just tell us everything you felt, no matter how strange, when you saw that card and the handwriting."

Sarah nodded, gulping in a breath. "I'll try." Her voice was timid and small.

"What was your first thought?"

"Run. I had to run."

"What were you running from?"

"I—I don't know. Everything's dark. Except… blood..." She gasped. "Tommy. I see blood. Blood everywhere. And I—I can't stay…I have to get out…I have to run. Now!"

She practically leapt off the couch with her final screech. TK's hands went up, ready to defend, but Tommy had the opposite reaction. He pulled Sarah back to him, the girl now decimated, a quivering mass of tears and wordless sounds of terror.

He hugged Sarah tight, palms stroking her hair, rocking with her as if she were a little girl caught in a nightmare. But his gaze was locked on to TK and his eyes were narrowed with worry.

TK nodded, her phone already in her hand. She grabbed the card from the floor and stepped into the bedroom, closing the door so Sarah couldn't hear her.

"Lucy? We have a problem."

CHAPTER 12

WHILE WASH BEGAN his work of combing through Sarah Brown's digital footprints, Lucy retreated to the back of the house to what Valencia called the "nanny's room." It was long and narrow with only one small window at the far end and was empty except for a few cartons of stray office supplies. Perfect for Lucy's needs.

At the FBI, she'd gotten used to surrounding herself with smart boards to visually represent a case, covering them with data as well as potential avenues of investigation. Here, she went low tech, but it still worked. She covered the walls with brown craft paper, grabbed a bunch of marking pens and sticky notes in various colors, and began deconstructing Charlotte Worth's last days.

On one wall, she created a timeline with documented facts: where Charlotte was, who saw her or was with her. On the other wall she organized hypotheticals—unverified sightings before or after the day she vanished, the various "possible" leads that law enforcement, the private investigators hired by Tommy and Charlotte's family, and Valencia had stumbled across—along with unanswered questions raised by the evidence: motives for her leaving voluntarily, reasons to question her mental health, motives for anyone to want to harm her, the stalled money trail she'd left in her wake, possible attempts to cover her tracks… There were so many questions that Lucy almost ran out of space.

When she was done, she stood back. No wonder both the police and private investigators had been so frustrated. Tommy was right. Despite the fact that they'd been able to discover a multitude of "facts" about Charlotte's disappearance, you could twist them into any story you wanted.

For instance, following the money—a time-honored law enforcement tradition, mainly because it usually did lead to answers—told a story of a woman who bought disposable cell phones, who had multiple accounts separate from her husband, and who, on the day she vanished, maxed out those accounts' ATM withdrawals. Cash in hand, she bought herself time by parking her car in a secluded scenic overlook, where it sat undiscovered for three days. Presumably she either met an accomplice or had another car waiting, then walked away from her life.

This was the story that seemed to please law enforcement the most. Lucy could understand why: it not only solved the case, but it had the most concrete, objective evidence to support the theory, and it meant that they hadn't allowed a murderer to walk around free to kill again.

Only problem: no one had been able to document any

motive or even a hint of unhappiness that might cause Charlotte Worth to abandon her life, including her husband and child.

The press had taken a different, more salacious view, following their own time-honored tradition of "if it bleeds, it leads." They speculated at first about possible motives for killing Charlotte—despite the fact that Tommy had an ironclad alibi for the day of her disappearance—setting their "investigative teams" to search for possible "thugs for hire" and tracking down would-be assassins he could have reached out to via Craigslist and other anonymous internet sites.

Lucy had to give them credit. For a story with almost no facts, they'd managed to create the illusion of a much wider conspiracy, as if husbands and wives throughout Pittsburgh were busy searching for nefarious partners to help eliminate their spouses, leading one paper to do a series on "how to get away with murder," while another online tabloid website tried to create a sting operation to snare potential hit men for hire. All of which no doubt brought much-needed eyeballs to their publications, but were of no help in finding Charlotte.

The last theory—suicide—was the least popular. And the one with the least concrete basis. But both Charlotte's family and colleagues had mentioned that she was stressed during the weeks before she vanished. No one said why, only that she'd seemed distracted and at times distraught. She was in good health, and at the time she went missing she hadn't been involved with any cases at work that would have been unduly stressful. Social workers rotated around various units at the hospital in an effort to avoid burnout, and when Charlotte vanished, she'd been working in the rehab department, one of the least stressful.

All of these hypotheses strived to create sense out of the devastation Charlotte had left in her wake. And odds were, none of them were right.

Lucy paced back and forth, her gaze darting from one wall to the other, letting the facts and questions whirl and spin, sparking off each other, without committing to any of them. Trying to be both neutral and involved, searching for what lay beneath the facts, seeking out new questions to ask.

Wash interrupted her with a knock on the door. "Found a few things on Sarah." He wheeled forward into the tiny room. "Wow. Isn't it kind of overwhelming? Seeing it all in one place like this?"

"It can be. Which is why I don't want Tommy stumbling in here." She glanced at the analyst to make sure he caught her meaning. "He doesn't need more on his plate right now."

"Sure, I get it. If you need me to help, just holler."

"I will. Thanks."

"So, what'cha think? Some crazy serial killer and she was in the wrong place, wrong time?"

The public always defaulted to random acts of senseless violence committed by strangers, but that was the least likely, statistically speaking. Especially with no evidence; most acts of spontaneous violence weren't clean and neat. And there was no evidence of anyone stalking Charlotte, targeting her. Which meant looking to those she knew and loved.

"C'mon," Wash continued when Lucy didn't answer right

away. "We know it wasn't Tommy. And why would she run off, leave her husband and kid? Had to be some psycho."

"What did you find on Sarah?" Lucy led him out of the room and locked the door behind her. They traveled down the hall back to the team's main work area.

"Got her birth certificate. Unfortunately her parents are named Robert and Mary..."

"How many Robert and Mary Browns can there be?"

"A helluva lot more than you might think. But based on the address listed, I followed the real estate transactions, and I think I tracked them down."

"Great. Where are they?"

He wheeled back in place behind his computer—Wash always seemed more comfortable with the computer and its screen serving as a barrier between him and the rest of the world—and clicked a key. The projection screen at the other end of the room lit up with two obituary notices. "Died in a car accident four years ago. I'm working on tracking the other relatives listed, but it'll take a while. And then we still need to make sure they're the correct Brown family."

"Right. We can't get Sarah's hopes up without being certain. She's been traumatized enough."

"TK sent over a copy of her lease agreement. Turns out she's a freelance photographer. I found several photographers named Sarah Brown with websites; I think this one might be hers." The screen flipped to a website with a wide screen slideshow of nature photos. "There's no personal profile picture, but the locations are all Pennsylvania and surrounding states, and it says the photographer is based in western Pennsylvania. The contact info leads to a Gmail account with a free phone number and answering system."

"So basically untraceable."

"Right. But, once we can prove that she is the actual owner of the Gmail account, we can ask them for access. Don't hold your breath, though."

Lucy knew that privacy reigned supreme when it came to tech companies, unless there were exigent circumstances like in a kidnapping or critical missing person—which was not the case here. Maybe since Sarah's wallet and cell were presumably stolen when her car was broken into, she could ask Burroughs to report her as a victim of identity theft. That would allow them access without needing court orders—although it would still be a slow slog wading through the bureaucracies surrounding Sarah's various accounts.

Lucy's eyes blurred as Wash flipped through Sarah Brown's photos, one image morphing into the next. "She really does have a thing for ferns and moss. Did the camera card's GIS info give you anything to go on?"

"No. It's all for the area around the trail she was found on. The first photo on the memory card is from earlier that same day, the trailhead sign—probably to help her organize her files when she downloads them."

"If you were a professional photographer, wouldn't you have a big computer and screen? They didn't find any in her apartment."

"These days, you can use your laptop, screencast to a hi-def TV, and the image is bigger than life, filled with all the detail she'd need to edit them. Same thing as what I'm doing here."

"So she could have had everything in the car and lost it all in the smash and grab. I guess I was just expecting all sorts of equipment at home—lights and whatnot. But Burroughs didn't mention anything."

"Look at what she shoots." He nodded to the image on the screen, which was filled with layers of thick, richly colored moss. "I'll bet she does it all in the field with what she can carry with her."

"Doesn't help us much, then."

Before she could ask anything else her phone rang. TK.

"Lucy? We have a problem."

Chapter 13

TOMMY HELD SARAH much as he'd become accustomed to holding his daughter, trying to comfort her the best he could. But holding Sarah felt so different—and yet, so very familiar, in ways he fought to deny.

The scent of her shampoo, the feel of her hair, simply having a woman lean on him, need him… He closed his eyes, and for a fleeting, searing moment it was Charlotte he held, not a stranger. He wanted to savor, to etch this exact second of time into his memory so that he would not lose it as he had so many other moments with Charlotte.

But something inside him refused to allow him even that small measure of comfort. He didn't push Sarah away in his need, but neither did he submerge himself in the intoxication of faux memory and denial.

Instead, as he'd done millions of times during the past 363 days, he relived those last moments with Charlotte.

He'd been pulling out of the driveway on his way to work. Nellie was waiting in the Pathfinder for Charlotte to drive her to school. Charlotte came out of the house, cell phone to her ear, her expression suddenly clouding, then growing—angry? Frustrated? Concerned? A mix of all three, maybe?

He hadn't kept on driving. No. He'd stopped, half in and half out of the driveway. Had been poised to shift into park, roll his window down, and ask her what was wrong. But she glanced up when he stopped the car, shook her head, and waved him off.

And he'd gone. He'd left. Never to see her again.

The vision of those final moments—the entire encounter less than four seconds by his estimate—brought with it so many questions. And emotions. It used to be denial. It wasn't his fault—he'd done everything he could. Then came anger, right on Kübler-Ross's schedule. Why hadn't she let him help? What had she been hiding from him? How could she have put herself in danger? What if something had happened when she had Nellie with her instead of later?

The questions raged on, unrelenting and never ending. Without answers, without even a body to mourn, he had gotten stuck in anger. Well, there was the occasional bargaining, and definitely some depression, but absolutely no acceptance. A maelstrom of grief consumed him from the moment he woke—when he did sleep—and followed him through the day and into his dreams.

And now, to have a woman in his arms once more. A woman who, for whatever reason, smelled like Charlotte, and who needed him, who was depending upon him.

A woman who had stopped sobbing and now was simply embracing him, her head nestled into his shoulder, hair hiding her face. The temptation was so strong—to steal this moment of comfort, transplant it over his own painful final memories of Charlotte.

No. He straightened, pulling his arm away from her shoulders. No. Sarah looked up, her expression wounded, as if he'd rejected her.

"It's going to be all right," he told her, using his best "I'm the doctor and know these things, trust me" voice. "Let me check with TK. We're not going to let anything happen to you."

She blinked, her eyes still wet with tears. Blinked again as she weighed his words. Finally, she nodded.

Tommy stood and went into the bedroom where TK was talking with Lucy.

"What's the plan?" he asked.

TK held a palm up, nodded, then said, "Got it." She hung up and pocketed her phone. "How's she doing?"

"Okay, I guess. What did Lucy say?"

"They found Sarah's parents. Dead. A few years now. Still working on locating any other kin."

"Seems like rediscovering her past is the least of our problems. What are we going to do to keep her safe now?"

"Wash is scouring court records, seeing if she was ever involved in any domestic violence cases or requested a restraining order. Hoping to get a name for whoever is stalking her. But since nothing showed up when the police ran her name, it means going county by county through their local databases."

"Maybe we should hand this back over to the cops?"

Tommy might not like Burroughs, but the man was good at his job.

"Lucy is updating Burroughs. But it's still not a crime—her feelings of being frightened when she saw someone's handwriting is not evidence."

"We can't penalize her because she can't remember who's stalking her with creepy messages and anonymous gifts. There has to be something we can do."

"Lucy is working on a place for Sarah to stay the night. In the meantime, we take the dress and card and everything over to Burroughs, and we watch over her."

"It's a start."

They returned to the living room. Sarah sat curled up on the center of the sofa, the empty space surrounding her making her appear even younger and more vulnerable. She looked at TK, then at Tommy, saying nothing. As if resigned to her fate.

That's when it hit him. Without her memories, Sarah had no idea who she could trust and who might be dangerous. She had no one. Except his team.

TK took charge. "I know you're scared," she said, surprising him with her empathetic tone. "But we're going to protect you. I'm going to stay with you while we find a safe place for you to go."

"You're leaving?" she asked Tommy. Her expression made it seem as if she was close to tears again.

"He's just going to take the evidence over to the police," TK rushed to assure her. "But I'll stay. All day and all night."

To Tommy's surprise, Sarah uncurled her legs and stood.

"No. That's foolish."

She strode past both of them to the kitchen, rummaging through the cupboards until she found a box of plastic sandwich bags. She handed them to TK. "To save the fingerprints."

"Right." TK exchanged a glance with Tommy before retrieving the card and carefully slipping it inside one of the bags. She was doing it more to appease Sarah than anything—they both knew there was little chance of any forensic evidence to be found, which was why Burroughs wasn't leaving his real cases to come himself. But if it made Sarah feel more in control…

"You're not planning on staying here?" Tommy asked Sarah while TK collected the dress and its wrapping.

"No. Of course not. It's not like this place has any meaning to me. I meant it was foolish for TK to insist on staying with me both day and night. What good is an exhausted bodyguard, right? She should take that," she jerked her chin at the wedding gown as if it were contaminated, "to the police and then go get some rest. While you help me pack. We can go someplace public and safe until we figure out where to go next. A cheap hotel would work for me, except I don't have any money or an ID—at least not until my replacement driver's license gets here. Detective Burroughs said it should arrive by tomorrow."

And that was that. No whining, no tears, just a plan. Tommy liked that. He only wished there was more to it. He knew Sarah wouldn't be safe until they caught her stalker—and she found her memories.

"Would it be okay for us to set up surveillance here?" he asked. "In case the stalker returns?"

"I think that's a great idea," TK added. "We can put a button camera overlooking your front door and another inside."

Sarah shrugged. "What do I care? I won't be here." She walked into the bedroom, leaving the door open so they could still talk. "Did you see any suitcases when you—oh, found it."

TK bundled her evidence. Tommy walked out with her, holding the door open for her.

"You okay with this?" she asked. "I know you were planning to head home early."

"I don't need to pick up Nellie from school until three twenty. That should give you and Lucy time to flesh out a plan, find a place for Sarah to stay."

"No problem." TK looked past him back into the apartment. "I don't know what to think of her. She seems all over the place, emotionally. Like she forgot what to feel and when to feel it, if you get my meaning."

"It's not uncommon in patients with concussions, even mild ones. Add that to the fact that her emotions are totally disconnected from any memories or life experiences..."

"Yeah, that makes sense. Feel kinda bad for her. It's a shitty position to be in, even without a possible stalker. Can you imagine? Losing everything?"

"Losing everything is easy. People do it all the time and start over. It's the losing every*one*—including yourself. That's a living hell."

TK paused, met his gaze. Seemed to realize maybe he

wasn't talking only about Sarah and her amnesia. "It'll be okay." Her tone made it sound so damn easy. "Give it time. It'll be okay."

With that she left. Tommy stood in the hallway, watching her walk away, and all he saw was Charlotte. Shaking her head and waving him away...right when she needed him most. And he'd gone. He'd left her. Alone.

Chapter 14

TOMMY RE-ENTERED SARAH'S apartment and closed the door behind him. He leaned against it for a long moment. He felt off balance, but that was nothing new—losing Charlotte had been like losing his gravitational center. He had to hang on with everything he had to keep from spinning off into the void. If it weren't for Nellie, he would have let go long ago.

What was taking Sarah so long? He wandered through the living room and into the bedroom, hoping he wouldn't interrupt her packing her underwear or anything else inappropriate. He found her sitting on her bed cross-legged, an open suitcase stuffed with clothing beside her. She was staring at the digital screen on her camera.

"I think I know where we should go," she said without looking up at him. "I want to retrace my steps, follow my path from Saturday."

Tommy considered. It was Monday morning; the trail would probably be deserted. "Last place anyone would be looking for you."

She glanced up, the camera rising with her as if it were part of her, and smiled. "My thoughts exactly. We can use the GIS info and these photos as a map. Maybe something there will trigger a memory—after all, it was the last place I chose to go, right?"

He didn't want to give her false hope. "Actually, with a traumatic brain injury, it's often those memories closest to the time of the trauma that remain permanently erased."

"Oh." Her mouth worked back and forth as she considered that. "Still, better than staying here staring at stuff that feels like it belongs at someone else's garage sale, right?"

"Sure. Finish packing and we'll get going."

She sprang off the bed, carefully returned her camera to its case, closed the suitcase, and zippered it shut. He hauled it off the bed—not very heavy; she really did travel light. "Sure this is everything you need?"

"No, but it's everything I could think of. Packing is easy when you have no clue what clothes you like or which shoes are the most comfortable." She spun around, taking in the room as if she'd never see it again. "I have no idea what I'm leaving behind. Everything feels so…sterile?" She heaved her shoulders in a sigh. "Leave your attachments behind. That's like Zen or Catholic or something? Right?"

"No idea. Sounds kind of like the Hare Krishnas."

"Hare Krishnas?" Her eyes closed as she concentrated. "I'm seeing orange, like wings flapping, swirling around…oh! I remember. They're a dance troupe?"

"Close enough. Let's go."

He ushered her out to the Volvo. Traffic was light, and a little more than thirty minutes later, they left the narrow two-lane highway that twisted around the mountain, turning onto a gravel drive leading upward. Passing beneath the shadows of tall hemlocks, they arrived at the parking lot at Fiddler's Knob.

During the drive they'd learned that Sarah didn't like rock, country, pop, or cool jazz, but preferred classical music or NPR. She knew some of the presidents but not all of them, remembered the major wars but wasn't sure who ISIS was—although to be truthful, who really was?—and she knew how to drive a straight stick, her left foot reflexively mimicking Tommy's movements as he shifted gears.

The parking lot barely earned its name. It was a simple hard-packed dirt clearing with space for maybe ten cars max. The sign for the trail was its only adornment—that, plus a notice with hunting regulations and the remains of the shattered car windows sparkling against the dirt. Apart from the Volvo, the lot was empty.

"You're sure about this?" Tommy asked while he undid his seat belt.

"Yes. It's better than sitting around worrying."

He couldn't argue with that. "Okay. But after a head injury you don't want to stress your body. If you get tired or dizzy or get a headache, tell me. And we go slow and easy."

"I'll be fine," she assured him. "I feel fine."

"It's strange. Most people after a concussion, they're fuzzy, little things confuse them. But you, you're so certain, so clear."

"Clear. I like that word. As if all those memories were a burden, blinding me, muddying things. I feel…light. Like I've shed a weight. Does that make sense?"

It did. But he didn't want to crush her mood with an explanation of *la belle indifférence* and the power of denial to protect a mind against overwhelming circumstances. So he merely nodded and got out of the car.

Sarah joined him, hoisting her camera bag over one shoulder as if it weighed nothing. It was almost noon, the sun not quite above the top of the mountain, leaving them in its shadow.

"I must have parked over there." Sarah pointed to the other side of the clearing as she peered into the camera's view screen.

"How can you tell?"

"Look at the angle of the shot of the sign. It's the first photo on the card." She thrust the camera at him. "Here. You follow through the camera while I see where my instincts take me."

The camera was heavier than he'd expected—and this was only the body with one small lens attached to it. She carried a selection of larger lenses in the bag slung over her shoulder. He quickly oriented himself to the camera's basic viewing functions, keeping his fingers away from anything that looked like it might alter her settings or take a picture, and followed her past the sign onto the trail.

The sunlight filtered through the trees in a cascade of pale gold ribbons that shifted with the wind. The forest was thick with pines, hemlocks, oaks, and maples, and the terrain on either side of the trail varied from moss-covered limestone ledges to spongy carpets of decaying leaves and pine needles. The scent was heavenly, waking Tommy up as if he'd been trapped within a long winter's slumber. In a way, he had been.

He pushed thoughts of his own problems aside as he focused on Sarah's photos, guiding them like landmarks on a tourist's map. Often they'd have to backtrack as Sarah's original path rambled back and forth away from the well-trodden main trail into the scrub and brush, searching out hidden gems of rock formations, plant life, and compositions of light and shadow.

"What's that?" He stopped to peer at the next photo. It was a close-up of a small, delicate flower—a pink lady's slipper. Beside it, on a bed of moss, was a bright metal object: a small, silver ballerina performing a pirouette. Except the leg holding her upright, the straight leg, had been broken off.

Tommy jerked upright, scanning his surroundings, feeling as if someone was watching him. That same sucker-punch feeling that came with being the butt of a sick joke.

No one was watching. No one was even near except Sarah, who was bent over examining a cluster of teaberry plants.

He sucked in his breath, bracing himself, and dared to glance back at the camera screen. It was still there. The charm, as broken as a promise, taunting him with impossible possibilities. He squinted, enlarging the image. How could this be happening?

"Sarah, look at this. Where did you take this?" His words

snapped through the air between them, but she didn't seem to understand his urgent need for answers.

Slowly she rose and took the camera from him. "Oh, I quite like that composition."

He tapped the screen, pointing to the broken dancer. "Where is it? The charm?"

"How should I know? Around here somewhere. Why?"

"My wife. She had a charm bracelet. When Nellie was born I gave her a ballerina charm exactly like that one." He crouched low to the ground, searching for the flower or any glint of metal.

She stared at him as if he'd gone mad. Maybe he had. "Tommy, there are millions of charms like that one."

"Not with the leg broken off. Nellie was playing with the bracelet and broke it just a few days before Charlotte went missing."

"There's no way—"

"Just help me find it. Please."

Without another word, she joined him in the hunt. It was backbreaking work, scouring the detritus beneath the trees. They went to the location of the next set of photos—an easily recognizable rock formation a few yards away—and Sarah worked her way back along one side of the trail while Tommy took the other.

Then he spotted it. A pillow of moss tucked in below a rotting log. The flower with its dark pink "slipper" dangling down between two shiny green leaves. And beside it, the charm.

He sank onto his knees, the damp from the ground

seeping into his bones.

Sarah came up behind him, taking pictures, the sound of the camera drowning out the rest of the world. Or maybe that was his shock, pushing everything else aside.

"Maybe you should leave it there," she said. "In case it really is hers?"

She was right. If this was evidence, he should leave it for the police. But he also knew there was no way in hell Burroughs would ever come out here. For what? A charm that was no doubt sold in thousands of stores across the country? Even the broken leg wouldn't convince Burroughs—he'd say that this charm design probably just had a weak, defective spot. If one broke, they probably all did.

He used a leathery maple leaf to coax the charm free from the moss. Up close, there was still nothing to indicate that it was Charlotte's. There was no special inscription, no unique markings other than the broken leg.

"Tommy." Sarah sank down beside him and rested her palm on his shoulder. She sighed. "It can't be hers."

"Why not?"

"Because look at it. It's pristine. Lying on top of the moss. If it had been out here a year, it would be all grimy and covered with leaves and dirt."

"Maybe you moved it? To compose your photo? Cleaned it up?"

She frowned, looked into the camera for answers. "I can't remember, but looking at all these, nothing appears to have been staged. In fact, there are a few that would have been better compositions if I had rearranged the elements. But I didn't."

"Well, then maybe it wasn't here a year." He dared to meet her gaze. "Maybe she was here. Herself. Maybe she's still alive."

Chapter 15

After her confrontation with Jesus-nailed-to-the-cross, Nellie couldn't stomach staying where his eyes followed her everywhere she went. She ran past the altar, barely remembering to genuflect and cross herself, and into the forbidden, secret room behind it.

It wasn't so much a room as a closet. There was a large T-shaped wooden thing that seemed to be a coat stand for the pretty priest coats they only wore during Mass. The one hanging there now, waiting for Father Stravinsky, was cream with gold trim and tiny flowers sewn all over it. There was also a table with two gold chalices, a wash bowl, pretty embroidered towels—the kind Mommy said were only for show, not to actually wipe her hands on—and a glass jug of wine. Another crucifix hung above the table, but it was small, not scary at all.

On the other side of the closet was a door leading out. Nellie opened it and peeked through. It opened onto a hallway that ran along the back of the church. There was a door going outside, and past it a set of steps leading down. The stairs looked like a good place to hide until her class finished Mass; then she could sneak back into the school.

Checking again that no one was around to see her, she left the closet and raced to the staircase. It led down to a musty hallway, illuminated by only a few naked bulbs. It smelled of cleaning chemicals and old paper.

The first door led to a room with a big furnace that looked scary, so she shut it and kept going. The next doors were storage rooms. One had boxes and boxes of paper—this was where the musty smell came from. Nellie wrinkled her nose; she'd be sneezing the entire time if she hid in there.

She found a room filled with athletic equipment stacked in racks, and across the hall was a room filled with folded canvas tents—even more smelly than the room with the papers.

The next door, though, opened onto a magical world. She stood in the doorway, stunned. The Christmas nativity scene—except for the straw and twinkle lights—was arranged before her, larger than life. Joseph stood behind his wife, protecting her and watching over their baby, just like Daddy did—only without the beard. The baby lay in the cradle, arms and legs kicking like he was laughing.

But it was Mary who held Nellie's attention. The Blessed Virgin Mother knelt, arms spread as if ready to hold her baby in her lap, smiling the same smile Mommy used to give Nellie. That smile was almost the only thing Nellie could remember every day; other things came and went before she could figure out a way to hang on to them, to keep them safe forever—or at least until Mommy came back.

She stepped inside the room, its only light the gleam from the hall and the wispy smudge from a tiny basement window high in the wall. She stopped and held her breath, half-expecting someone—the angel or one of the wise men—to tell her to leave, that bad girls like her didn't belong here, didn't deserve a mommy and daddy to look after them. But no one moved. No one said anything.

She closed the door behind her. Her eyes adjusted to the dim light and she carefully crept over to the Blessed Virgin—Mary looked so much happier before she became the Lady of Sorrows and someone pierced her heart with a sword—and crawled onto her lap. The statue was wood, hard, with tiny ridges where they'd carved the folds of her dress, but Nellie didn't care. She twisted her body, fitting just right, head resting against one of Mary's arms. Mary beamed down at her as if she'd been waiting forever for just this moment to hold Nellie.

Nellie had promised herself a long time ago that she wouldn't cry anymore. Crying meant people asking questions she had no answers to. Like why was she crying, and when was her mother coming back, and didn't she want to be a big, brave girl?

Or worse, crying meant seeing her father blink back his own tears before he'd pretend to be big and brave and strong. He'd wrap his arms around her, pulling her tight against his chest to where she felt his heart beating, and she knew it was breaking and she'd only cry harder for them both.

But here, that promise held no power. Joseph seemed to

nod to her, the light coming from above and behind him, telling her it was all right: he'd watch over her and no one would know. And Mary cradled her and smiled Mommy's secret smile that was just for Nellie. Everything was going to be okay, that smile said. After all, she was the Mother of God; she should know.

Nellie missed that smile so much. She curled up and sobbed, until finally she fell into an exhausted sleep.

LUCY AND WASH were on the phone with Burroughs, reviewing the credit card reports Burroughs had run on Sarah after he'd verified her social security number and identity.

"Her car getting broken into was a real blessing," he told them. "Since her wallet was stolen, we can investigate her as a possible identity theft victim, which gives us access to her recent transaction history."

"You're placing a hold on her credit for her, right?" Last thing Sarah needed was to regain her memory only to find her finances ruined.

"Yeah, what little there is. Only two credit cards, both with the wrong address, one with her name spelled B-r-o-w-n-e and the other with Sarah spelled without the H. Like she's leaving a false trail for anyone looking for her."

"Fits with her fleeing a stalker," Lucy told Burroughs, looking over Wash's shoulder while he scrolled through the credit card statements Burroughs had emailed.

"They both were used for small purchases," Wash said. "Less than twenty-five dollars. Mainly magazine subscriptions—

sent to two more false addresses."

"What the hell is she hiding from?" Burroughs said.

"You mean *who* the hell. Anything on the dress and card TK brought you?"

She could almost hear his eye roll over the phone. "You're joking, right? A few smudged prints, but I'm certain they're all from Sarah and your people." She noticed he avoided mentioning Tommy by name. "I tagged and bagged them just to preserve chain of custody, but there's nothing helpful. I sent TK back to stay with Sarah."

Interpretation: to relieve Tommy so he wasn't left alone with Sarah. While she appreciated Burroughs' help and his protective instincts, it was her team, and she'd run it the way she thought best. She was about to tell him exactly that when TK walked in the door. "Thanks, Burroughs. Let us know if you turn up anything else."

"You, too." He hung up.

"That was Burroughs?" TK asked. "He about laughed me out of the station house when I showed up with that damned dress."

"Don't take it personally. He's just frustrated. Hard enough to help a woman who has lost her memory, but looks like Sarah was deliberately hiding her tracks even before she hit her head."

TK flounced into the chair beside Wash, angling herself so she had a good view of his screens. "I know. You should see her place—everything she owns fits into one suitcase."

"You're one to talk," Wash said.

"That's because I was homeless," she retorted. TK wasn't ashamed of her past; she saw it as a failing of society when a decorated veteran working two jobs couldn't pay for a roof over her head, not a failing of her own. "Sarah has a home. Only it sure as hell doesn't feel like one."

"So you and Tommy didn't find anything."

"Not a takeout menu, no pizza coupons, not even a fridge magnet. Only thing in her trash was the receipt Tommy sent to Wash."

"Yeah, about that..."

Lucy turned to the analyst. "What?"

"Well, I'm not sure if it means anything. The receipt is from the same Sheetz Tommy's wife was last seen at. I mean, I know it's a year apart, but isn't that kind of weird?"

TK stretched her legs out and crossed them at the ankles. "I doubt it. That stretch of highway, your choices are limited. Sheetz or keep going to the interstate with that skeevy truck stop. If you're a woman, you always go for Sheetz."

"Cleanest restrooms around," Lucy explained. "TK's right. I've been there myself."

"Okay, so just a freaky, small-world thing." Wash shrugged and cleared his screen. "Then we've officially got nothing."

He and TK looked to Lucy as if expecting her to conjure a woman's life from thin air. "Not nothing," Lucy said. "We have a vulnerable victim who is a potential target."

"And who would have no idea if she came face to face with her stalker." TK shuddered. "I can not even imagine being that powerless."

"Thoughts on the best way to protect her while we keep running the databases and track down any family?"

"What about having her bunk here?" TK said. "If it's okay with Valencia. I'll crash now, pull guard duty tonight."

"Guard duty?" Wash sounded alarmed. "You really think someone could track her back here? And get through Valencia's security?"

"The police put her out there on every screen in the area with the public service announcements before Burroughs canceled them," Lucy answered. "Anyone looking for Sarah knows she's working with us, that she has no clue who's stalking her. What better time to strike?"

CHAPTER 16

TOMMY ROLLED THE tiny ballerina over in his palm, still protected from his flesh by the maple leaf. Sarah was right: there was no way to be certain it was Charlotte's charm. Hell, he couldn't even be one hundred percent certain it was the same size and pose as Charlotte's dancing girl. Had she had both her arms up like this one? Or had one been stretched out and the other curved into the air?

He blinked back his confusion. A year was simply too long for a man's mind not to lose grasp of essential bits and pieces. It was hard enough to keep hold of Charlotte's laugh, the special sly smile she had for him when they were alone in bed, the way her hands and feet were always moving, dancing to invisible music...

"What should we do?" Sarah asked.

"I don't know." He shoved the charm, leaf and all, into his jacket pocket and stood. "Keep following your trail, I guess."

She kept hold of the camera—a good thing, the way his

hands were trembling—and led the way. They both moved more slowly now, searching for...what? If he didn't know, how could she?

They entered a tunnel formed by centuries-old mountain laurel. Dark foliage and intertwined branches created the walls and roof, and thousands of pale flowers hung from stems, like stars showered across the night sky. The air was still here, noise muffled as if they stood apart from the rest of the world. Sheltered.

Sarah stopped in the middle of the tunnel to look around, both through her camera and her eyes. "It's so beautiful. How could I have forgotten this?"

Tommy could only nod; he didn't trust his voice. All he could think was how much Charlotte would love this place.

"I'm sorry." Sarah turned to him, touching his arm. She did that a lot. Whoever she was, she was the touchy-feely type. Not that he minded, it was just that he wasn't used to anyone touching him. No one had, not like that, gentle, familiar reminders that he wasn't alone—not since Charlotte.

"My missing memories must seem so small compared to losing your wife," she continued. "I'm so sorry. Are you okay?"

"You're right," he said after a pause. "That charm can't be hers. She wasn't here."

"You mean she wasn't here now, without you? Does that mean you're giving up? You think she's dead?" Sarah raised her camera, framing his image, then lowered it quickly. "I'm sorry. I don't mean to—"

"No, no, it's fine. I just, I haven't—there hasn't been

anyone I could talk to about this. I mean, I don't know what's more painful. Hoping she's still alive out there, somewhere, living her life, or..."

"Maybe she's like me?" she said brightly. "Maybe she has amnesia. That's why she hasn't come home. As soon as she remembers..."

"If she's like you, she'd have people like me and the police to help her. Someone would have recognized her from the missing persons reports. Someone would have found her, brought her home."

Sarah hung her head. "You're right, I guess."

"Funny thing is, the police, except for Burroughs, think she is still alive. They think she ran away." He hauled in a breath. Here, sheltered by an otherworldly cocoon of green, he could speak the truth. Finally, for the first time in a year. "Maybe she did."

"Really? Why?"

"I don't know. But when I look back, she was acting strangely in the weeks before she vanished. Nothing I can be certain about, nothing I could ever explain to the police. She wasn't sleeping well. I'd find her talking on the phone at strange times, a strange look on her face. A few times, I came home from the ER and she wasn't home yet. She'd always show up later with a bag of groceries, saying she stopped at Giant Eagle, but, it never felt…right."

"Doesn't sound like a lot to go on."

"I know. That's why I never told anyone else. Maybe it's all in my imagination, grasping for hints that aren't there, searching for any kind of explanation."

They passed through the tunnel and back into the light. The forest came alive around them once more, and Tommy blinked as a ray of sunshine angled through the treetops. The trail grew steeper here, but Sarah didn't seem to mind.

They were almost at the plateau halfway up the mountain where the old iron furnace stood. The trail forked at the furnace, one path leading up to follow the steeper ridgeline along the top of the mountain, the other winding down the backside of the mountain and circling around, ending up just above the parking lot where they'd begun.

"Could she have been having an affair?" Sarah asked in a soft tone as they walked.

"Now you sound like the cops. That was the first thing they asked. Well, second. Right after they asked if I killed her." He stepped over a fallen branch. "No, I don't think so. I think if it was something like that, if she really wanted someone else, she would have just told me. One thing about Charlotte, she didn't pull punches. And she never would have left Nellie to be with another man. That much I'm certain of."

"Okay, then. Something at work? You said she was a social worker, right? Maybe a case got too personal?"

"No. She'd been working with the rehab unit the past three months. A nice break from rotating through the ER or with the trauma team or OB-GYN."

"Hmm. Her family?"

"Solid. And I don't have any, not local, so no meddling in-laws for her to worry about. She did volunteer with the women's shelter, but that was mainly answering phones, putting together care packages, arranging transportation and logistics like visits to attorneys and the like."

"Still, working with victims of domestic violence—don't they worry about abusers coming after them? I heard about a shooting where the man broke into the shelter his wife was staying at, killed four women and then himself."

"It's the one thing Charlotte didn't talk about. She was very serious about confidentiality, for just those reasons, to protect the women and children at the shelter. But she's volunteered there for years; she wouldn't have continued if it was dangerous."

"Then what else could it be? If not something at home or work? Unless—" Her eyes grew wide. "Maybe she saw something she shouldn't? Like a drug deal or mob hit or something? Or maybe someone was stalking her, like whoever that creep is who sent me that dress? Sneaking around so she wasn't even certain herself, not until it was too late."

Tommy had no answer. Those and a thousand other scenarios had been suggested and examined by him, the police, the press, Charlotte's parents, the private investigators they'd hired, and everyone he'd ever met, it seemed. "What-ifs don't help," he said. "Not when there's no evidence."

They reached the old stone iron furnace standing at the center of the plateau. The pyramid-shaped structure had crumbled with time but still stood a good thirty feet high. On two sides, arched openings as tall as Tommy led into the central area below the chimney, where the heat would have been concentrated. A waterfall above created a stream that trickled down past the furnace before continuing down the backside of the mountain. When the furnace had been in use, the trees had been cut to burn inside it, leaving the area clear except for a few bold saplings now taking hold among the limestone.

The views were stunning. Western Pennsylvania this time of year was a glorious carpet of lush greens and golds.

But all of it was lost on Tommy. He slid his hand into his pocket and grasped the maple leaf with its lost dancer. Hope was dangerous. He'd learned that this past year, following false lead after false lead.

But, like any junkie, he just couldn't help himself.

His phone rang, the sound an intrusion, shattering the tranquility of their surroundings. It was Gloria, Charlotte's mother. She usually checked in with him around lunchtime to solidify plans for Nellie's pickup from school.

"Where have you been?" she demanded, with none of the gentle calm she usually radiated. "The school's been trying to call you."

He glanced at his phone. One bar—which meant probably none while he'd been below the plateau. "What's wrong? Did she start another fight?" Nellie's tantrums at school had been almost as bad as her ones at home. "What did Sister Agnes say?"

"Tommy." Anguish flooded her voice. "She's missing. Nellie's gone."

CHAPTER 17

TOMMY TURNED IN a circle, still clutching the phone, scanning the horizon as if he'd suddenly developed superpowers and could see Nellie from the mountainside. This couldn't be happening. Not again.

"No," he gasped. "What—how—"

"We're at the school, Peter and I. Searching the grounds with the teachers and staff. Sister Agnes is certain Nellie is still on campus, but there are so many places a small child can hide—"

"Did you call the police?"

She hesitated. "Do you want us to call the police? Sister Agnes thought we should wait. You know how Nellie's been acting lately. Running off and hiding, sulking—"

"Sister Agnes is worried about the school's reputation," he snapped, starting for the trailhead then stopping when the reception grew fuzzy. He backed up a few steps to avoid losing the call. "Call the police. Now."

He glanced up, trying to fight the garrote tightening

around his throat, forcing himself to take slow, deep breaths. He wanted to hurl the phone, to howl at the brilliant sun overhead, to hammer his fist into the stone of the iron furnace. But instead he swallowed, forcing his emotions aside. For Nellie. He had to stay calm, had to think, focus. He was all she had.

No, that wasn't true. She was all *he* had.

"What's wrong?" Sarah asked, her face a blur until he blinked and focused.

He didn't answer. Leaning against the lichen-covered furnace, the hard limestone biting into his back and the smell of ancient charcoal escaping the structure to choke the air, he blinked at the sun. Then he called Lucy. "It's me. I just heard from Nellie's school. She's missing."

Lucy didn't waste any words on sympathy. Good thing, because he probably would have snapped if she had. "Any signs of forced abduction?"

"No. Her teachers think she's still on campus, probably hiding. She's been acting out, throwing tantrums."

"Still. She's only five. Are the police involved?"

"Not yet, but I told them to call them. Will you—"

"I'm on my way. Our Lady of Sorrows, right?"

"Right. I'm with Sarah at Fiddler's Knob. It'll take us a while—"

"Try not to worry. I've got it covered."

"Thanks, Lucy." He hung up. The phone was a weight, heavier than a black hole, pulling him to his knees, pain spiraling through him. He fought the panic attack, the elephant sitting on his chest, smothering the life out of him. No time to fall apart. He had to go, had to get off this damn mountain.

Sarah knelt in front of him and eased the phone from his numb fingers. "Look at me," she coaxed. "It'll be all right. Just come with me."

Their trip down the mountain was a blur. She moved fast, always holding his elbow as if guiding a blind man, steering him around obstacles he was oblivious to, talking in a calm voice that became his touchstone. Finally they reached the parking lot, where the Volvo sat all alone in the shadow of the mountain.

"I'll drive," she said, taking the keys from him.

He stumbled around to the passenger door, barely able to get into the car and fasten his seat belt.

"You sure?" he asked, although it was already too late, she was turning the key in the ignition.

"Muscle memory," she answered, zooming them back out of the lot and shifting gears without the clutch slipping. "But I've never driven a car as ancient as this one. At least, I don't think I have."

"It's not ancient, it's a classic. Only has two hundred thousand on it." His reply was automatic. Another milestone Charlotte had missed—they'd been planning to do something fun to celebrate the Volvo's "car birthday," as Nellie had called it. But sometime last month, the day had come and gone without anyone—including Tommy, who must have been driving—even noticing.

Nellie...if he lost her, too......

Sarah kept talking, filling the silence, but Tommy wasn't listening. He was staring at his phone, willing the bars to stabilize. As soon as they turned onto the main highway, reception looked solid once more, and he called Lucy. "Anything?"

"I just got here. The school is on lockdown and they're taking roll call of all the students. With the fence surrounding the school, the convent, and the church, the place is fairly secure. The only point of access would be the church since it's open to the public."

"They take the children to Mass every day."

"Okay, that complicates things. Wait, here's the principal. What's her name again?"

"Sister Agnes."

"Give me a minute."

Tommy's body was rigid as he clutched the phone, the scenery rushing past like a freight train barreling down on him. Sarah placed her hand on his thigh. "She'll be all right."

"Don't say that." The words emerged like a slap, but he didn't apologize. He'd lived through too many warm thoughts and prayers and empty platitudes—useless, all of them. He still returned home each night to an empty bed, a house that had been bled dry of its joy, a child he could not comfort with the truth.

Sarah nodded and returned her gaze to the road. She was a fast driver, and they made it to the Parkway in record time. Still on the phone, Lucy was now arguing with several people; he recognized Sister Agnes's voice, but now two men had joined in on the conversation. Something about permission or rules, private versus public property...the words blurred into meaningless noise until Lucy cut through them, taking control with a tone of command he'd never heard from her before. Was this what she'd been like at the FBI?

She got back on the phone. "We got the search organized. I have the cops setting up road blocks and a perimeter, but turns out the teacher isn't quite sure how long she's been gone, so that might be problematic."

"I don't understand."

"Whether she left on her own or was taken or even picked up by a Good Samaritan after getting lost, we have no way to know how far she could have gotten without knowing when she left. I think we need to declare her a critical missing person."

From her tone, Tommy knew she would have already done that if he hadn't been on the phone with her. Was fairly certain she wasn't even asking his permission, just taking the extra twenty seconds to warn him. Because he knew exactly what happened when word of a critical missing person—especially a child, but it also happened with their pretty social worker mothers—was made public.

A media feeding frenzy. And Tommy would be the chum in the water.

They couldn't hurt him any more than the pain slicing through him now, the pain of not knowing that Nellie was safe. Pain he barely felt as his mind returned to the cold, numb vault he'd buried himself in after Charlotte had gone.

How can this be happening again? What if she's gone, what if some madman has her... One last shred of panic, before he swallowed it whole, knowing he'd pay the price later—nothing stayed buried forever.

"Tommy?"

"Do it. Make the call."

CHAPTER 18

DURING THE COURSE of her career, Lucy had noted that during any critical missing person case, especially those involving children, two emotions invariably surfaced: fear and anger.

The fear she understood. A missing child was any parent's worst nightmare. The anger usually took the form of guilt and blame—also understandable. But as she marshaled the police and school staff to effectively search for Nellie Worth, she encountered an emotional response that was unusual: denial.

It came from the school principal, a middle-aged nun whose stern countenance radiated a steadfast refusal to relinquish control over the situation.

"There is no 'situation' here," Sister Agnes told Lucy. "This is totally unnecessary. The girl isn't missing. Eleanor is a willful, stubborn child crying out for attention. I tell you, she's hiding."

"But you searched the school and didn't find any sign of her." They sat in a dark-paneled office with one narrow window that cast Sister Agnes in a reddish glow that was less halo and more hellfire. The principal had offered Lucy a straight-backed wooden chair with uneven legs, as if designed to force whoever occupied it to spend all their energy on not toppling. It was an interrogation technique Lucy was well aware of, dating back to the Gestapo.

"Mrs. Guardino, do you have any idea how conniving and inventive a five-year-old girl mad at the world can be? By responding in such a dramatic and excessive manner, you are merely reinforcing her immature and inappropriate behavior."

"You make her sound like an unrepentant convict. She's five. She has no idea where her mother has been for the past year or even if she's still alive."

"Exactly. The child must learn to place her faith in God's plan and accept His will."

Cold comfort. Lucy wondered if maybe Sister Agnes saw herself as a prison warden, shouldering the burden of rehabilitating young sinners before releasing them into the world at large. She tried a new tactic. "Perhaps I could speak with her teacher? Gain some insights into Nellie's behavior?" The nun hesitated. "After all, the sooner we find her hiding place, the sooner we'll be gone and you can resume your normal routine."

"Very well." The nun rose in an abrupt motion. If she'd been wearing an old-fashioned habit with the veil and skirts that fell to the ground, the sweeping movement would have created a fine bit of drama. As it was, her actions merely caused the cross hanging at the front of her turtleneck to shudder.

Sister Agnes led Lucy down a hall decorated with art

projects and posters celebrating school events, saints, and martyrs. Sister Agnes opened a classroom door and entered without knocking.

A circle of children sat on mats on the floor listening to a young woman read them a story. *Daniel in the lion's den,* Lucy recognized before the woman stopped and everyone looked up.

"Miss Cortez, this is Mrs. Guardino. She'd like to talk to you about Eleanor Worth."

Miss Cortez leapt up from where she sat cross-legged on the floor, stretching a hand to take Lucy's. "Ava, please. Thank God you're here. We're all so worried."

Sister Agnes made a hrumphing noise at that. "I'll leave you to it. I'd best oversee those police trampling through the convent and rectory. When Monsignor returns from Harrisburg, he is going to be extremely unhappy." Her glare at Ava Cortez made it very clear who would be taking the blame.

Ava flushed and looked down. She didn't glance back up until the door had shut behind Sister Agnes. "She's right. This is all my fault."

The children behind her sat obediently, watching the two adults with appraisal—except for two little boys and a girl who were busy exchanging glances and smirks with each other.

"It's nice to meet you, Ava. Would it be okay if I spoke with you and the children about when and where everyone saw Nellie last?"

"Of course. That will be easy, because we do everything together as a class, don't we, class? We stick together, right?"

"Yes, Miss Cortez," came a well-rehearsed chorus. The

three children in the back were practically snickering their response.

"Class, this is Mrs. Guardino. She's here to help find Nellie. No one is in trouble, we just need to know if you saw or heard anything."

"Thanks," Lucy told Ava. Then she turned to the children, who all had their heads tilted back, staring up at her wide-eyed as if she were a visitor from another planet. "I'll start with those three, in the back."

"Matthew, Glinda, and Joseph," Ava replied. "Why don't you show Mrs. Guardino our art corner?" She turned to Lucy. "We've been creating stained glass windows with tissue paper."

"Wonderful. Show me." Lucy inserted the slightest tone of command into her voice, aiming it at the trio of troublemakers. The two boys stopped smirking and shut their lips tight. The girl, however, grinned back and looked Lucy straight in the eye. Ahhh...the leader of the pack.

The girl, Glinda—really? What were her parents thinking?—simpered, stood, and took Lucy by the hand to lead her to the back corner near the windows. She wore a pink dress that flounced and made rustling noises as if she wore old-fashioned crinolines. Perfect Princess type, Lucy thought. Megan had skipped that phase, except for playing the occasional dress-up and a few months of ballet before she discovered soccer and decided she was a tomboy at heart.

The art corner was behind a waist-high partition of shelving that contained supplies in labeled bins. No rugs here, just easy-to-clean linoleum. There was a low, round table stained with paint and glitter, with colorful child-sized chairs around it. Glinda took a seat in front of the window, arranging herself like a queen taking her throne. The two boys stood to one side, watching warily.

Glinda folded her hands in front of her and nodded to the chair opposite, as if daring Lucy to fold her adult-sized body into the tiny chair. Lucy didn't take the bait. Instead, she perched herself on the radiator that ran in front of the window, placing her body between Glinda and the boys, effectively dividing their forces. The boys sat down in the chairs on Lucy's left. From her seat higher than them, she could see all three while shifting the boys' attention from Glinda to her.

"You guys are Nellie's friends, right?"

The boys nodded glumly while the girl beamed. "Of course we are. No one else would be," Glinda said. "But Jesus teaches us to have compassion for those less fortunate."

"And Nellie is less fortunate?" Lucy kept her tone neutral. Glinda seemed the know-it-all type. "How so?"

Glinda leaned forward and dropped her voice. "Her mother's gone. And she lives with a monster."

"A monster?"

"That's what my mother told Mrs. Kersavage. She said the poor, poor girl should be taken away from that monster of a man."

"Is that what happened today? Did someone come take her? Rescue her, maybe?"

The boys squirmed and looked at each other. Glinda glared at them, and they stilled. "Maybe."

"What do you guys think?" Lucy turned to block the boys' view of Glinda so they had no choice but to focus on her. "You seem pretty smart to me. I'll bet you know what happened. Where is Nellie? Is she with anyone?"

Both boys looked down as if mesmerized by the paint stains on the table. Matthew shifted in his seat and mumbled something.

"What was that?"

"It was his fault." The mumbling turned into a whine.

"Nah-uh. Glinda dared me to kick it over the wall."

"So you guys were playing? That's okay. No one's going to get in trouble for that." Lucy leaned forward as if part of the conspiracy. "What happened?"

"It was Nellie's fault," Glinda said from behind Lucy. Couldn't resist regaining the spotlight—exactly what Lucy had hoped. "She didn't have anyone to play with—she never does—and we told her she could play with us but only if she played ball-fetcher."

"So you guys were kicking a ball around and Nellie ran to retrieve it?"

"We were having a kicking contest," Glinda explained, as if that made it legit.

Joseph finally spoke up. "And I won," he said. "I kicked it all the way over the wall."

"But then the bell rang and we had to come back to class." Glinda leaned back and crossed her arms over her chest, daring Lucy to challenge her. "It's not our fault that Nellie didn't get in before the doors closed."

“And she hasn’t been in class since?”

“No. Miss Cortez would have noticed, but Sally Richards tripped and got an ouchie and was crying and then it was time to get cleaned up for Mass and then when we came back after lunch she said where’s Nellie? But we don’t know where Nellie is *now,* so we couldn’t bear false witness. Because that’s a sin.” Glinda finished with a jerk of her chin, her story, alibi, and rationalization all solid.

“Where was Nellie when you saw her last?”

Matthew answered. “She’s skinny. Was trying to get through the fence—I thought she was stuck, but when we got inside, I looked out the window and she was gone.”

“You looked out these windows? Can you show me where she was?”

He stood and marched up to stand beside Lucy, pointing out the window and across the playground to the wrought iron fence that wrapped around the compound. There was a gap in the hedge, just wide enough for a skinny girl to slide through the arborvitae and shimmy between the iron bars.

Beyond the bars was the church’s parking lot. And beyond that the street. Where anyone could have stopped for a little girl searching for a lost ball.

CHAPTER 19

THE STREETS AROUND Our Lady of Sorrows were blocked by police cars and barricades. Tommy had to repeat his story three times and show his ID before they finally waved Sarah into the parking lot beside the playground. He was out of the car before she turned it off, running toward the wrought iron gate at the school's entrance.

TK was waiting for him there.

"Did you find her?" he asked as TK led him and Sarah into the playground. He spotted Don Burroughs standing with several other policemen, and from the expression on the detective's face, he knew the answer.

"No," TK said. "Lucy was able to find witnesses who saw her leaving the school grounds several hours ago."

"Wait." He spun to her but felt disconnected from his movements and his words, as if the entire world lagged a second behind. "Nellie *left?* How? Why?"

"The kids said they were playing, kicked a ball over the

fence, and she squeezed between the bars to chase after it."

"Which way? I need to start there—" He'd already turned to leave, anxious to do something, but she grabbed his arm and pulled him back.

"You can't, Tommy. They need you here. We've a lot of people searching for Nellie, but we need to follow procedure so we don't miss anything." Her tone was gentle, as if instructing a child how to perform the complex act of standing still.

Every cell in his body strained to be released to join the hunt, but he took a breath and nodded. How well he remembered this, having a role to play: the stalwart, helpless family standing by, anxiously waiting. A role he despised for its absolute powerlessness. He needed to do something, anything, not stand around doing nothing.

He scrubbed his face, turning in a full circle, not remembering what came next.

TK seemed to understand, filling in the blanks for him. "Burroughs asked if you have a recent photo he can use. We're still searching here—between the school, church, rectory, and convent, there's a lot of ground to cover. But in the meantime, he's getting the ball rolling on a public appeal. He'll need a description of what she's wearing as well."

Tommy nodded, his lips suddenly too numb to form words. Sarah touched his arm in that way she had, but he barely felt it. "I'd like to help," she told TK. "Maybe I can join the search?"

"Of course. Check in with Burroughs. He'll tell you where to go."

"Will you be okay?" Sarah asked, squeezing Tommy's arm then letting go.

He hauled in a breath. "Yes. Thanks for helping."

She left to join Burroughs. Tommy watched her, his vision dark around the edges.

"Tommy?" TK said. She might have been saying more, but he missed it. "The photo?"

He slid his phone free, his fingers hitting the wrong spots on the screen as he tried to pull up the photo gallery. TK took it from him, tapped the screen for a few moments, then held it up for his approval. "How's this one? Okay?"

It was Nellie dressed for Easter. He had more recent photos, but he understood, somewhere in the dim recesses of his mind, that TK wanted a photo that clearly showed Nellie's height and full face. Next she'd choose a close-up to accompany it. And then she'd be asking about distinguishing marks...

Time fractured, folding over itself as he remembered giving Burroughs Charlotte's details, finding the right photos for the missing person flyers and then choosing different ones for the media and website her father set up, never knowing if choosing the wrong photo might somehow lead the public to not recognize Charlotte.

"A mole," he said before TK could ask. "On her left ankle. About a centimeter in diameter. And a small scar below her chin from when she fell off the swing set last year."

"Okay. I'll let Burroughs know." She left him to approach the detective.

Tommy stood alone. Alone amid the chaos. Helpless.

Worthless. Lost.

In the ER his job was to control chaos. He was no miracle worker, never had a surgeon's ego, fantasizing playing at God. He was simply a man who healed what he could as best he could.

Life and death decisions. Allocating resources and stretching them to meet overwhelming demand. Facing the families of the patients he lost. All of these he dealt with everyday. But that was life BC—before Charlotte went, when he'd been in control, before his power was stripped.

Even now, in his new, fragile life AC, after Charlotte, he thought he'd managed okay, fooled most people, played his new roles well. And always his priority was Nellie. Protecting her at all costs, even if it meant leaving the job he loved, forging a new dependency on Charlotte's parents, living in limbo.

But limbo was a temporary dwelling. Sooner or later, you had to ascend into Heaven or fall into Hell.

As Tommy stood there, activity swirling around him, he closed his eyes and felt the flames singe him.

AS NELLIE SLEPT in the arms of Holy Mary, Mother of God, she dreamed of Jesus raising the dead. They'd learned about Lazarus and how his family had to wait days before he returned to them.

Lying in the embrace of the smiling Virgin, somewhere in the deep recesses of her mind, Nellie found new hope. Miss Cortez had told them about how when God created the world in only six days, it didn't mean six human days, but six of God's days, which could have been a really, really long time. Well, maybe being missing was like waiting to be raised up by Jesus—and maybe three days in Jesus-time was like a year in Nellie-time.

In her dreams, she chased after her mother, playing tag in a large field of wildflowers so bright their colors ran together like a rainbow. But as fast as Nellie ran, she could never quite catch up...her mother was always just out of reach.

"Mommy!" she screamed, waking up so fast it was like a slap, stealing the breath from her, leaving her gasping as she fought free of the wooden embrace of the statue.

"Nellie, it's okay." A woman's voice soothed her.

Nellie blinked. The door was open; a woman knelt in front of her. Before Nellie could say anything, the woman pulled Nellie into her arms. "Oh, my poor baby. Are you okay?"

Still groggy from her restless sleep, Nellie wrapped her arms around the woman. She smelled so good. "Mommy?"

The woman—not Mommy, Nellie knew, but she also didn't want to know—pulled back the tiniest bit, although she kept one palm on Nellie's head, smoothing her hair, banishing the last trace of the nightmare. "Oh, sweetie, I'd love to be your mommy. We'd have so much fun. And I know how much you miss her. Is that why you came down here?"

It was too much to put into words, so Nellie just nodded and buried her head in the woman's hair again. The woman held her, patting her back. "My name's Sarah. I'm a friend of your dad's. He's very worried about you."

"Daddy's here?" Sarah asked the woman's hair.

"Yes. He was scared something happened to you."

"Like going missing? Like Mommy did?" That was just wrong. Nellie crinkled her face, thinking. "I wouldn't do that."

"But sweetie, you kind of did. You've been gone hours. Everyone is worried."

"Sister Agnes knows?" Sister Agnes was about the only person who scared her more than Jesus-nailed-to-the-cross.

"Yes, she does. But don't worry. I'll handle her. You're not in any trouble."

Nellie wasn't sure if she should trust the strange woman, this Sarah. But she hugged just like Mommy and she smelled just like Mommy and she was a friend of Daddy's… "Are you sure?"

"I'm sure." Sarah set Nellie on her feet and brushed off her dress, wiped her face. "Let's go find your daddy and tell him all about your adventures. Okay?"

Nellie took Sarah's hand—if she was going to face Sister Agnes, it was better to have an adult close by her side—and led the way out. She couldn't help pausing one last time at the door to look back at the Virgin Mother, but the magic was gone. The statue was just a hunk of dead wood.

Chapter 20

TOMMY STOOD ROOTED to his spot just inside the school's gate. In his haze, people came and went, asking questions, trying to get him to move inside where he could sit down, offering him water, distraction, privacy from the press who'd arrived and were camped beyond the fence. He barely heard them. All his attention was fixated on Don Burroughs. Any news, good or bad, Burroughs would get it first.

The detective was the center of a constant swirl of activity, speaking on his radio or cell phone, getting reports in person, scrutinizing a tablet computer screen. Occasionally he'd glance over to Tommy, give him a nod of acknowledgment. Not encouragement or false hope, just letting a terrified parent know that everything that could be done was being done.

Tommy wasn't sure if he nodded back or not. The world spun beneath his feet, oblivious to the petty concerns of the humans who trod upon it, and he was dizzy with powerlessness. There was nothing he could do to bring Nellie back. No thing.

His heart wasn't just broken by the thought. It was emptied. Cracked down to the foundation and bled dry.

"Daddy!"

He jerked his head up. Had he imagined the voice he'd been praying so desperately to hear?

"Daddy!"

Tommy saw Burroughs track to the church's back steps, delight filling his usually sour face, and he knew it wasn't a mirage—it was truth. He followed the detective's gaze just as a whirlwind of purple and pink raced across the playground and tackled him.

"Daddy!" The exclamation was muffled as he lifted Nellie into his arms, hugging her tight, her face against his shoulder. He opened his mouth but had no words.

Burroughs came over with Sarah.

"Where was she?" the detective asked. Before Sarah could answer, he clicked on his radio to recall his men and pass the word of the happy resolution.

"Church basement. She found the storeroom where they keep the holiday altar decorations," Sarah explained. "Was asleep in Mary's lap between the shepherds and Baby Jesus."

Tommy wiped his tears on Nellie's hair, blinked back more. Through their rainbow haze, he saw Sister Agnes approach to face Burroughs. "Detective, you have my most sincere apologies over this unnecessary disruption of your routine. I assure you, it will never happen again."

"I'm glad the girl was found, but—"

"I told them she wasn't lost. There will be consequences,

rest assured." The last was accompanied by a glare at Tommy and Nellie.

Tommy turned away, shielding Nellie from the nun's wrath, and came face to face with Sarah, who stood looking uncertain and very much alone. "Thank you," he told her. The words were cliché and meaningless, but he had no better to offer. "Thank you."

She blushed. "I was glad to help."

"I had an adventure, Daddy," Nellie announced, squirming to be let down. Tommy reluctantly placed her feet onto the ground, but kept a firm grip on her hand. She grabbed Sarah's hand with her free one, swinging between them. "Can Sarah come home with us?"

Tommy was so surprised, he didn't know what to say. Thankfully, Lucy appeared with Gloria and Peter, Charlotte's parents. Nellie squealed with delight as they rushed over to her. While her grandparents embraced her and fussed over her, Tommy tuned in to the conversation beside him. Burroughs was berating Sister Agnes for the slow response to a missing child.

"If this had been a real child abduction—" Burroughs started.

"But it wasn't," the nun interrupted, obviously on the defensive.

"Precious time would have been lost," Lucy added. "Time that could have meant a life lost."

The nun shook her head, her face flushed, eyes narrowed. She squared off her shoulders. "Very well. I will take it under advisement. Now that the situation is resolved, will you please leave so that we can resume our normal routine?"

"We'll make sure the school's board of directors and the bishop get a copy of our report and security evaluation," Burroughs said. Tommy was pretty sure the detective had enough real cases on his hands that he'd never go through with writing an actual report, but when he spotted the frown on Lucy's face, he knew *she'd* follow up. For sure.

After checking to see Nellie still safely ensconced between her grandparents, telling them of the wonders she'd found in the storage room, he turned to Burroughs and extended a hand. "Thank you."

To his surprise, Burroughs took it. Not a friendly handshake, just a quick acknowledgment. "You're welcome. I'm glad everything worked out. How's it going with Sarah's case?"

"We were interrupted," Lucy answered, "obviously. But we have a few leads."

Tommy's hand closed around the broken ballerina charm that had ridden in his pocket all the way from Fiddler's Knob. He almost told Burroughs about it, but hated looking the fool and distracting the detective, not after the man had already been pulled away from his duties to search for Nellie. Sarah was right. The charm was meaningless. A desperate man's misguided attempt to find a sign, any sign.

Lucy led Burroughs away to update him on Sarah's case, leaving Tommy with Sister Agnes and her wrath. "Mr. Worth," she started. "You need to take Eleanor home now."

"I'm sorry this happened. I'd like to keep her out of school for the rest of the week. Especially with all the attention on the anniversary of Charlotte's disappearance."

"No. I'm afraid you don't understand. Eleanor is expelled. This behavior simply will not be tolerated. We only have three weeks left in the school year. That will give you all summer to find an alternative placement for her. Perhaps one that is more suited to such an unruly and recalcitrant child."

"Wait, no—you can't seriously be blaming Nellie?"

She raised an eyebrow at him. "Of course not. I blame you. Please leave. Now. I'll send her belongings later. We've suffered enough disruption for one day on your account."

Before Tommy could modulate a reply that didn't include the kind of language that he would not use in front of Nellie, much less to a nun, the woman stalked away.

"Are you okay?" It was Sarah—she'd heard everything.

He glanced past her to where Nellie was showing her grandparents her escape route. Nellie's laughter washed over him, erasing his anger. "I'm fine. Excellent, in fact."

He covered the distance between him and his daughter in two oversized steps and scooped her up into his arms, twirling her as she giggled and beamed. "Come on, Nellie. Let's go home."

Chapter 21

LUCY WALKED WITH Burroughs out to his vehicle, a white departmental Impala. "You know I'm looking into Charlotte Worth's case, right?"

He shrugged, turning to lean against his car door, glancing past her to the schoolyard. "More eyes the better, I say. Worth hired a few PIs—or rather his in-laws did. They got to the same place we did. Nowhere."

"Just didn't want you to think I was going behind your back." The first case they'd worked together she'd had to fight to win his acceptance—that had been a critical missing person as well, a girl who could have been a runaway but who had actually been abducted by a serial killer.

"Honestly," he released a sound that would have been a sigh coming from anyone else, "I'd appreciate your opinion. I don't buy that Charlotte left of her own accord. Something about her case doesn't sit right. Hinky. Not sure if it's the husband or what..." Another shrug as he trailed off. "Anyway, let me know your thoughts. Oh, and TK told me about Sarah's possible stalker, so I cancelled the PSAs. No reason to put her face out there in public until we're certain of her safety. You got someplace for her to stay?"

"She's going to stay at Beacon Falls, at least for the next few days."

"Good."

"I was wondering—" She stopped, knowing that she was just speculating, but it would be nice to have another trained law enforcement officer's opinion. Not that she didn't value what TK and Wash thought, but… "Did you know we found a receipt at Sarah's place? Dated Friday night."

"So?"

"It was from the same store that Charlotte Worth was seen at the day she went missing." She stopped, waited for him to weigh the evidence—or lack thereof.

"Hundreds of women go to that store every day. And Sarah wasn't attacked, wasn't a victim of a possible abduction. Odds are it's random chance."

"Right. That's what Wash said. He even ran some probability calculation algorithm, whatever." Analytics were absolutely not her strong suit. For her, instincts trumped data—an approach that had led Lucy down the wrong path more than once, but that's why she had a team to balance her weaknesses with their strengths. "But, don't you think it's strange? I mean, what if our actor," police slang for bad guy, "followed Charlotte from there? And maybe that's how he picked up Sarah's trail?"

"You mean her mysterious wedding dress stalker is involved in Charlotte Worth's case as well?" His face contorted as he puzzled through the scenario. "Stalkers take their time, love the watching, the insinuation of themselves into their victims' lives. Rarely do they escalate to violence or abduction—certainly not over the course of a few hours, if the store was ground zero for their very first encounter."

"You're right, you're right. It just feels…hinky."

"Told you. Not much we can do but keep working the leads. On both cases."

"Right."

Tommy, his in-laws, and Sarah appeared at the parking lot entrance, Tommy carrying Nellie piggyback. Her laughter carried effortlessly across the pavement to where Lucy and Burroughs stood.

"Thanks, Burroughs." She didn't just mean his advice and help with the Sarah Brown case, and he knew it.

"No problem. Nice to have a happy outcome." He nodded to Lucy. "Take care now."

He drove off, and Lucy glanced over to see Sarah staring at her, an undecipherable expression on her face. Then she smiled and waved, leaving Lucy wondering what she'd just seen.

TK rejoined Lucy, and they watched Tommy, Nellie, and Sarah leave together in Tommy's Volvo. "I asked Sarah if she wanted a ride back to Beacon Falls, but she said Tommy invited her to dinner first. Or rather Nellie did. He's going to have his hands full with that one, isn't he?"

"This is going to be a rough week for him," Lucy answered. "We can handle Sarah's case without him."

TK stared at her. "I meant Nellie, not Sarah. What's

wrong with Sarah?"

"Nothing. I'm just trying to keep things simple, uncomplicated."

They strolled across the lot to Lucy's Subaru. The police had all left, the media as well, and with the children still in classes for another twenty minutes, a sudden hush embraced the property.

"You were the one who thought working this case would be good for Tommy," TK said.

"Maybe I was wrong. I didn't realize how much he's juggling." Lucy unlocked the Subaru and slid into the driver's seat.

TK got in on the passenger side. "Did you find something while reviewing Charlotte's case?" she asked as they pulled out of the parking lot.

"Didn't have time to do more than organize the files. But there are a few things I want to follow up on."

"Anything I can do to help?"

"Did we get the cameras placed at Sarah's apartment? Any stalker who goes to so much trouble, sending that dress, will want to see her reaction."

"Wash has one of his friends on it. He would have called if anyone showed up."

"Unless he's already been and gone." Lucy frowned. She hated cases dealing with stalkers—they were far too unpredictable, especially the ones caught up in delusions, denying reality.

"Maybe he saw us, got spooked?"

Before Lucy could answer, her phone rang. She clicked the hands-free speaker. It was Wash, back in Beacon Falls. "Boss, I think I got something."

"On Sarah?" TK asked, leaning toward Lucy.

"No. At least, I don't think it has anything to do with Sarah. More like an unhappy accident. I could use another pair of eyes."

"What is it?" They stopped at a red light, the afternoon sun glaring through the windshield. Lucy reached for her sunglasses.

"I'm not sure. I've been scanning through Sarah's photographs, enlarging them, looking for anything that might help—"

"You mean besides a bunch of dead leaves and flowers?" TK obviously was not a nature enthusiast.

"What did you find?" Lucy asked.

"I'm not sure, but there's a picture with a tiny silver charm, a little ballerina. But it's not the charm—it's what's under the log behind the charm."

Afternoon traffic was already snarled. At this rate, by the time they got TK back to Beacon Falls, it would be time for Lucy to turn around and go home. "Just tell us what you found, Wash."

"Well, could be, maybe, bones? Like human hand bones?"

"Shit." TK exhaled the syllable.

"Send TK the photo and the exact coordinates," Lucy ordered as she eased into the other lane and signaled for a U-turn.

"Should we call the cops?" Wash asked.

"Which ones? Scotia County's sheriff's department only serves papers. So it'll be the staties, and the nearest barracks is twice as far away as we are. By the time they get there, it'll be dark. I don't want to send them on a wild goose chase after a bit of deer antler or the like."

"What should we do?"

"You keep scanning those photos. Bodies in the wild have a habit of getting spread out over a large area. TK and I are going for a walk in the woods."

CHAPTER 22

AS TOMMY DROVE them home, Nellie chattered with Sarah, bombarding her with questions, telling her all about school—anything to prevent Tommy from getting in a word, much less attend to the actual discussion they needed to have. She was using Sarah as a human shield to avoid Tommy's wrath, and with a typical five-year-old's logic obviously thought the longer she kept the conversation flowing, the less chance she had of Tommy remembering how much trouble she was in.

Fat chance. He kept his eyes on the road. Not because he was ignoring Nellie but because right now he could still taste his fear, and anger burned through his belly. He couldn't afford to lose control and unleash those emotions. Another reason why it was good Sarah had come along to buffer the conversation.

As he stewed, reliving those minutes of terror and helplessness, he realized that, as upset as he was with Nellie, it was Sister Agnes he was most furious with. She was an adult, it was her job to care for children, and she'd put her own needs before his daughter's. No way in hell would he take Nellie back there. No way would he trust those idiots with his daughter ever again.

A horn startled him, and he realized he'd drifted slightly over the line into the other lane. He veered back to his side of the twisty two-lane road that followed the creek on its way toward Route 51.

They arrived home in one piece. Gloria and Peter were already waiting, their Lexus parked at the curb to give Tommy room to pull into the driveway in front of the Craftsman's single car garage. It was a small house, with an inviting front porch resting on a foundation of river rock, and two bedrooms occupied the space originally intended as the attic, but it had fit them just right.

Gloria went to start dinner, while Nellie tugged Sarah upstairs to show her her room and toys, leaving Tommy with Peter. Tommy and his father-in-law had always gotten along well, despite the fact that Peter didn't understand half of what went on in a hospital ER and Tommy didn't understand any of what a software engineer did—other than make a nice living. One thing about being a pediatrician, it meant the very bottom of the medical pay scale, and Tommy and Charlotte both had student loans to pay off. Their neighbor who drove a snowplow for PennDOT made more money than Tommy did. But between the two of them they'd managed all right.

At least, he thought they had. Until they lost Charlotte's salary and he'd left the ER to work with the Beacon Group. He'd refused to let his in-laws bear the costs of the private investigators by themselves. He hadn't told anyone, but he'd had to borrow from his 401K when that bill came due.

"Rough day, eh?" Peter said, taking a Yuengling from the fridge and patting Gloria on the shoulder as he gestured for Tommy to join him on the back deck. Tommy hesitated, a primal instinct urging him to stay close to Nellie, but he knew she was home, safe, and well protected. And the idea of a cold beer—anything to calm this agitation he couldn't shake—sounded perfect. He grabbed one and joined Peter.

Peter relaxed in his usual chair, the one that faced Charlotte's rose garden. Tommy had no gift for gardening, not like she had, and no idea what the plants needed, so when they'd begun to grow twisted and brambly, their thick thorns scratching Nellie, he'd pruned them back—a bit too severely. They were only now daring to show some fresh branches and green buds.

Tommy tried to sit, but couldn't stay still, so he abandoned his bottle of beer on the arm of his Adirondack chair and paced along the edge of the deck.

"Maybe the two of you should come to the farm, stay with us," Peter suggested. "At least for the week." The farm was the twelve-acre spread halfway up a mountain out in Forward Township where Gloria and Peter had built their dream home and kept a few horses. Peter called himself retired but was too restless to ever fully stop working, taking on private clients when the project appealed.

Tommy didn't answer; all he could think of was the night before Charlotte's car was found, when Peter had stayed up all night building a website to use for the public appeals. Then the next day, after the car was found with no signs that she hadn't left voluntarily, everything had changed. Peter and Gloria grew distant, and more than once he overheard them asking Nellie if everything was okay, if she was scared of anyone, did Daddy ever scare her? Then, when the extent of Charlotte's deceptions came to light—hidden bank accounts, credit cards, a post office box, multiple cell phones—her parents began to question how well they knew their own daughter. Tommy asked himself those same questions. It was this shared confusion that actually cemented their bond, with Nellie at the heart.

What if tonight, Tommy thought, what if they hadn't found Nellie? What if instead of sharing a beer and moment of peace, tonight he and Peter had to build another fruitless website? Tommy's hand trembled. He shoved it into his pocket, found the dried leaf now beginning to shred, felt the solid mass of the charm wrapped inside it.

Hold it together. He just had to hold it together… for how long? When would this stop?

"I think Nellie needs to stay here," he heard himself saying, not quite sure if they were the words he'd intended or not. But he had to fill the silence with something—what did it matter which words he chose? They were all empty noise, vanishing into the void as soon as he spoke them. He was so sick and tired of words. He wanted more. Something solid. Something real.

Before he could figure out what that something was, much less how to get it, Gloria called out, "Dinner's ready."

They went inside, Peter exchanging a glance with Gloria

and shaking his head, an entire conversation in shorthand. Usually Tommy loved watching them together—he used to nudge Charlotte and whisper to her, "That'll be us in twenty years"—but tonight he knew he was the topic of their silent conversation.

Get used to it, he thought. He was lucky the media wasn't already camped out on his front stoop after what had happened today.

"Nellie," Gloria called upstairs.

Clumping footsteps answered her, and Nellie appeared, tugging Sarah behind her—the stranger in their family drama. She looked a bit stunned and overwhelmed. Tommy regretted allowing her to join them.

"We were washing up," Nellie said, letting go of Sarah's hand long enough to raise her own for inspection. Only a few smears of magic marker and paint. She took her seat beside Tommy. The dishes were on the sideboard waiting for Gloria to dole out servings of pasta and sauce direct from the pots on the stove. Gloria's maiden name was Burgoyne, and it was from her that Charlotte had gotten her auburn hair, but when she'd married into the Callabrese family, Gloria had quickly learned how to cook proper Italian food.

Sarah pulled back the vacant chair at the foot of the table, preparing to take a seat, when Nellie cried out, "No. That's Mommy's chair."

Sarah flushed and glanced down at the place setting. They always set one for Charlotte, a habit that had turned into a hopeful ritual. Magical thinking, the trauma counselor called it.

"Sorry. I didn't—"

"It's all right," Tommy reassured her, using that fake-too-bright voice he despised. "Sit beside Nellie."

"Is that all right with you, Nellie?" Sarah bent down to Nellie's eye level as she asked.

"Yes, please sit here. And if you don't like your meatballs, it's okay, I'll eat them for you."

"How can I resist an offer like that?" Sarah said with a smile, the tension broken.

Gloria began to place steaming bowls of pasta before them, and everyone began to talk, complimenting the cook and talking about Nellie's adventure. From his spot at the head of the table, Tommy closed his eyes, absorbing the feeling of family. It was an intoxicating illusion, but it was broken as soon as he opened them again and his gaze fell on Charlotte's empty seat.

CHAPTER 23

WITH TRAFFIC, IT was almost an hour later by the time TK and Lucy reached the parking area at Fiddler's Knob. There was one other vehicle in the lot, a dusty Ford pickup. TK was feeling a bit carsick from squinting at the photos Wash sent to her phone during the trip, but they'd found three possible areas to investigate.

Lucy parked her Subaru and popped the trunk. TK watched as she balanced on the rear bumper and changed into a pair of hiking boots. It was the first time she'd seen Lucy's brace, a molded piece of plastic designed to keep her foot from drooping and dragging on the ground. It was also the first time she'd seen the extensive braid of scar tissue extending above the brace and Lucy's sock—and she knew there was worse hidden below.

"You going to be okay on the trail?" she asked. "It looks pretty steep in places."

Instead of answering, Lucy surprised her by hesitating. TK would have felt better if Lucy had snapped at her for questioning her fitness; uncertainty in Lucy was not something she was comfortable seeing. It made her seem too vulnerable, human.

After lacing the boots tight, Lucy reached into the trunk for one more item: a hiker's walking stick with a wide rubber tip. "I'll manage."

TK smiled. Leave it to Lucy to find a workable compromise without admitting weakness.

Then Lucy handed her a small knapsack. "Flashlight, gloves, other gear that might come in handy."

TK glanced up the mountain. She'd been raised in West Virginia, had gone fishing and hunting with her father when she was young, but that was to put food on the table, not because she liked the woods.

"Other gear? Like bear spray? Maybe that shotgun?" Both she and Lucy carried nine-millimeter Berettas, but TK doubted that would stop a rampaging bear. She'd much rather have the Remington pump-action Lucy kept stowed in her trunk.

"If I were you, I'd be more afraid of snakes," Lucy said, slamming the trunk closed and leaving the shotgun behind. She moved toward the trail, using the walking stick to offset her limp. "Rattlers and copperheads are both common around here."

Oh, great, TK thought as she followed, keeping one eye on the ground and the other on her phone, where Wash had overlaid Sarah's photos onto a topo map. "We've got four areas Wash tagged," she said.

"We only have maybe two hours of sunlight. Let's start at the top and work our way down."

"Then we'll be staring at the first place he spotted—the one with the ballerina charm."

They entered the forest, and the light was already cut by half. TK took the lead, surprised that Lucy didn't lag too far behind despite the obvious pain her ankle caused. Not for the first time, she thought that Lucy would have made a decent Marine. It was the highest compliment TK could give anyone, and she didn't give it lightly.

"If we do find something," TK continued as they climbed the trail, "what then? I mean, I've read reports and seen the photos, but I've never been involved right from the start. With a body."

"Lucky you. First, we'll call the authorities—in this case the state police would have jurisdiction. They'll send a trooper who will secure a perimeter and call their sergeant or corporal to dispatch an investigator and CSI team. If it is skeletal remains, they'll call in a forensic anthropologist, probably from Pitt or Penn State, depending on who's available, and together with their team they'll work on searching the entire area and documenting it. Then they'll excavate any remains they do find, and begin their analysis."

"So how long before we actually know anything? All that doesn't happen overnight."

"I wish. But sometimes you get lucky—personal belongings to provide a preliminary ID, medical equipment with serial numbers like breast implants or orthopedic plates. Finding a jaw is always a help."

"Because of dental records."

"Not just them. Remember, you need to have a name to start with in order to pull records for a comparison. But molars are also a good source of DNA."

TK slowed as they approached the coordinates where Sarah had taken the photo of the pink flower and the silver charm.

"Okay, we should be near." She squinted in the fading light, searching for a reference point, but it was Lucy who spotted the log about eight yards off the trail.

"Wait there," Lucy said as she carefully picked her way through the leaves and underbrush.

"I know how to not disturb a crime scene," TK protested.

"It's not that. Just wait."

TK didn't care for Lucy's tone—the kind of tone that implied that something was off. "Why?"

"Because this log is a fallen tree trunk."

Well, duh. "We're in a forest."

"It's a pine tree." Lucy crouched down a few feet away from the moss growing around and under the tree trunk. She held out her phone, recording everything. "You see any pines this size around me?"

TK looked up. "No. They're all oaks and maples. Nearest pine tree I see is over here, on the other side of the trail."

"Exactly. Know any deer or wild animals that drag a fallen log over to weigh down something they've buried?"

"Shit." They hadn't even seen the maybe-could-be bones yet, and Lucy had already figured out that they had a crime scene. "Should I call the staties?" She glanced at her phone.

"Wait. I can't—no reception."

"The charm in the photo, it was right beside the orchid, right?"

"Yep. About four inches, I'd guess. Between the flower and the log."

"It's gone."

"Do you see the bones Wash spotted? They were at the far edge of the photo, in the shadow of the log." She was still amazed Wash had seen them at all. Guy had a hell of an eye for detail.

"Yes." Lucy leaned forward, bracing herself with her walking stick to get as close as possible without disrupting or touching anything. TK saw the flash from her phone fill the shadows with bright light. "Can you carefully follow my tracks? I need more light."

TK pulled the high-intensity flashlight from the pack and joined Lucy. The gathering shadows were quickly banished by the LED beam. She knelt in the damp leaves beside Lucy and angled the light under the log. There she could make out three not-quite-parallel rows of grayish-tan colored material stained by dirt and moss. They didn't resemble the polished ivory of bones from an anatomical skeleton. Maybe they were just twigs? Or pebbles? Whatever they were, they'd been exposed to the elements for a while.

Lucy took TK's hand and aimed the light at a slightly different angle, revealing a flash from something metallic. Two rings fallen into a gap between the gray bits. Okay, not twigs. Not pebbles or bits of debris. Bones.

"A woman," TK breathed, craning her head, trying to see if there was anything more. Was that a piece of cloth or just a brightly colored leaf? Impossible to tell without moving the log, and they couldn't disturb the crime scene.

"Let me try something before we go down to call the staties," Lucy said. She stood and readjusted her angle, aiming her phone from the opposite side, zooming in on the rings. She took several photos with TK moving the light, then sat back on her haunches to examine them, zooming in even more with the photo editor.

"Are you seeing what I'm seeing?" TK asked, looking over her shoulder as Lucy scrolled through the photos. One of the rings was becoming visible thanks to the bright light. "Are those hands?"

"It's a claddagh." Lucy breathed out, then blanked the phone as if she couldn't bear to see any more. She used her walking stick to haul herself up, wincing as she put weight on her leg. "I spent the morning reviewing Charlotte Worth's case. Her engagement ring was a claddagh design. Two hands holding a heart made of green agate."

TK remained on the ground, still staring at the rings caught in the flashlight's beam. The stone between the hands definitely looked green, but maybe that was from the moss? "No. It can't be. I mean—what are the odds? Tommy and Sarah were just up here today. And Sarah—her amnesia, coming to us—it's impossible, right?"

"Most cops don't believe in coincidences," Lucy replied in a grim tone. "Tommy is in for a rough time."

TK pushed herself up to standing. "No way. Not Tommy."

"Then who? Someone who targeted his wife, and then a year later, Sarah Brown? Someone who chased Sarah down this mountain, and when he didn't catch her, somehow arranged for her to be sent to us for help? How exactly does that work?"

"I don't know. But dammit, it did."

Lucy stared at TK for a long moment, shadows clouding her expression, then finally nodded. "Okay. Then it did. Which means we have a lot of work and little time to do it. I'm going to wait here while you run down the mountain and call the staties. Ask their permission to call Burroughs in as well, since Charlotte is his case."

"Maybe it's not Charlotte. You said yourself, it'll take days to confirm an identity."

"Then I'll owe Burroughs. But I want to get our part over with as soon as possible."

"Should I call Tommy?"

"No," Lucy snapped. Then she softened her tone. "No. I'll go, tell him myself."

"Right. We shouldn't upset him, not until we're certain."

Lucy sighed. "I don't think we have the luxury of waiting that long. But we can at least give him a few more hours. Now go, hurry."

CHAPTER 24

AFTER DINNER, GLORIA took Nellie up for her bath while Peter cleaned up the kitchen. Tommy found himself in the living room, slumped in his usual place on the worn, overstuffed couch. The night was chilly and he debated starting a fire, but didn't have the energy. Just as he had no energy to protest when Sarah sat down at the other corner of the couch, unknowingly taking Charlotte's place.

"Why'd you leave the ER to work with the Beacon Group?" she asked. "All those cold cases with no answers…doesn't seem a good fit. You seem like someone who likes to be doing, taking care of problems, not plowing through ancient history."

"If you had any idea what I see in the ER—"

"*See.* Present tense. You miss it." She tucked her legs under her and leaned toward him, squeezing a throw pillow on her lap. "Why don't you go back?"

He turned away.

"You're awfully young to leave everything you trained so long for behind forever."

He started to give her the same story he gave everyone else. The story he told himself every morning when he looked in the mirror. That it was too hard being a single father working rotating shifts, that Nellie needed his full attention. All true.

And all lies.

"Ever hear of the term poleaxed?" he asked her. She looked up, puzzled, not realizing that he'd answered her question more truthfully than he'd answered that same question asked by anyone else in the past year.

"No. I don't think so. Is this a memory test?" A shy smile. "You know I'd fail."

"When I was a kid I thought it meant something to do with pole vaulting. Those guys fascinated me, how high they went, closest thing to flying."

"What does it really mean?"

"I'll be fine. Look fine. Act fine. Even my thinking will feel fine. Like I'm functioning normally. Like life is normal again. That's one second. Then the next, no warning, no hint, it's like someone flips a switch. I'm in the dark, lost. Absolutely lost. Sinking into a black so complete I'm suffocating—I can't even find the strength to keep fighting to breathe. My body goes numb, like it's not even my own. And my mind—it's a fog so thick I struggle to remember my own name, much less who I am or why I'm here. Forget making any kind of complex decision. Like how to save a life."

His shoulders slumped. He hadn't told anyone this before:

not his friends, not the counselors, none of the well-meaning well wishers constantly asking how he was but not really wanting the answer.

"I simply," his voice dropped to a whisper, cowering against the weight of the truth, "disappear."

"Poleaxed," she whispered back.

They sat in silence for a long time. Somehow her hand ended up on top of his. He didn't pull away. Since Charlotte left, Sarah was the first person with whom he'd felt comfortable enough not to raise up defenses and retreat behind a facade.

"What about—I mean, there are drugs, medications?"

He stopped her with a shake of his head. "Single dad, remember? Can't risk adverse reactions. I need to stay alert in case Nellie needs me."

"You can't take care of her unless you take care of yourself," she argued. Then to his surprise, she smiled. "Ouch. I'll bet you tell all your patients and their parents that. Sorry."

Not for the first time today he wondered if she was a mother. He had a feeling she might be. Or maybe if she didn't already have children, she'd make a good mother in the future.

"When's the last time you slept?" she asked.

A sigh escaped him at the thought of sleep. A distant memory. "Sometimes when Charlotte's folks have Nellie I'll take a pill. But when Nellie's home I can't sleep. Can't risk it. I wander the house checking the doors and windows, checking in on her. Then I work at the computer, following up any leads on Charlotte. I'll hear a noise—the furnace turning on, the fridge defrosting—and I'll know it's Nellie and something awful has happened and..."

"You panic." Her hand clasped his. "I don't remember having those feelings, and yet, when you talk about them, I feel it. Here." She raised her free hand to beat against her chest, then closed it into a fist and pressed it against her throat. "And here. Like I can't breathe, my body's too heavy."

He nodded grimly. "Yep, that's about right." He sagged against the sofa. Damn, it was comfortable. This was where he and Charlotte sat together and finished each day. In silence that wasn't silence but something so much more. He could almost imagine...

"You're safe here," Sarah said quietly. "Go to sleep. Just a short nap. I'll watch over you. Wake you if anything happens." Her voice was soothing, hypnotic. And he was so damned tired...

His eyes closed against his wishes. He tried to will them open, but they were heavy, too damned heavy...

THE FIRST STATE trooper arrived just as the sun set. After Lucy explained the situation, he took a quick look at the scene, then radioed for backup. Lucy had always thought of the state police as the unsung heroes of law enforcement: as more and more municipalities closed down their own police departments, the staties stepped in to fill the gap, stretching their own resources thinner and thinner.

Like now. With an unexpected, rural crime scene to

protect, assignments would need to be shifted, investigators called in—whether on duty or not—and a forensic team scheduled, not to mention additional help to search the mountain for more evidence, a painstaking, tedious job.

"At least most of it can wait until morning," Lucy told TK after the trooper sent her down the mountain and she returned to the parking lot.

"I'm more worried about Tommy. They're going to think he did it."

"If it is Charlotte up there."

"It is. It has to be. Right?"

Lucy had no answer except a shrug. "It might be days or weeks before we know for certain."

"Burroughs won't wait. He'll go after Tommy. And the press, they'll crucify him."

Lucy was silent, busy rearranging her own priorities. They still needed to help Sarah, but now her review of Charlotte's case had become urgent.

"You think he's guilty, don't you?" TK said, her tone biting. "How could you?"

"It doesn't matter what I think. What matters is what we can prove. To answer your question, no, I don't think he killed his wife." At least she hoped not. She liked Tommy. But she didn't know him, not well enough to let it cloud her judgment. "But I need—*we* need—to stay objective, investigate every possibility. That's the best way to clear Tommy, prove that he didn't do it."

"You can't prove a negative," TK grumbled. A new set of

headlights entered the parking lot. Burroughs' white Impala. "Oh look, your partner in the lynch mob."

"I warned you," were Burroughs' first words as he barreled out of the car, despite the fact that there was no urgency, not at this crime scene. "Didn't I tell you not to trust him? Not to let him near Sarah?"

"You can't seriously think Tommy had anything to do with Sarah's accident?" TK stepped forward, squaring off with Burroughs.

"Maybe it's not an accident," he answered. "A new witness came forward before we closed down the public service announcements. Guy who left before the smash and grabs, didn't know about what happened to Sarah until he read it this morning."

"What did he see?" Lucy asked, her gut tightening as if preparing for a blow.

"Said Sarah wasn't alone on the trail. Said he saw a man with her—they were talking and she seemed upset." He paused. "Description sounds a lot like Worth."

"I don't believe it," TK said. "How good of a look did he get?"

"He only saw his back and profile," Burroughs admitted. "But if those remains up there are Charlotte's, then—"

"Let's not jump to conclusions," Lucy urged. "The staties have a lot of work to do before we know anything for certain. In the meantime though, we should prepare Tommy and his family. Update them on what's happening. I can do that if you want to stay here."

"No," Burroughs said. "I want to see his face when he hears. And like you said, they won't be doing much here until morning." He tilted his head to look up at the dark mountainside now awash in headlights. "I'm not sure if I want it to be her or not."

"I know how you feel," Lucy admitted. Families always said they wanted closure—until you gave them answers they weren't prepared for. Answers that destroyed their worlds and reshaped their lives forever. "TK and I will come with you to tell Tommy."

"You're a civilian now." His tone warned her to tread lightly when it came to his investigation.

"Right. And Tommy is on my team. I'm going to be there for him."

"*We're* going to be there," TK amended.

Burroughs stared at them both with narrowed eyes, then shrugged. "All right then. Best get to it."

CHAPTER 25

TOMMY WASN'T DREAMING, but neither was he awake. He lay in a languid half-state, his body paralyzed while his mind raced. And he wasn't alone. *Charlotte.* He felt her heartbeat as she held him in her arms, her breath stirring his hair, her scent filling his lungs. Not a dream. It had to be real...

She smiled down at him, her fingers dancing through his hair. "I miss you," she whispered.

He tried to speak, but he couldn't. Every muscle in his body was weighed down with exhaustion. He fought to open his mouth, to move a limb. He felt her slipping away and he was powerless to stop her. The paralysis that gripped him was terrifying, but even more frightening was the thought of losing her again.

No! He tried to scream but still couldn't move. *Don't go!*

"Tommy." It was a voice almost exactly like Charlotte's. A hand shook his arm. "Tommy, you and your friend need to wake up."

Gloria, Charlotte's mother. Disappointment washed over

him, freeing his body from the sleep paralysis. He opened his eyes. Gloria was frowning in disapproval—and behind her stood Peter, TK, Lucy, and Don Burroughs.

Pushing himself up, he realized he *had* been sleeping in a woman's arms: not Charlotte's, but Sarah's. Sarah. He'd forgotten all about her. As he disentangled himself from her embrace, her eyes fluttered open. "What?" she asked with a yawn.

"We fell asleep," he said.

She reached for him with half-closed eyes, the way a lover would reach for their partner.

Gloria made a noise and stalked out, followed by Peter. Tommy pushed Sarah's hand away and scooted down on the couch, beyond her reach. He knuckled his eyes, still not quite awake, but took his hands down when he realized there could only be one reason why TK, Lucy, and Burroughs would be here together.

"You found her. You found Sarah's past," he said excitedly. "Does she have family?"

Sarah's eyes popped fully open and she sat up. "What did you find?"

To Tommy's surprise, Lucy touched TK's elbow and nodded to Sarah, giving a silent command. TK moved forward. "Sarah, why don't we wait in the kitchen?"

Confusion clouded Sarah's face, but she stood and followed TK from the room. Lucy took her place on the couch, facing Tommy.

"We need to talk," she started, and he realized he'd been

wrong, so very wrong.

The world grew dark around the edges, and for a moment he wondered if he was still asleep. He shook his head, trying to ward off her words, yearning to retreat back behind the protective shield of denial. Once the words were said—words he'd dreamed a thousand times, words that colored his every thought throughout the day—once spoken, those words could not be unsaid. His glance ricocheted from Lucy to Burroughs. Even the detective wore a mask of sympathy.

"You found Charlotte." The words tasted of ash. They sounded foreign, like another language.

"We think so." Lucy's tone was soft and gentle. She'd done this before, he could tell, because it was the same tone he'd used in the ER when he had to give families bad news.

Reality crashed down on him. Charlotte *had* run away, hidden, hadn't wanted to be found—by him. Tears choked his throat. She'd abandoned him and Nellie. She'd never loved them.

"Where is she?" he asked, the words feeling sharp, painful. "Is she all right?"

Burroughs made a low noise in the back of his throat and stepped back, leaving Lucy to take the lead. Lucy hesitated, didn't meet Tommy's eyes. And he knew.

Cold slapped him, stealing his breath—the truth asserting its cruel grip, tearing away his final shroud of denial. "She's not alive?"

"No," she confirmed. "We found skeletal remains that might be hers. It's too soon to tell. We'll need to finish searching, get the forensic anthropologist and medical examiner..."

He nodded. He knew the routine. He also knew she was spelling things out both to give him time to process and because a mind numbed by shock could not retain information.

"Where?" he asked. "How did she—did the woman—die?" Maybe it wasn't Charlotte. They'd been wrong before—like in December when they'd found a body in the Ohio River, ruined their Christmas until they confirmed it wasn't Charlotte. "Why do you think it's...her?"

Something in him refused to use his wife's name to reference a corpse.

"You were with Sarah today at Fiddler's Knob. Had you ever been there before?"

Her question puzzled him. "I think so. A few years ago—Nellie was young enough I carried her in a baby backpack gizmo. Charlotte wanted to see the mountain laurel in bloom. But we were too early—late frost or something."

He knew he was rambling but couldn't help it. Anything to delay dealing with reality. No matter how much he wanted answers, an equal part of him desperately wanted to avoid the truth. Because everything would change once he knew. Not just for him, but for Nellie.

"I remember thinking today when Sarah and I were there, how much Charlotte would have loved it. There's a tunnel, twenty feet high, made from mountain laurel. It's so beautiful."

Lucy and Burroughs exchanged a glance. "Have you been there more recently?"

"No. Not until today." He sat up, stretching his fingers

into his pants pocket—no, the charm was in his jacket. "Wait." He left the couch and went to the coat rack beside the front door where his jacket hung, fished into the pockets. He emerged with the tattered leaf and its treasure. "We found this. Today."

He held the leaf and charm on an outstretched palm for their inspection. Burroughs reached for it and Tommy flinched, hating the idea of anyone else touching something that he'd imagined had a connection to Charlotte.

"It was in one of Sarah's photos," Burroughs said.

"Right. It looks a lot like one Charlotte had—I think. Of course, it couldn't be. Look how clean it is. No way it was on that mountain for a year." Hope infused his tone, turning his statement into a question. A question he did not want answered.

Lucy slid her phone from her pocket while Burroughs took both the charm and the leaf from Tommy. To Tommy's surprise, the detective pulled an evidence bag from his own pocket and slid them inside.

"No. Charlotte can't be—" His voice faltered and his legs began to swim out from under him. He slumped down into a chair before he fell.

Lucy crouched beside him, holding her phone. The image was blurry until he blinked a few times, bringing it into focus. "Does this ring look familiar?"

Her voice had dropped even lower. Soothing, comforting, and preparing him for the worst. He glanced away from the image immediately, but it wasn't fast enough.

"No." The syllable emerged not as a word, but a primal warning. "No."

"Look again. Please."

He shook his head, looking past her to the stairs leading up to where Nellie slept. Blissfully unaware. How would he tell her? How *could* he tell her?

"No." The word lost its magic, and somehow his gaze returned to Lucy's phone—with its ugly, disastrous, heart-breaking, life-ending image of despair. "It's the ring I gave Charlotte when I proposed. It belonged to my grandmother."

Then he paused and waved his own words aside, denying them as traitors. "Maybe. It could be. Hard to tell with all the dirt. Who knows? There could be thousands of those rings sold every day in tourist traps across Ireland."

Lucy nodded slowly, as if willing to grant him the asylum of denial for one last night. "We'll get it cleaned up, show it to you again."

She stood, looked to Burroughs.

The detective did not look pleased. "I'll be back tomorrow with any more information we have. In the meantime, I'd ask you not to talk to the press, and stay here where we can find you if we need you."

Tommy didn't even bother nodding his agreement. Numbness had overtaken him. It was as if he floated above his body, watching the three of them play out their little drama on a stage. Nothing to do with his reality. He sat there, hands between his knees, head bowed, unable to look up at Lucy and Burroughs. They were too real, with their evidence bags and photos and tales of bodies found. How he wished he was still asleep, Charlotte's arms wrapped around him, never letting go.

"Did she—" He hated himself for asking, but he had to know. "Did the body, the woman… Was it an accident? How did she die?"

Again Burroughs made that noise like a dog scenting a threat. Leaving Lucy to answer. "We're not sure yet." She touched Tommy's shoulder, and he suddenly felt very small, like a child sitting in church, avoiding the gaze of an angry, all-knowing God, his sins revealed for all to see. "But it wasn't an accident."

CHAPTER 26

LUCY DROVE TK and Sarah back to Beacon Falls. The drive felt longer than normal as all three of them sat in silence, each enveloped in her own thoughts. Lucy was relieved when at last she dropped them off at the house and Xander, Valencia's assistant who ran the household, met them at the door.

As she drove away, she called Nick. "I'll be late, don't wait for me."

"Your amnesia victim? Anything I can help with?"

"Not her—Tommy's missing wife." She filled him in on Charlotte's case and the events of the night, using the opportunity to organize the facts in her own mind.

"Is he a suspect?"

"Of course he is." TK had asked the same thing. Was Lucy not being objective enough? Why were people questioning her ability to work the case as a neutral party?

"But he's also on your team, and you feel protective." As always, Nick nailed it.

"So you think I should stop working the case? I mean, it's not as if I have any jurisdiction." Hell, she had no police powers at all—a fact she was still getting used to.

"No. I think the opposite. You *should* work the case. You're in a unique position to search avenues the police might ignore."

"You mean if they get too focused on Tommy." They both knew that one of the pitfalls of any investigation was investing in one narrative, developing tunnel vision, blocking out any evidence that didn't fit that theory of the crime.

"That, and you have a chance to work an angle no one else seems to be investigating. The victim's point of view."

Of course. In the FBI, starting with the victim had always been Lucy's opening salvo when jumping into an investigation. But here she'd gotten distracted—by helping Sarah, by worrying about Tommy's feelings, by Burroughs and his obvious suspicion of one of her team members.

"Have I told you lately that you're brilliant?"

She practically heard his smile over the airwaves. "Wake me when you get home," he told her. "I want to hear everything. Good luck."

It was almost nine o'clock and traffic was light as she drove back to Tommy's house. She knocked softly, but he had the door open almost immediately, as if he'd been expecting her.

"Any news?" he asked, his face pinched with anxiety.

"Sorry, not yet. Can we talk?"

He thought about it, then moved aside to allow her in. His movements were stiff, guarded.

"I noticed your in-laws' car is gone—did they take Nellie to stay with them?" They both knew that it wouldn't take long for the press to learn of the discovery of the body at Fiddler's Knob and connect it to Charlotte.

"No, she's already asleep. They're coming back in the morning and will take her home then." He glanced up at the ceiling, whether praying or searching out his daughter's room, she wasn't sure. "Hopefully we can shield her from all this. But..."

"Sooner or later you'll need to tell her."

"After we know for sure. We've been down this road before. First, when they found her car at that overlook beside the Yough and dragged the river. Took a week before they gave up. And since then, every unidentified female body in the area…it's like holding your breath when you're drowning. You can't tell if it's better to let the water in or deny it."

He sank into the couch, hands propped on his knees, face buried in his palms. Silence filled the room, but Lucy didn't rush it. Instead, she took a seat on the chair closest to him and waited.

Finally he scrubbed his face against his palms and looked up, eyes bleary with despair. "What if it is… what will I…how will I tell Nellie?"

Lucy had no good answer, so she didn't try to offer a poor one. She sat in silence, giving him time. After the pain had eased from his face, she said, "Tell me about Charlotte."

He jerked up at that. "I've already told the police everything."

"I don't care about what you've told the police. I want to

know her. Tell me about her. How did you meet?"

Tommy simply sat there, hands hanging between his knees, staring into nothing. But then slowly, very slowly, the faintest hint of a smile lit his face. He shook his head, shrugged, and met her gaze. "Best damn day of my life."

"Tell me."

"July first. Most dangerous day of the year. Because that's the day all the new interns start work and new residents and fellows. So you can imagine that July fourth isn't a whole lot safer. My first week running the peds ER as a fellow. I was so damn hot to trot, to prove myself—especially since I didn't do my residency here, so none of the nurses or first responders knew or trusted me. Anyway, we get this kid. Five-year-old. Depressed skull fracture, epidural hematoma—that's a small bleed between the skull and the brain. And a big old goose egg on his scalp to go along with it. Dad brought him in, saying he was washing the car while the kid was washing the puppy, and next thing he knew the kid had the goose egg, but the kid didn't fall or anything. Then the kid started acting goofy and Dad freaked, brought him in. Good thing—for the kid. But me and the nurses, we're looking at Dad."

"You thought he hurt his son?"

"Sure. I mean, could you ask for a more vague story? A puppy? Seriously? But Dad never budged. Kid was already up in the OR with the neurosurgeons, so we couldn't ask him for confirmation. And no way in hell was I going to let a possible child abuser walk, not when the nurses are telling me to call social services and I'm trying to look good to them."

"Charlotte. She was the social worker?"

He nodded. "Charlotte was the social worker. Comes down, fire in her eyes like Joan of Arc, ready to defend and protect—until she sits down with Dad and listens, really listens to his story. She comes out from talking to him and I can see she's not at all convinced, so I get all high and mighty about how we have a duty to report any suspicion of abuse. And she...she just laughs so hard, she can't even talk. Which, of course, only makes me more mad and eager to prove that I'm right."

"What happened?"

"She calms down long enough to invite me to join her and the dad. We all sit down in the family room, knee to knee, me seething about having to put up with this bullshit from a child abuser. When she puts her hand on my knee and suddenly there's this feeling of calm like I'd never felt before. Like her hand touching me was something meant to be. And then she asks Dad to show me a picture of the puppy." His smile turned wistful as he gazed past her. "It was a Lab that was only eight months old but probably weighed at least a hundred pounds. With a tail on it that you could only imagine. Easily enough force from that tail wagging to crack a skinny little kid's skull if it hit the right place. Which it did."

"So Dad was saved, the kid was okay, and—"

"And Charlotte let me take her out to dinner so I could apologize." He shook his head, his expression growing serious. "Ironic. We got together because I believed the evidence more than the truth, and now everyone's looking at me like I'm a monster for the same reason."

CHAPTER 27

TOMMY WOKE TO Nellie's frantic shaking, almost rolling off the couch. After spending most of the night talking with Lucy, he hadn't had the energy to climb upstairs to bed. Not that he'd gotten much sleep, although it had come more easily than it had in months. Something about reliving the good times, talking about them out loud, had given his mind a chance to rest.

"Daddy, Daddy," Nellie whispered in a voice so loud it would have wakened a sleeping elephant. "There's strange men looking at me."

That brought Tommy fully awake and up to a sitting position. "What? Where?"

Nellie tugged him to his feet, gripping his hand fiercely. She wore her favorite nightgown, the purple one with the yellow bananas and lime green monkeys, and was clutching Magpie, her tattered rag doll. She pulled him to the bay window in the dining room, the one without curtains because it overlooked their backyard with its trees and the creek that ran along the property boundary.

Two men pressed their faces against the glass. One held a phone up, and the other a large, professional-looking video camera. When they spotted Tommy, the one with the camera began to pound on the window and shout.

"Dr. Worth, do you know about the body—"

Tommy pulled Nellie back into the living room before she could hear the rest. At least he hoped it was in time. "How about you run upstairs and get dressed?"

"Who are those men? Why are they so mad at us?" She trembled, her lip pulling in and out.

"They aren't mad at you, sweetheart." He folded her into his arms. "I'll never let them hurt you. I'll never let anyone hurt you. You know that, right?"

Finally she nodded, her head bobbing against his chest. He kissed the top of her head and scooted her toward the staircase. "Get dressed and I'll get rid of those men."

She ran up without a word, but stopped at the top banister and looked down at him anxiously. "Daddy, will you be okay? They won't hurt you, will they?"

"I'll be fine," he called back, fighting to keep his fury out of his voice. "You might hear me shout, but it's just to scare them away."

"Are they monsters?"

"No, sweetie. They're reporters. Not as scary, but harder to get rid of."

That seemed to satisfy her because she turned and left for her room.

Tommy went to the door, gathering his strength. Through the skylight he saw a local news van parked on his front lawn. The early birds, the ones who woke, ate, and slept to the sound of their police scanners. Others would be here soon, he knew.

He'd learned the hard way that dealing with the press was much like dealing with a recalcitrant toddler: you needed to set firm boundaries, ignore their tantrums, and never negotiate with terrorists. He hauled in a few deep breaths, fatigue buzzing through every cell, straightened his posture, and opened the door.

Before he could do or say anything, the cameraman from the bay window was there—a hyena scenting prey—joined by a woman dressed in a suit. The cameraman turned a high-powered light on, shining it directly in Tommy's eyes, making him wince and squint—all the better to make him look either pitiful or menacing, depending on how they decided to edit things later.

"This is private property and you're trespassing," he said in a level voice, swallowing back his anger. "Also, there is a restraining order in effect, so if you don't leave in the next thirty seconds, I'm calling both the police and my lawyer. I believe the judge set a fine of fifty thousand dollars?"

Peter and Gloria had helped with that after an overzealous reporter had stalked Nellie and tried to question her while she was playing in the sprinkler in their backyard. When she'd try to run inside, screaming, the reporter, a man, had grabbed her, and she'd fallen on the flagstones. With all of it caught on film, the lawyer was able to go to the family court judge seeking to file charges of child endangerment.

It was a stretch—games lawyers play—but it had bought them some relief as the judge created a "no press" zone around Nellie. Tommy was still fair game, but as long as Nellie was protected, he didn't care.

"Leave now," he told the reporters. "You can't come within fifty yards of my daughter—which means you'll be reporting from the middle of the creek."

He slammed the door in their faces. Out of their sight, he turned his back to the solid oak door and slid down to the slate floor, burying his face in his hands. He heard them drive off but didn't look up.

It was happening. All over again. He'd barely survived it the first time. How was he going to find the strength to do this again—and protect Nellie?

A knock came at the door and he jumped up, adrenaline fueling his rage, ready to do serious harm to any reporter on the other side. He yanked the door open. "I told you—"

It was Gloria and Peter.

"Oh. Sorry. I thought you were reporters."

"They were here? At the house?" Peter said as Tommy let them in. "What about the judge's order?"

"Apparently reporters have a short memory. Don't worry, I got rid of them."

"You know there'll be more," Gloria said, straightening the rumpled couch pillows. She glanced back at Tommy. "Where's your friend?"

He frowned. “Who? Lucy? She left hours ago to check on the state police and their progress.”

Her frown matched his. “No. Your special lady friend. Sarah.”

“Gloria,” Peter said, clearly uncomfortable with his wife’s insinuations.

“She’s not a friend of any kind,” Tommy protested. “She’s a client. We were just both exhausted and fell asleep on the couch. There’s nothing more. Besides, with everything going on, I’ll probably never see her again. Lucy and the others will deal with her case. It’ll all be over by the time I get back to work.”

Gloria twisted her lips in suspicion. “Okay. It’s just that Nellie seemed especially attached to her and I don’t want to see her hurt.”

How could Tommy argue with that? Impulsively he gave his mother-in-law a quick peck on the cheek. “That makes two of us.”

LUCY SHUFFLED BLEARY-EYED into the kitchen. Nick wordlessly handed her a cup of coffee. She’d stayed up with Tommy until around three, then spent another hour talking things through with Nick once she’d arrived home. After that, she’d tried to get some sleep while Nick had left for a pre-dawn run. He was now freshly showered and appeared ready for anything.

Unlike Lucy. Resilience. That was maybe the greatest

hidden damage her leg injury had cost her. More than the pain or the inability to trust her balance was the new realization that she simply couldn't bounce back the way she had before. As if agreeing with her, her foot dragged, catching on the floorboards, sending a fresh strike of pain racing from her toes up to her teeth.

She sank into the nearest chair, her breath escaping in a rush while she tried to pretend that she was simply blowing to cool her coffee. Didn't fool anyone. Megan, who was eating a bowl of cereal while watching a video on her phone, glanced up.

"Want me to run up and get your brace, Mom?"

Before Lucy could tell her no, she was gone. Leaving her with Nick, who leaned against the counter, observing her over his own cup of coffee.

"Don't say it," she muttered. Her coffee was still a touch too hot, but she needed it, so she gulped down a scalding mouthful, feeling the burn tangle with the pain from her leg. Funny how pain worked—sometimes different types blocked each other; sometimes one would swallow the other, growing and multiplying; sometimes they'd spar and end up shattering, ricochets spraying out across her entire body.

"Say what?" Nick asked after she'd taken a second sip of coffee.

"That I should stay home and take it easy. That I was foolish to climb that mountain yesterday." Although the climb wasn't strenuous at all, and her ankle had been fine on the way up—it was coming down that had done it in. "That I'm getting too involved."

He rocked his head as if considering her words. Then he set his mug on the counter and came over to wrap his arms around her from behind, leaning down to rest his head against hers. "I was only going to say that I'll be working at the VA today, and if you need me, just call."

"Why do you put up with me?" she asked with a sigh.

He kissed her, then straightened, his back sounding tiny creaks that made her feel better—petty, she knew, but she couldn't help herself. "It's your cooking," he answered. "I'll never have to worry about getting fat."

"If you didn't make such good coffee I'd throw this cup at you."

He held his hands up in surrender.

Megan returned with Lucy's ankle brace. It was designed to keep her foot from dragging and to support her ankle where she'd lost the muscles meant to do the job. Lucy had a love-hate relationship with it—it was hot and chafed, and she could only wear certain shoes, but it did its job and she couldn't do without it. The last was probably the biggest reason why she despised it. Not only was the brace a constant reminder of what she'd lost, it was also a reminder of how powerless she was. Her rehab had helped her to regain far more than the doctors had anticipated, but she was nowhere near her old idea of normal.

"Thanks, honey." Lucy strapped on the brace. "I saw Oshiro yesterday."

"I know. June texted me. She was wondering if I could babysit for them this weekend."

"Don't you have that English paper due? The one that's a

third of your grade?"

"Already finished. Just need to polish it—and I can do that there after the baby goes to sleep."

"All right, then."

"Great, thanks." In a flash of movement Megan took her bowl to the sink and rinsed it, put it in the dishwasher, and was gone, clattering back up the stairs to finish getting ready for school.

Lucy watched her go with wistful eyes. "I can't believe she's so excited about taking care of someone else's baby. She never even liked playing with baby dolls."

"I think it's the money," Nick said with a laugh. "Not to mention the feeling of responsibility, independence."

"Getting away from us, you mean."

"I think, given our jobs, we both tend to be a bit overprotective. She's a good kid, though."

Lucy thought back to the stupid stunts she'd pulled when she was Megan's age, rebelling against her own mother. Miracle she'd lived past that tumultuous stage. "We are so lucky."

The phone rang. Nick handed it to her

It was TK. "Sarah's gone."

Chapter 28

Despite Tommy's protests—he actually enjoyed cooking—Gloria fixed breakfast for all of them. He couldn't help but notice that Nellie didn't ask for Sugar Loops, not even once. And she cleaned her plate.

Ah, the way a mercurial five-year-old could play mind games. It was as if she sensed exactly where he was vulnerable and pushed at those soft spots without mercy. Not because of any overarching well-considered plan to manipulate him. No. It was simply that Nellie was screaming in silent pain and needed to know he heard her.

As he moved to get coffee refills for the adults, he paused behind Nellie and brushed her hair with his hand.

"What?" she asked, squirming to look up at him.

"Nothing. Just I love you."

That earned him a squinched nose. He pinched it, twisted his fingers in the age-old "got your nose" gesture, and she smiled. "I love you, too, Daddy."

"After you put your dishes in the dishwasher," Gloria told Nellie, "I'll help you pack. Are you excited about coming to the farm for the week?"

Nellie loved Gloria and Peter's farm with the horses—including a pony they'd bought for her, over Tommy's protests—and the land to run free. Not to mention the shopping trips that invariably happened and the other assorted spoiling. But lately she'd been reluctant to leave Tommy's side, whether for school or overnight visits with her grandparents. "Is Daddy coming, too?"

"Of course. He deserves a vacation, doesn't he?"

Nellie leapt off her chair and took her plate to the dishwasher without prompting. "Daddy, can we bring apples for the horses? And Misty?" Misty was the pony, or as Nellie liked to call her, "my horse."

"If we have any. Go look."

She opened the refrigerator and began removing apples and other potential horse treats, like the baby carrots he'd bought for her lunches, and placing them on the counter.

"You'll want to empty the fridge anyway," Peter said. "Don't want to come back to spoiled milk."

The doorbell rang, startling them all. Nellie dropped an apple and it rolled under the table. "Are the monsters back, Daddy?"

"Don't worry, I'll take care of them."

He marched to the door, Peter behind him. But when he looked through the sidelight, it wasn't a reporter, it was Burroughs. Tommy opened the door, a feeling of dread sloshing the scrambled eggs he'd just eaten, dissolving them to sour acid. With it came a strange feeling of déjà vu as well.

During the initial investigation, once it had become clear that the job would require multiple investigators from several jurisdictions and the state police, Burroughs had been assigned as the main point of contact for Tommy and the family. He'd been the one keeping them updated when the staties dragged the river. And again each time another body or lead surfaced that required follow-up.

But this time, it felt different. Final.

"Detective. Have they found anything more?"

Burroughs glanced past Tommy to where Peter stood. "We should talk in private."

Peter stepped forward, keeping his voice low so it wouldn't carry to the kitchen. "Is it her? Is it my daughter?"

Tommy noted that he also shied away from using Charlotte's name in conjunction with a dead body. Guess even engineers weren't immune to magical thinking.

They both waited for Burroughs' answer. The detective shook his head. "No positive ID. They're going slow so they don't miss anything."

"Did they call in a forensic anthropologist?" Tommy asked.

"A team from Pitt are starting later this morning. As soon as we've finished retrieving the other evidence."

"What other evidence?"

"Artifacts found near the scene. Most of it debris left by hikers, but we're collecting it all." He hesitated, again glancing at

Peter. "That's actually why I'm here. I brought a crime scene unit tech. We'd like to examine your vehicle, if you'll give us permission."

Tommy frowned. "Of course. But the state police already went over it."

After Charlotte's Pathfinder had been found abandoned, the police had impounded it as evidence and kept it for months before returning it to Tommy. It had sat in Charlotte's spot in the single-car garage ever since, while Tommy kept the Volvo outside on the driveway. He still started the SUV occasionally to keep the battery charged, and often he'd sit in it, trying to absorb any essence of Charlotte remaining, but he hadn't had the heart to drive it, despite the fact that it was almost two decades newer than his Volvo.

"I'll just be a minute," Tommy told Peter as he grabbed his keys. He escorted Burroughs outside via the front door, taking the long way around to the garage instead of going through the kitchen to the inside door.

As they walked down the path, he saw that Burroughs had not just brought the crime scene tech but also a flatbed tow truck. He also spotted two news vans parked down the street, just beyond the fifty-yard limit. A few neighbors watched from their windows. Tommy turned away from their questioning glances. He knew from experience that engaging curiosity only created more grist for the neighborhood rumor mill.

He raised the garage door and handed Burroughs his keys, selecting Charlotte's electronic key fob. But to his surprise, Burroughs chose the key to the Volvo instead.

"Actually, it's your car I'd like to examine. With your permission, of course."

"Sure, but why? What are you looking for?" He'd driven the Volvo to Fiddler's Knob yesterday; was there something they thought he might have picked up while there?

Burroughs handed the keys back to Tommy. "If you wouldn't mind opening it?"

Tommy opened the driver's door and gestured to Burroughs, who in turn waved the tech over to join them. They both stood aside as the tech, clad in overalls and wearing gloves, climbed into the car.

"And the rear compartment?"

"Sure, but it's a mess." Tommy lifted the latch. The back of the station wagon was cluttered; it was where everything ended up when he had no time to return it to its proper place inside the house.

Burroughs leaned in, looking without touching. "Do you have a spare tire?"

"It's under everything." Tommy pushed aside his first aid kit, Nellie's bag of toys, books, and puzzles that she kept for "emergencies" like getting stuck waiting for Tommy with nothing to do, a blanket, tarp, box of garbage bags, and a box of wet wipes, and was finally able to raise the top of the spare tire compartment. "There you go."

Burroughs craned his head in, scrutinizing the spare tire and jack. "What about the tire iron? And the lug nut wrench?"

Tommy lowered the lid to the spare tire compartment. "Volvo included a tool box, here in this side compartment." He opened the compartment to reveal the tool kit.

"Okay if I open it?" Burroughs asked.

"Sure."

To Tommy's surprise, the detective donned nitrile gloves—the same type Tommy used to wear in the ER. A cold feeling in the pit of his stomach warned him that he'd made a mistake, that this was all wrong, but there was no going back now. All he could do was maintain a facade of normality. Even though it was clear from the way Burroughs was acting that everything was very much not normal.

Burroughs unclipped the lid of the tool kit and opened it. The kit had molded inserts to keep each tool in its proper place. While the crescent wrenches and a pair of screwdrivers were secured in their compartments, there was a gaping void slashing diagonally across the tool kit. "Looks like the tire iron is missing."

"Should be in there."

"When's the last time you saw it?" Burroughs asked.

"I don't know. Years? I've never had a flat, so I've never used it. Want to tell me why you're so interested?" He had a sinking feeling but could not admit the possibility, not even as a question—best to let Burroughs do the talking. Anything Tommy asked would just be misconstrued and used against him.

Burroughs shined his Maglite through the spare tire well once again, as well as the side compartment where the toolkit was housed, then gestured for the tech to move in. He motioned for Tommy to stand aside, then joined him. "There's no tire iron in there anywhere."

Tommy shrugged and shoved his hands in his pockets, hiding fists of frustration. The cops wouldn't be asking about a tire iron unless they already had a tire iron and wanted to tie it to him...which meant... "It was Charlotte, wasn't it?"

"Like I said, we don't know for certain."

"But you think it's her, right? Why are you asking about a tire iron? Is that how—" The ground felt uneven, and a wave of nausea forced Tommy to look away without finishing his question.

Before Burroughs could answer, the tech alerted. "Found something!"

Burroughs moved forward, Tommy looking over his shoulder at what the tech pointed to, tucked deep into the shadows, wedged behind where the spare tire sat. A silver charm bracelet.

Tommy's legs swam out from under him and he steadied himself with a hand on the top of the car. His entire body flooded with ice water. He stretched a second hand out, gripping the luggage rack with what little strength he had left. Head sagging down, he focused on a crack in the driveway below him, a dandelion thrusting through it in an act of defiance. He hauled in one breath, then another, but couldn't get his vision to focus past the tiny yellow flower.

"Dr. Worth?" Burroughs had his hand on Tommy's arm. Tommy shook his head and his vision cleared. He raised his head. "Do you recognize this? Is it your wife's? It seems to be missing a charm."

CHAPTER 29

"SARAH'S GONE." TK felt so foolish, calling Lucy to tell her. How could she have messed up so badly? All she'd done was take a shower, and she'd lost their client.

"What happened?" Lucy asked.

TK ran her fingers through her still dripping hair and reached for a towel before it stained any of Valencia's antique furniture. She wished she'd stayed back at her own place; the gatehouse was simple, basically a studio apartment, but more than enough to serve TK's needs. Unlike this sumptuous guest suite where Valencia had ensconced TK and Sarah last night.

"I'm not sure. We both stayed here at the house last night. She was fine when she went to bed. I checked on her this morning and she was still sleeping, so I jumped into the shower. And when I came out, she was gone."

"Did she talk to anyone? Was anyone there?"

"No, but she left a note. Says she went to pick up her car from the shop and that she'd be fine. Says we should concentrate on helping Tommy."

"You told her about the remains on the mountain."

"She overheard last night at Tommy's and asked, so yeah, I told her all about Charlotte." She hesitated. Had that been a mistake? Usually she'd never have violated operational security, but Sarah had seemed more concerned about Tommy's well-being than the facts of the case.

"Transportation?"

"Xander said she called a cab. Want me to go after her? I saw which repair shop her car's at when Burroughs gave her the paperwork."

"No. She's a grown woman, can make up her own mind."

"But her stalker—"

"*If* there is a stalker. Plus, if we don't know where she's going, odds are a stalker won't either."

Which could be exactly what Sarah had planned. Someone who traveled as light as she did was probably used to making fresh starts.

"I feel responsible," TK admitted. "At least let me and Wash keep tracing her past. If we find anything helpful, Burroughs can track her down and let her know." After all, Sarah had never asked them to babysit her, only to help her find her previous life.

"Go ahead," Lucy said. "I'll be in the field most of the day."

"Are you with the staties? Did they find anything?"

"No, they wouldn't let a civilian like me anywhere near the crime scene." A wistful hint of regret shaded Lucy's voice.

"Where are you going?"

"To walk in a dead woman's shoes."

TOMMY STARED, MESMERIZED by the tiny bracelet that sparkled in the sunlight. Then the crime scene tech turned away, taking Charlotte's bracelet with him.

"I have no idea how that got there," he stammered, acutely aware that he sounded like any stupid criminal from any reality police show. "Burroughs. What the hell is going on here?"

But the detective had turned aside to make a phone call. He pulled his phone away from his ear for a moment. "Wait for me inside, Dr. Worth. I'll be with you in a moment."

"No. I deserve to know—"

The detective walked away, his back to Tommy's protests. Tommy raised his head to see that a small crowd had gathered where the news trucks were parked down the road. Lips tight as he held back his anger and frustration, he stalked back into the house.

Only to be confronted with Gloria and Peter. "What was all that about? What were they looking for?" Gloria asked.

"What did they find?" Peter added, his tone low and laced with a touch of menace.

"They asked to look at the cars, so I let them." Tommy tried to make light of his apprehension. How the hell had that bracelet gotten there? And what did his tire iron have to do with anything?

Worst of all was Burroughs' reaction. Forensic tests or not, the detective seemed certain it was Charlotte dead up on that mountain.

Tommy walked away from his in-laws, desperate to marshal his emotions. "I think…I don't know, but I think…that body they found is Charlotte."

Gloria's sudden choked sob wrenched through him. She fled up the stairs, leaving Tommy alone with Peter.

"Tell me you had nothing to do with this."

Tommy whirled to face Charlotte's father. "What? No, Peter, I swear—"

"No. Say the words. I need to hear you say them."

Tommy usually forgot that Peter was taller than him, and despite the older man's sedentary occupation, he was in good shape. Now, with Peter leaning in, fists raised level with his heart, eyes blazing with pain, there was no mistaking who would win any physical encounter between the two of them.

Tommy met Peter's stare head on. He was so sick and tired of people assuming the worst—and being helpless to disprove them. But he'd thought he was past it with Gloria and Peter. "I had nothing to do with Charlotte's disappearance. I have no idea what happened to her." He stepped forward, chin jutting up. "Does that satisfy you?"

Peter held his gaze for a long moment. "No. Not at all."

The door opened. Burroughs. "Dr. Worth, we're getting a search warrant for your vehicle. In the meantime, I'd appreciate it if you accompanied me to the station for an interview."

With Burroughs on one side, blocking any escape, and

Peter on the other, blocking access to the stairs and Nellie, a sudden wave of claustrophobia hit Tommy. Trapped. He was trapped, inside his own home.

"I didn't do anything," he protested. "Why would I let you search the cars if I had?"

His attempt at reason failed miserably. "What choice did you have with your in-laws right here, listening?" Burroughs countered. "And if you refused, it wouldn't have mattered. Based on what we found at the scene, we would have sat on the car until I had enough probable cause for a warrant."

"So then why—"

"More I see you in action, Dr. Worth, the more chance you have to trip up."

Tommy was silent after that. Last time Tommy had gone through this, after days of interviews, Peter had insisted he get an attorney. And the attorney had told him he was a fool to answer any questions.

At least ten separate police officers, state police troopers, detectives, and investigators, and one FBI agent who had been called in to assist, had all questioned Tommy. And despite the attorney's admonishments, he'd told them everything he knew—or didn't know—certain that this was the best way to get them to take their focus off him and instead concentrate on the search for Charlotte.

Tommy noticed that this time Peter didn't offer to provide an attorney. Instead, Charlotte's father moved up the steps, calling to his wife. "Gloria, get Nellie's things. We're leaving. Now!"

Halfway up, he paused and turned back, looking down at Tommy. "We're taking Nellie. You'll stay here until this is cleared up. She's better off not seeing you, not like this."

"No," Tommy said. "You can't—"

"It might be the best way to protect her," Burroughs said in a voice that sounded almost human.

Tommy closed his eyes, wishing he could open them again and he'd have his life back. No such luck.

"Let me say goodbye." He turned to Burroughs. "Then I'll go with you, tell you anything you want." The sooner he finished with the police, the sooner he could rejoin Nellie.

He didn't feel safe being away from her. Yes, Peter and Gloria would shield her from the reporters, but it wasn't the same. They didn't know how to quiet her night terrors or where they were in the book he was reading to her or which socks she liked to wear with which outfit. She needed him. Even more, he needed her. Needed to know she was safe.

Burroughs nodded his assent, and Tommy rushed up the steps, ignoring Peter's glare. Nellie's room was the first one at the top of the stairs and he barged through the door, startling Gloria, who stepped in front of Nellie as if to block Tommy's access to his daughter. As if he might hurt Nellie. The thought stopped him dead—that and the obvious fear in Gloria's eyes.

Peter and Burroughs crowded the doorway behind him while Nellie bounced off her bed and rushed into his arms. "Daddy, I don't want to go. Can't we stay here?"

Tommy crouched down to her level and bundled her tight, his face pressed against hers. "You need to go with Papa and Gramma now, sweetie. I'll be along later."

She shook her head violently, almost breaking free of his grasp. "No. I want to stay with you. Don't make me go, Daddy!"

Her voice rose, not in the tantrum screeches she'd been using all too often lately, but in pure terror. She grasped his arm with both of her hands. "Stay with me, Daddy. I'm scared. I don't want you to go. You need to stay with me."

Gloria approached Nellie from behind and rested a palm on her shoulder. "Everything will be all right, Nellie. Your father just needs to help the policemen out. But we'll go to the farm, play with the horses, roast marshmallows, and make s'mores. We'll have fun."

Nellie whirled on her grandmother. "No! You can't make me. I won't go. I want to stay with Daddy."

What little control Tommy had left was fast escaping. "Eleanor Rose Worth," he said sternly. "You do not speak to your grandmother like that. She loves you very much and only wants to take care of you."

"But don't you want to take care of me, Daddy? Or I can take care of you. Just please don't go." Her voice held a tremor that pierced his heart.

He stood and gently pulled her hands, one finger at a time, away from his arm. He nodded to Gloria, who rushed in to wrap her own arms around Nellie, giving Tommy space. "I love you, sweetheart."

As Peter and Gloria fought in vain to comfort Nellie, her cries followed Tommy down the stairs until he and Burroughs closed the front door behind them.

He couldn't help it; he glanced back at the house one last time. He couldn't shake the feeling that nothing would ever be the same again.

CHAPTER 30

LUCY DIDN'T BOTHER driving all the way out to where Charlotte Worth's vehicle had been found abandoned along the banks of the Youghiogheny. The police would have covered all the routes in and out of the secluded overlook using better tools than she had at hand. Instead, she drove to the last place Charlotte had been seen alive, the same convenience store where Sarah Brown had stopped the day before she went up Fiddler's Knob and came down without her memory. No matter what anyone told her, it still felt like an unnatural coincidence.

As she parked her Subaru in front of the Sheetz, she had the weird tingling along her spine that her grandmother used to call coffin chills. Someone, somewhere, was walking over Lucy's grave. At least that was the old wives' tale her granny had teased her with.

She mixed a coffee at the well-equipped coffee bar and waited until the cashier, a twenty-something who had a nose stud and wispy goatee, had finished with the other customers. As he rang up her coffee, she explained who she was and why she was there.

"You mean the lady from last year?" he asked.

"Yes. I noticed your security cameras and thought—"

"Oh, the cops took all that. Huge manhunt, they looked through everything. Even searched our garbage."

Given that the first case she'd worked with Burroughs involved a body stuffed into a drum for discarded fast food frying oil, she wasn't surprised.

"Didn't find nothing," he continued. "Lady just vanished."

"You know it happened again." She leaned in and dropped her voice to a conspiratorial level. "Just Friday night a lady was in here, and Saturday morning she developed total amnesia."

"No shit. Like she can't remember her name, anything?"

"Exactly. We're working to trace her steps, help her figure out who she is." She showed him her copy of Sarah's receipt.

"Friday? Like four days ago?" He shook his head. "Sorry, I wasn't working."

"Would you keep the security footage that long?"

His expression brightened. "Hell yeah. It's all on computer, so it just keeps recording until the drive is full. I think it holds like a month or something. Hang on." He gestured to a clerk who was mopping the floor near the restrooms. "Hey, take over for me, will you?"

As he escorted Lucy into the manager's office, she asked, "You sure your manager won't mind?"

He flashed her a smile. "Lady, I am the manager. Well, assistant day-shift manager. Which means I'm the boss until eleven when the day-shift manager arrives." He sat down at a desk and began to type at the keyboard. "Do you think they were abducted by aliens or something? I mean, two ladies, one vanished without a trace and one with her mind wiped..." He leaned back and gestured for her to join him behind the desk. "Here we go. Friday. Same time as on the receipt."

Lucy watched Sarah pay for gas and a soda, then walk out the front door. "Can you follow her on the other cameras? See her car?"

"Sure, hang on." A few more clicks, and the view changed. "That's her. Parked at the side of the building. A lot of kids like to park there, think it's more private because they're behind the ice machine, they never see the camera. You wouldn't believe the things it picks up."

"I'll bet," she said absently, leaning forward to get a better look. Sarah was getting into the passenger side of a vehicle, but it was an SUV, not her Prius. "Can you freeze it there?"

He clicked, and the image froze. The car was a silver Jeep Cherokee. And the driver was a man. Caucasian, nothing really to distinguish him. Not for the first time she wished Pennsylvania had front license plates.

"Can you send me that one frame?"

"Sure thing." She gave him her email as he grabbed a screen capture. "Is he our bad guy?"

"Not sure. Can you see the car's license plate when it pulls out?"

He forwarded the video, but it was useless. Still, it was more than she'd had when she walked in. He escorted her back through the store and out the front door. "Hope that helps."

AT LEAST BURROUGHS didn't handcuff him, Tommy thought as they drove past his neighbors. Some of them had their cell phones up, recording his humiliation for posterity—or to make a quick buck with the tabloids. Seems like nowadays everyone was a paparazzo, like the guy he'd caught earlier trying to take pictures through his dining room window with his cell phone. It'd been obvious he wasn't a reporter. Maybe a neighbor? He'd looked kind of familiar.

Tommy didn't turn away from the stares; he faced them all. He had nothing to hide, he told himself. Nothing to hide. It became his mantra, his last line of defense.

"Just tell me one thing," Burroughs said as he steered the Impala around the throng of onlookers and the news vans. "Is Sarah safe?"

Tommy jerked his head around. "Sarah? What's she got to do with this?"

"You tell me. I mean, at first when I met her at the hospital and she suggested using you guys to help—"

"Sarah suggested the Beacon Group? I thought it was because you and Oshiro know Lucy."

"No. The nurses lent her a laptop to surf the web, try to jar her memory. She saw a story about that Texas case you guys've been getting a lot of press about." He gripped the wheel, chin jerking as if he'd just now realized something. "But it wasn't the Texas case that caught her attention, was it? There was a picture of the entire team in that story—including you. She recognized you, didn't she? Wow. What must you have thought when she showed up at Beacon Falls yesterday along with me and Oshiro. Tell me, Worth, were you about ready to shit yourself? I mean, the girl who knew your secret shows up at your work?"

"I never saw Sarah before yesterday," Tommy protested. "And I have no secrets."

The smile that creased Burroughs' face was not a kind one. Menacing would be more like it. "Sure you do. We all do."

"What do you think Sarah knew?"

"For one thing, I'm guessing you attacked her on that mountain. She wasn't running *to* the parking lot like everyone else when the car alarms started blaring. She was running *away* from you. Too bad the smash and grab interrupted things. Would you have bashed her head in like you did your wife's?"

Fury mixed with pain as he visualized what had happened during Charlotte's final moments. His mind was filled with the image of her face twisted in agony. "Go to hell, Burroughs."

"You first, Worth. You first."

Chapter 31

LUCY'S NEXT STOP was a nearby Eat 'n Park to meet with the director of the domestic violence coalition that ran all the county shelters and the woman in charge of the shelter Charlotte had volunteered at. In the police materials detailing Charlotte's work as a domestic violence counselor, Lucy had found that all the names and addresses and any other pertinent details about the women Charlotte had helped had been redacted. When she called, the shelter director had refused to meet Lucy anywhere official and insisted that their discussion be "off the record."

By the time Lucy arrived, the director, Thelma Pierce, and Charlotte's immediate supervisor, Fran Wainwright, were already sipping coffee and waiting for her. The family-style restaurant was almost empty at this after-breakfast-not-quite-lunch hour, and they had chosen a quiet booth far away from any eavesdroppers.

"We already shared with the police all that we could

about Charlotte's work with us," Pierce began as soon as Lucy had placed her order and the waitress had brought her a cup of coffee. Her posture was defensive and her attitude seemed to be that Lucy was wasting her time.

"I saw their notes, scant as they were," Lucy said. "Am I correct in understanding that since you're shielded by confidentiality, as are your clients' identities, that none of Charlotte's clients were actually interviewed?"

"We spoke to them," Wainwright answered. She was younger, mid-thirties, and seemed eager to please. "On behalf of the police. With their consent, of course. No one had seen Charlotte since her last shift, a week before she went missing."

"I saw that in the report."

"Then the matter is closed." Pierce set down her cup and seemed ready to leave.

"Not quite. What about any contact with Charlotte outside the shelter? Beyond her regular duties as a volunteer?" Lucy raised her cup and stared at Pierce.

"I'm sure I have no idea what you're talking about. Our shelters follow the guidelines set forth by the state—"

"I'm sure they do. But we both know that there are occasional clients who require additional services, above and beyond counseling."

Wainwright jumped in to answer. "Charlotte was more than a counselor. She was a whiz at helping our clients navigate the state bureaucracy. Helped them get official non-residential addresses that the government would recognize but that couldn't be traced to their real address. A few of them she even walked through changing their name and getting new social security numbers."

Lucy knew that the tools available to help victims of domestic abuse had come a long way in the past few years, with a greater emphasis on protecting victims' locations and identity. Ironically, much of the progress had occurred as a result of the epidemic of identity theft, a crime which had left its victims requiring similar governmental procedures.

"We loved Charlotte," Pierce said. "She was more than a co-worker, she was our friend. She is dearly missed. But really, Ms. Guardino, I don't think we have any information that might be helpful."

Between the two of them Lucy felt like she was playing Red Rover. Time to tag someone else. She chose Wainwright, who seemed the more pliable of the two. "I'm not asking you to break any confidences. But we all know that every now and then a woman leaves an abuser who has the resources to find her despite the protective services you offer. And every now and then, those women need a little extra, off the record, type help. Like cash, disposable phones, maybe transportation, a way to start a new life. You both know Charlotte spent her last day buying disposable phones and collecting a nice nest egg of cash. Any idea who it was for?"

"The police seemed to think it was for herself," Pierce said.

"Really? I thought she was your friend. Surely she would have come to you if something was wrong at home."

"Confidentiality precludes me from—"

"It doesn't preclude you from answering a simple question. Did she come to you or give you any hint that she might be leaving her husband?"

Pierce's mouth twisted as tight as a lock missing its key. But Wainwright finally looked up from whatever had fascinated her at the bottom of her coffee mug and met Lucy's gaze. "No. She did not."

"If you knew the police believed that she was leaving her husband, why didn't you—"

Pierce shifted her glare from her younger subordinate to Lucy. "Because we can never be suspected of breaking confidentiality. These women have placed their faith in us—they trust us with their lives. We cannot break that trust. Not ever."

"Not even to help find whoever killed your friend?"

"Not even—" Pierce stopped herself, her cup rattling in the saucer. "Wait. Killed?"

"We think we found Charlotte's body. Decomp would put her time of death at about a year ago." Lucy wasn't basing that on any official report—much too early for that at this point—but she'd seen enough dead bodies to make an educated guess. "So while the police were chasing a false trail, thinking she left voluntarily and covered her tracks..."

"The killer had her." Wainwright's eyes went round, and her hand stroked her throat. "Was she killed right away? Could she have been alive? I mean—did we, could we have—"

"It's not our fault," Pierce said, enunciating each word precisely. "We had no indication of what happened to Charlotte then, and we certainly don't now. I'm sorry it's ended this way.

She will be missed." She stood to leave, waiting for Wainwright to follow.

"I need a moment," Wainwright said.

"Very well. I'll see you on Thursday at the regular staff meeting. We can discuss a memorial for Charlotte at that time."

"Actually, please wait until the police release the information to the public," Lucy said. She couldn't help but add, "I'm sure you understand how important confidentiality is in these cases."

Pierce gave her a stiff nod, then pivoted on her heel and stalked away.

Wainwright held her coffee cup in both hands but didn't drink any of it. She simply stared for several long moments. "You're right, you know."

"About what?" Lucy asked softly, approaching her as timidly as she would a wild doe.

"About the clients who sometimes need extra services. Thelma doesn't like or want to know about them—she needs to keep everything aboveboard for the state regulators. But there's a group of us who have banded together to help them." She finally looked up. "It's ironic. Most of them are afraid for their lives because their husbands are in law enforcement."

"Which means you can't use any of the official procedures to change their identity or address."

"No. Government officials, the courts, and law enforcement still have access to those records. They're sealed from the public, of course, but sometimes even banks and other private institutions can access them. Heck, in some counties, it doesn't matter if the woman gets a new name and the judge seals the records. They'll just cross out her old name on the birth certificate and write in all her new info—where anyone can access it if they know where to look. Happens more often than you'd think."

"So around the time Charlotte went missing, was she helping one of these special clients?"

"Because the police know the locations of the shelters, clients like these tend not to come in in person. They'll make contact via phone, and we'll give them advice on how to best stay safe." She glanced up and met Lucy's gaze. "We don't break the law. It's just circumventing standard procedure."

"Did Charlotte mention anyone who might need extra help?"

"Well, a few weeks before she left, she was asking a few of us questions."

"Questions?"

"More like scenarios. Hypothetical worst cases."

"Like?"

"Like what would we do if we were helping a client and the abuser was someone with access to law enforcement databases. Or, our absolute nightmare scenario—an IRS agent."

Of course. You could change your name, address, get a new driver's license and social security number, but none of that would hide you from the tax man. If Charlotte was facing a challenge like that, she might have been forced not just to bend the rules, but even break the law to help her client. A good reason for her not to share details with anyone else.

Lucy tried a different approach. "Where would you meet someone who needed help?"

"We've each set up a few bank accounts so we can access cash without arousing any suspicion. Bankers have a ton of access to information, so we try to be very circumspect. We'll gather what cash and supplies we can, like disposable cell phones, and arrange to meet the client at a pre-arranged location. Usually someplace public but out of the way where three women chatting wouldn't be noticed. And we always go with a partner to watch out for trouble."

"So a convenience store off a highway might be used to meet a client?"

"Exactly. A lot of clients want to meet in really private places, but we have to protect ourselves. I mean, what if they weren't for real and it was an abuser trying to get to us?"

"I'm glad you don't take chances."

"Well, I don't. But Charlotte—sometimes we had clients who were just so terrified, truly fleeing for their lives, that she'd bend the rules."

"Could she have been helping a client like this the day she died?"

"That's what I don't understand. If she was, why didn't she tell anyone? That's why we work together, so we can watch each other's backs." She gave a shake of her head. "I don't think she could have been. Unless..."

Lucy raised an eyebrow and waited.

"Unless she thought the abuser was someone so dangerous that it might put us at risk. Then I can see her going it alone."

"Has that ever happened before? Charlotte helping a client on her own?"

"Not that I know of—and certainly someone would have said something after she went missing if they'd suspected it." Her lips tightened as if she was debating with herself. Finally she glanced up. "No. I think maybe Thelma was right. Charlotte's disappearance has nothing to do with her work with the shelter." She pushed her cup and saucer away and slid out of the booth. "I'm sorry I couldn't be more help. Please tell her family they're in our prayers."

CHAPTER 32

THEY ARRIVED AT the Zone 3 police station on the Southside, an old brick building that squatted on a busy corner wedged between a coffee shop and a vacant lot. Burroughs led Tommy upstairs to an interview room, explained the recording procedures and that he could leave at any time, had him sign paperwork saying he understood everything, asked if he wanted coffee—he didn't—then left.

The wait began.

Tommy sat in silence with nothing to distract him. Memories of the last time he'd been in a room like this kept flooding over him, swamping him as the past filtered over the present for a few moments, coloring it gray. Different room, he thought, yet exactly the same, except for the graffiti scratched into the plaster walls. Same molded plastic chair that felt rickety and was too lightweight and flimsy to ever use as a weapon. Same steel table bolted to the floor with a bar across it to secure handcuffs to if necessary. Same fluorescent light with its interminable buzz that would drive any man to confess any sin if he were left confined with it for long enough.

Same silence. With nothing to fill the void except memories.

He'd lost count of how many times he'd been interviewed those first days, and then re-interviewed when the trail went cold, over and over and over again. Good cop, bad cop, kind cop who came to the house and sat at his very own kitchen table hoping for a confession, competent cop, foolish cop, polite cop, angry cop…he'd met them all, played all their cop games.

Last time he was here—maybe in this very same room—last time, he'd been so anxious to leave, had felt like a caged animal, filled with the need to be out there, searching, doing something, anything to find Charlotte.

This time, there was nothing more to be done. So he sat. And waited.

Finally, Burroughs returned, accompanied by a petite dark-skinned woman who, despite being dressed in civilian clothing like Burroughs, had a military-like bearing. "You remember Corporal Harding from the state police?"

Tommy nodded. A year ago, it had been "call me Liz" as Harding sipped Charlotte's favorite tea at his kitchen table.

They both regarded him in silence for a moment—the way a surgeon studied a patient one last time before he plunged his scalpel into the patient's flesh.

Harding broke first, stepping forward to toss a stack of photos onto the table, face down.

"Do you recognize anything from those photos, Dr.

Worth?" She scraped the seat out across from him, pulled it around so they were sitting side by side instead of opposite each other, and sat down, leaning forward so close he could smell her shampoo. Nothing floral or exotic, just simple and clean.

He slid a finger toward the photos, itching to turn them over, yet dreading what they would reveal. They had to be from the mountain grave. He pulled back, crossing his arms over his chest and pushing away from the table. It was a childish impulse, this deep-seated fear that once he saw, he could never go back to the way things were before the photos, before this evidence of the truth invaded his world. But it was an impulse he could not conquer.

Harding reached forward, selected a photo—seemingly at random, but Tommy was certain it wasn't—and turned it over.

He'd braced himself for a view of a decomposing corpse. But that's not what she showed him. Instead, it was the tattered remains of a yellow baseball jersey. The Falcons, his old softball team from Three Rivers' ER.

"Do you recognize this jersey, Doctor?" Unlike Burroughs, Harding always used Tommy's title.

"Yes. That's the softball team I played on—until last year when I left the hospital."

She flipped another photo over. Once again Tommy clenched his muscles and relaxed again when he saw it was simply the back of the jersey, where his name and number were imprinted. "Is it your shirt?"

"Yes. I had several. Charlotte often wore them to my games. We had one that night, the day she…but you already know that." He glanced to Burroughs for confirmation.

"That's all right. Feel free to repeat anything you already told us." *All the better to trip you up and hang you with,* Burroughs' expression said.

"Last time you saw your wife, she wasn't wearing this jersey?" Harding asked, catching Tommy off guard by flipping another photo over. Again, he tensed and relaxed when he saw it was simply a close-up of his name on the back of the jersey.

They were conditioning him, he knew. He had to guard against it, because those photos hid much, much worse than an old softball jersey.

"No," he answered. "She was dressed for work. Blue slacks, ivory colored blouse. Like I've told you."

"What time was your game that day?"

"Seven. I was working the eight to four shift, but it always runs late, so we'd planned to meet there, at Frick Park. Her folks had Nellie, so we were going to make a night of it, go out with the team after." He hadn't made it; a multicar pileup on 376 involving a school bus and twenty-two kids had kept him until almost eight.

"When did you realize Charlotte was leaving you?" Burroughs asked, his tone matter-of-fact when he had no facts.

Tommy twisted away from Harding to glare at the detective. "She wasn't leaving. She wouldn't. If she was wearing this jersey, doesn't that prove it? She would never have worn it anywhere else, certainly not if she was trying to run away."

Burroughs leaned against the wall, arms crossed, tossing away Tommy's alternative theory with a flick of his eyes.

"Unless she didn't know you knew. Thought she still had a few days to finish preparing. Maybe you convinced her to leave the game, meet you somewhere else. Wait until you got there. And then..."

Then it hit Tommy. Eyes wide, he looked up, first at Harding, then at Burroughs. "Leave the game?" Based on the time Charlotte had been seen at the convenience store and the time it would have taken to drive to where her car was found, the working theory had been that she'd never come back into the city or made it to Frick Park. "Does this mean—she was there?"

Harding waited a long moment before answering. As if hoping Tommy would fill the silence with words of his own. "We're not sure."

"One of the private investigators we hired, they talked to everyone at the game," Tommy said. "No one saw her."

"We know. We spoke to them as well. In addition to shop owners in the area." Regent Square was a haven for coffee shops, cafes, and eclectic art galleries.

"But, if she was there and her car ended up thirty miles away at the Youghiogheny, and..." His voice trailed off as he stared at the backs of the other photos.

"Now that we've tied Charlotte to the area around Fiddler's Knob, we accessed the CCTV for anywhere near there. A Toyota Pathfinder with a partial plate matching her vehicle's was headed south on Route 51 at two thirteen that morning."

Seven hours after he was supposed to meet Charlotte at Frick Park. Tommy couldn't make sense of it; he stared at them both bleary-eyed. "You think she was taken at the game? While waiting for me?"

If so, then it was all his fault. She'd been there, alone, without him to protect her. Because of some stupid softball game on a warm spring night with no reason to rush home. It was supposed to have been a romantic timeout from adult responsibilities; instead it had turned into a nightmare.

"The Pathfinder spotted by the traffic camera was driven by a man." Burroughs nailed the coffin shut. "Unfortunately, it was too foggy to get a good look at him."

"Where were you at that time, Dr. Worth?" Harding asked in a gentle tone.

"You know where I was. At home, waiting." He'd called the police after he'd gone to Frick Park, the game almost over, and hadn't found Charlotte or been able to reach her cell. "Exactly where the police told me to be. In case she called or came back."

More silence as they waited. He filled in the blanks for them—even though he knew they already knew the answer. "And no, no one can prove it. I didn't talk to anyone or see anyone."

Not until the next morning when he'd driven over to the police station— to this very building—and insisted on them updating him with everything they'd found during that long, long night. But it had boiled down to nothing. They promised to keep looking, but reminded him repeatedly that Charlotte was a grown woman, free to come and go as she pleased, and that there was no evidence of foul play or any criminal activity.

They'd told him that even if they found her, if she didn't want him to know, she had a right to privacy and they wouldn't be able to tell him anything.

He'd left feeling more alone than ever. Frustrated and frightened and with no idea what to do to find his wife.

Now, both detectives remained silent. Harding eased back in her chair as if in no rush—as if the truth was sitting right in front of her and all she had to do was listen.

Interrogation 101: give them enough rope and they'll hang themselves. He was so damn tired of their games, treating his life, Charlotte's life, as if they were puzzles with pieces missing.

He wasn't going to play anymore. If that was Charlotte up on that mountain, then everything changed. Right here, right now.

Tommy stretched out his hand and whipped one photo over, then another, flipping them onto the table so fast they became a whirl of dirt and bones and more clothing, a tire iron, close-ups of a wedding band and the claddagh ring, and finally, a skull and the full skeleton. Shot *in situ*, just the way it had been buried.

Face down. Arms and legs shoved together to take up less room. Like garbage tossed aside.

Then he turned over the last photo. The skull alone, a frontal view. Nothing of Charlotte's face remained, the soft tissues long ago rotted away. A few wisps of hair clung to the skull, lackluster and robbed of their coppery shine. The bones were broken; even in this view he could see the gaping cleft of a wound to the right temporal region, along with a shattered zygomatic arch—cheekbone—and eye socket.

Someone had hit her. Over and over. Venting their rage.

His entire body trembled with fury. At the animal who'd done this. At the police with their callous mind games. At God, at Fate, at life itself.

How could this have happened? To Charlotte, beautiful, joyous Charlotte, who'd spent her life helping people?

He swept the photos off the table, banishing them to the floor, refusing to acknowledge the truth they held. Except one truth. The one he could no longer avoid.

"It's her. It's Charlotte."

Burroughs ignored the photos to step forward and press his palms on the tabletop, leaning forward until he filled Tommy's vision. "How do you know? How can you be so certain? DNA testing isn't back."

"I'm sure. It's her."

"Seems to me there's only one person who could be that certain. The person who put her in that grave."

"Are you saying I don't know my own wife?"

The two men stared at each other. Harding didn't interrupt—rather, Tommy felt her studying him. They all seemed to understand that whoever spoke first lost.

Tommy was finished playing their damn games and following their damn rules.

"I'd like to call my lawyer now." It felt like an admission of guilt, but he was drowning here. The more he tried to explain, the worse things got.

"You mean the suit your in-laws paid for last time we had you here?" Burroughs said. "Good old Gloria and Peter going to keep footing the bill now that we have you dead to rights?"

Tommy ignored him, trying to remember the lawyer's name. Seth something-first-name-son. Thompson? Williamson? No. Michaelson, that was it. But Burroughs was right. He couldn't involve Gloria and Peter, get them caught in the middle. Not if Burroughs was serious about actually arresting him.

How had it come to this? He tried to think of any other lawyers he knew. Only one came to mind. All he had to do was swallow his pride and make the call. She would understand. Plus, she already knew everything about both Charlotte's and Sarah's cases.

Valencia Frazier.

Chapter 33

Despite Lucy telling her not to worry, TK still called the body repair shop to confirm that Sarah had arrived safely to pick up her car. And then she returned to Sarah's apartment building to canvass her neighbors. She hated feeling as if she'd shirked her duty, letting Sarah leave, but Lucy was right: the woman wasn't a prisoner.

Still…she'd been given a mission, to find the truth, to watch over Sarah. And she'd failed.

Now she paced behind Wash as he worked his magic with the computers.

"No matter how much she loves lichen and rocks, I can't believe a woman can live with no people in her life," she said as she paced. He rolled his chair into her path and she changed her route, circling the table instead. "All she wanted was the truth. How hard can that be?"

"Sure you didn't miss any of the neighbors?" From his tone, he wasn't asking for information but rather searching for an excuse for her to leave.

"Nope. Not a single one remembers her. A few thought I was crazy, said her apartment was empty. How can she have not touched anyone's life?"

"Relax, TK. Now's the time for the machine to come up with the answers."

"She's a person, Wash. I mean, even when I was living on the streets, people knew me, people looked out for me, would have noticed if I'd vanished. But with Sarah—nothing. No one."

"You said yourself she might have worked hard to keep it that way."

"Still." A red icon flashing at the corner of the projection screen caught her eye. "Hey, one of your thingies. What's that for?" She rushed back behind his workstation to watch over his shoulder.

"When we got no joy from the local database search I extended it to the mid-Atlantic states."

"So what is it?"

He clicked a few keys, and the monitor filled with a birth certificate.

"I thought you already found Sarah's birth certificate."

"This isn't hers. She had a baby. A son. Born in Washington, DC two years ago."

TK reeled back. "A baby?" She shook her head. "Definitely not at the apartment. Not with her on the trail. Where is he? With the father? Grandparents?"

"The father's name is listed as Walter Thomas Putnam. Says they're married. Address in DC." He kept typing. "No Walter Putnam at that address now though."

"Sarah was married. She has a son." The implications spun through TK's mind. "And she has no idea—" Then another thought occurred to her. "Wait. What if this Walter Putnam is who she's hiding from? We need to learn everything we can about him."

"I'm on it. But while we have Sarah's consent to search the databases for *her* information, there are privacy issues if we look for anyone else. Birth certificates and death certificates and the like are protected. I only got access to this one because Sarah is listed as a parent." TK's glare stopped him. "Okay, you don't care about privacy issues. But I can't break any laws. Let me see what I can do."

She leaned over his chair, toes bouncing. Finally, something concrete. Once they untangled Mr. Walter T. Putnam's life and his relationship to Sarah, they could give Sarah back her life. Or at least a start to reclaiming it.

And if Mr. Walter T. was the reason why she was on the run, then TK would make sure he answered for his actions.

VALENCIA HAD ARRIVED twenty minutes after Tommy's call, striding into the interview room like a mother bear, fierce and protective. "Any questioning will cease until after I've had adequate time to confer with my client."

"We simply requested Dr. Worth's assistance—" Burroughs said, his tone markedly deferent compared to the way he'd spoken to Tommy.

"Are you charging my client with any offense?"

Burroughs looked to Harding, who merely frowned in return. It was clear they wanted to arrest Tommy but also wanted a rock solid case. Good to know he still had a little wiggle room. But it felt as if whatever time he had left to enjoy his freedom was quickly slipping away.

"No," Burroughs answered. "We're not prepared to arrest Dr. Worth at this time."

Valencia gestured for Tommy to join her. Burroughs returned his key ring—all except the key to the Volvo—and escorted them out of the station. On the way, Tommy caught a glimpse of Harding talking on a phone but watching them leave, her gaze one of suspicion and appraisal. It was obvious the police had already made up their minds about what had happened to Charlotte. Which left it to Tommy to fight for the truth.

Valencia led him to her Audi, where Xander waited. Valencia never went anywhere without Xander. He was more than her personal assistant, more than a driver or bodyguard, but how much more Tommy had no idea.

Valencia slid into the front passenger seat while Tommy climbed into the back. Once they'd turned onto Arlington, she twisted in her seat to address him. "I'm going to make some calls, get you a criminal defense attorney."

He scowled, feeling as petulant as Nellie during one of her Sugar Loops tantrums. "I don't need one. I have you. Besides, I'm innocent."

"Innocent men are arrested every day. Innocent men go

to trial every day and are convicted every day. We need to get ahead of this."

He nodded, his mind still reeling at the memory of the photos Harding had shown him. What a horrible way to die. It wouldn't have been fast. He closed his eyes and slumped back in his seat. "Burroughs has it in for me."

"Even police officers are only human."

"The man hates me." He opened his eyes. "If he's in charge of the evidence, I'll never get a fair shot at clearing my name."

"In his own way, Detective Burroughs is just as protective of Charlotte as you are." Tommy started to protest, but she continued, "You need to move past your personal feelings about the man and concentrate on protecting yourself."

"But whoever did that to Charlotte is still out there, running free!"

"I know. And I know it's difficult, maybe the most difficult thing you've ever done. But now's the time to focus on your daughter, on your public image. It means a lot, more than people think, especially if it ever comes to a trial. You need to take care of yourself, Tommy. That means working with an attorney, telling them everything, good or bad, whether you think it might hurt your case or not."

"I've already told you everything. The cops as well, not that they believe me."

They turned down Tommy's street. Thankfully, the news crews had gone and the street was empty. So was his driveway; Gloria and Peter had left already, taking Nellie to their home. He remembered how upset Nellie had been, how angry Peter and

Gloria were. Valencia was right. He had to focus on protecting his family first.

Then he could deal with Burroughs and all the rest.

Xander parked the Audi and Tommy climbed out. "I'll call you as soon as I have the name of an attorney," Valencia promised. "In the meantime, take care. Get some rest. You'll need it."

He nodded glumly and watched them leave. Then he trudged up his front walk, up the steps, and into his home. The house felt cold and empty. As if all the life had been sucked out of it.

What to do next? Taking a shower and changing his clothes would be a start; he was still wearing what he'd had on last night when he fell asleep on the couch after talking with Lucy. And then packing. Both Nellie's things and his. If Peter and Gloria would have him, they could hide out at the farm, away from the press. If not, then he'd take Nellie to a hotel or rent an apartment. Any place but this suddenly lifeless house that used to be a home.

He climbed the steps and passed Nellie's room, then stopped. The door was ajar. He pushed it open. Her bed had been stripped. All her stuffed animals and toys were gone—not just her favorite, couldn't-spend-the-night-without ones, the ones she usually took to Gloria and Peter's.

Stalking across the room, he opened her closet door. Everything, even the hangers, had been taken. The dresser drawers were also empty.

He stood frozen, his hand gripping the edge of the

dresser, the wood biting into his palm. All the rage that had been building during the long morning finally burned its way to the surface, coalescing into a single spike of fury.

He'd lost his wife. He was not about to lose his daughter.

Whirling, he ran down the stairs and out the garage door. His car was gone, so he had no choice but to take Charlotte's SUV. He wrenched the driver's door open and climbed into the seat. It was already adjusted for him, because this was his silent shrine to Charlotte. On long, weary nights he would come out here and sit where she'd last sat, touch the steering wheel—maybe the last thing she'd touched—and listen to her music.

Opera. He hated opera, but she'd loved it. One of her favorites was Maria Callas singing *Tosca.* She'd tried to explain the story to him, translated the Italian, but in the end, it was all a mystery to him. Part of the mystery that was Charlotte. He had loved that even after all these years she could still surprise him, still had hidden depths to be explored.

Until last year, when those mysteries had turned into nightmare questions, taunting him. How many nights had he tried and failed to put himself in her shoes, to figure out why she'd gone or how or where? Mostly why. He'd hated feeling so sorry for himself, despised the weakness and powerlessness it brought with him. He'd thought if he understood the why, he could regain some semblance of control instead of faking his way through every moment of every day.

He jabbed the Pathfinder's ignition switch, ignoring the silver fingerprint powder that still covered it and every other surface of the car. He'd planned to get the car detailed or clean it himself, but had never found the strength to face the job. It was too much like cleaning Charlotte out of his life, erasing the last known traces of her.

The SUV roared to life, anxious to hit the streets, the plaintive voices of lovers facing tragedy filling the air. It still stank of chemicals—Luminol or some other forensic testing compound, he guessed—but the engine worked just fine. He backed out of the driveway, tires screeching as he yanked the wheel and shifted into drive, then sped down the street.

Nellie was the one thought that drove him, unrelenting, insistent. He had to get his daughter back. With him she was safe.

A faint whisper of doubt forced its way through his rage. Was that really what he believed? Or was he using Nellie as a crutch, a way to avoid facing the truth?

Maybe it wasn't he who kept Nellie safe. Maybe it was Nellie who protected *him.* With her he could deny the truth, pretend that everything would be all right.

Pretend he still had a family.

CHAPTER 34

LUCY ORDERED LUNCH and reviewed her notes, still at the booth at the Eat 'n Park. The waitress was now giving her the stink eye, one patron taking up a table that could seat four during the lunch rush, but Lucy ignored her.

Finally, after scouring the files for a third time, Lucy conceded defeat. If Charlotte had been helping one of the shelter's clients that last day, there was no record of it, no one to question about it. The trail was long cold and dead.

Her phone rang. Valencia. "I wanted to update you on Tommy's situation," she started in her cultured tone. "The police brought him in for questioning. Apparently something they found at the crime scene may link him to the dead woman found there."

"Like what? Did they arrest him?"

"They showed him photos of a baseball jersey that belonged to him and that had been in the grave. Also they searched his car for a tire iron but didn't find one. They did, however, find Charlotte's charm bracelet—the one she was wearing when she vanished."

"Damn." More than circumstantial. Once forensics were in, Burroughs would be arresting Tommy, no doubt about it. Unless the state's attorney wanted to wait for a grand jury indictment; sometimes with potential capital crimes, they liked to hedge their bet that way.

"Have you found anything that might help?"

Lucy slid her plate with its half-eaten burger aside and began to gather her stuff. "Not yet, nothing concrete. But we'll keep hammering at it."

"I'm counting on you, Lucy. So is Tommy."

Lucy hung up, paid her bill, and retreated to her Subaru. As she drove to Beacon Falls, she called Burroughs. "What the hell? You arrest one of my people and don't even give me the courtesy of calling?"

"We didn't arrest him. Not yet anyway. And you know how it gets when a case is finally heating up. Calling friends of the main suspect isn't part of my job."

"I had to hear it from my boss. My boss, Burroughs."

"Tough shit. This is a homicide investigation. I'm sorry you've been out of the field so long you've forgotten how the job goes."

Ouch. She'd only left the FBI last month.

"Besides, how do you think I'll feel, having to tell my boss that I trusted a witness to the suspect we're getting ready to arrest?"

"Witness? You mean Sarah?"

"Where is she?" Burroughs asked.

"You don't think she has anything to do with Charlotte?"

"Of course not. But that hiker who came forward says Sarah was arguing with a man. And from his description of their location, they were near Charlotte's grave."

"You think it was Tommy? That he chased Sarah off that mountain? Why?"

"Maybe she saw something she shouldn't have. After all, we would have never found Charlotte without her photos."

"You're talking like it's definitely Charlotte."

"Yeah. This isn't for the public, not yet, but you'll hear it soon enough anyway. Dental records and the ring, her clothing, everything so far is a match. DNA should confirm it soon."

"Did the witness positively ID Tommy?"

"Didn't get that far. Not yet anyway." They both knew that eyewitness identification was a minefield if not handled properly—if the witness didn't ID Tommy, the defense would use it to decimate Burroughs' case.

"Valencia said you were searching for a tire iron?"

"The probable murder weapon," he replied grudgingly. "Buried with the victim. Wrapped in a baseball jersey belonging to Worth. State's attorney wants to wait for forensics, but they'll give us him, I'm sure."

Aw, hell. Tommy was so in over his head. Funny, she'd started reviewing Charlotte's case trying to be objective, to rule out Tommy based solely on facts, but it felt like her gut instinct had done that for her instead. If only she could find some hard evidence to prove his innocence.

"Where's Sarah?" Burroughs asked again. "I'll find

someone else to help her. Someone without a conflict of interest," he added, in case Lucy hadn't gotten the point.

She had. It just didn't help. "I don't know," she confessed. "She left this morning."

"What? How could you—"

"She's a grown woman. We had no right to stop her."

"She has no memory. And a stalker. Not to mention Worth. Who knows what they said during their argument? He might go after her."

"Tommy would never—"

"Sure he would. If he killed his wife, why not a witness? In fact, maybe that whole wedding dress-stalker thing is a smoke screen? Worth could have set the whole thing up."

"In the little time he had after you brought Sarah to Beacon Falls? Now you're reaching."

"No. Think about it. There are tons of thrift stores between Beacon Falls and Sarah's place. He stops in, grabs a wedding dress, pays cash, has them wrap it up, slips in the card—after wiping his prints, of course—and leaves it before he goes into her apartment. Then when she and TK show up and find it, surprise! Oh my, how did that get there?" The last came in a mincing tone that sounded nothing like Tommy but revealed just how invested in his guilt Burroughs had become.

"You've no proof."

"But it's a damn good theory. Even you have to admit."

"Like hell I do. I think you're too emotionally involved—in both Charlotte's case and Sarah's."

"He used me, Guardino. Wake up. He's using you, too. If

anything happens to Sarah, we blame her so-called stalker and never look at Worth. And it's all my own damn fault. I can't believe I ever let a bunch of amateurs mess with my case."

"First of all, we 'amateurs' have a better closure rate than any department in the state—including yours. Second of all, Sarah isn't a case. She's a civilian—"

"A civilian with a traumatic brain injury and amnesia. Not competent to—"

"A civilian cleared by the doctors to return to her own life. Which makes her actions out of our control."

"Damn it, Guardino. I trusted you. I trusted her with you."

"And we're doing our best. TK and Wash are still piecing together her past. When we have something, we'll send it to you."

"Send me everything you have."

He hung up before she could tell him about Charlotte's extracurricular activities with the shelter. Lucy considered calling him back, but decided to wait until she had something more concrete. After all, according to Burroughs, she was a fumbling amateur and he already had his man.

CHAPTER 35

AS TOMMY DROVE Route 51 south past suburbs and strip malls, storm clouds glowered from the sky overhead. When he reached the turnoff for two-lane road that corkscrewed its way up the mountain to his in-laws' house, the first drops of rain began.

He made his final turn and steered Charlotte's Pathfinder up their driveway. Their house was modern, all glass and timber, perched in the center of a clearing near the top of the mountain. The fields around it were either fenced in for the horses' grazing or seeded with wildflowers, with a sturdy metal-roofed barn a short walk down from the house.

By the time he ran up the flagstone path to the front door, the rain had drenched his clothing and doused most of his anger. Peter opened the door and stood on the threshold as if considering refusing Tommy entrance.

"We need to talk," Tommy said, surprising himself with how calm he sounded. As if he actually had any answers to this insanity that had devoured his life. "Where's Nellie?"

Peter nodded past Tommy's shoulder. "In the barn with Gloria."

"Good. She doesn't need to hear this."

Peter considered that, then finally stood aside to allow Tommy to enter.

The foyer followed modern angles, sweeping up two stories to the roof, and opened onto the dining room and behind it the kitchen to the right. On the left was a wall that soared up to the ceiling, creating a dramatic archway into the living room. An open staircase led to a loft that ran along the back wall, overlooking the living room to the left and leading to the hall to the bedrooms on the right. Rain slashed at the foyer windows, casting strange shadows against the light oak floors as if beasts swarmed in the storm outside.

Tommy wiped his shoes on the mat and followed Peter into the living room, where a fire was going. When he'd left with Burroughs earlier he'd left his jacket behind, and now with his shirt soaked through he was shivering. He didn't bother with one of the comfortable leather club chairs or the couch, but instead sank down right on the stone hearth, the fire's warmth at his back.

Beside him stood a large armoire—no, Gloria insisted on calling it a "chifferobe" because it could hold hanging clothes inside its vast expanse. She collected big heavy pieces like that, loved to paint them with folksy designs then partially strip the paint to make them look battered and older than they actually were. Given how expensive the damn things were, he'd never understood that, but Charlotte said it was because all he cared about in furniture was how comfortable it was for napping.

Peter regarded him with a stony stare. "I know you're angry..."

Tommy shook himself from his distracted musing about Gloria's decor. It took an effort to focus—he was just so damn tired of everything. And everyone. Burroughs. His in-laws. Everyone. "I was. I am. That was a lousy thing to do." Peter opened his mouth but Tommy raised his hand. "But I know why you did it. You're worried about Nellie. So am I. This is going to get bad, Peter. We need to protect her."

"Then why are you here?" Peter poured himself a drink at the bar that separated the den from the kitchen, then raised a glass in question to Tommy, who shook his head. "We just calmed her down. She's only going to get upset again if she sees you."

Tommy was silent for a long moment. The heat of the fire crackled at his back while Peter's chilly countenance measured him from across the room. He finally looked up and said, "I'm here because she's my daughter and I made her a promise."

"This is bigger than a promise," Peter said, lowering his body into one of the chairs facing the fire. His face sank and he stared into his whiskey, the glow from the fire etching new lines Tommy hadn't noticed before. "Even if you're innocent," Tommy didn't waste energy on protesting, "we still need to prepare for the worst."

"Which means Nellie needs to stay with you and Gloria."

Because on the list of worst-case scenarios, Nellie watching the cops haul him away in handcuffs was near the top.

"So I'll ask again: Why are you here, Tommy?"

"To say goodbye." A sigh heaved Tommy's shoulders. "I don't know what the cops think they have, but it isn't enough for them to arrest me. Yet." The words left the bitter taste of defeat in his mouth. "All I'm asking for is one night. Time to give Nellie a memory, something she can hold on to."

Before Peter could answer, the back door opened, releasing a blast of rain and cold air along with the whirlwind of energy that was Nellie. She raced through the kitchen and tumbled into Tommy's arms, almost knocking him into the fire. "Daddy's here!"

Gloria followed in Nellie's wake, a towel in her hand. "Nellie, leave your father be. We need to get you dried off and clean up the mud you tracked in."

Nellie bounced on Tommy's lap before facing forward. "Daddy's here. Now we can go to Pizza Joe's."

"I don't think so, sweetie," Gloria said, her face uncertain as she glanced from Tommy to Peter.

"But you promised. You said if I was a good girl we could go to Pizza Joe's, and I was a good girl, wasn't I, Papa?"

"Yes, but that was before the rain," Peter said. "We'll do Pizza Joe's tomorrow night. Tonight we'll eat here. All of us. As a family."

Nellie shook her head. "No. That's not fair." She twisted in Tommy's lap to clap her palms on either side of his face, shutting out the rest of the world. "You'll take me, won't you,

Daddy? I was a good girl, and you shouldn't ever break a promise, right?"

Her face was so close that their foreheads almost touched. Those eyes. Exactly like her mother's. Same with the determined, never-surrender twist of her lips.

He stood, taking her with him, sliding her weight to sit on one hip, despite the fact that she was getting too big to carry for long. "I can't argue with that. A promise is a promise."

"But Tommy—" Gloria gestured to the rain, although Tommy knew that wasn't really what she was protesting.

"Special father-daughter dinner at Pizza Joe's," he said. "Then it's back here, where you will be a good girl and listen to your Papa and Gramma. Deal?"

Nellie squinched her face in consideration. "Are you coming back here, too?"

"No. Daddy's going to be busy. So I'll need you to be a big girl and help your grandparents out here."

"Like with the horses?" From the spark in her eye, it was clear that idea held some appeal.

"Exactly. And I'll come when I can. Deal?"

She scrutinized him. "Deal. After you take me to Pizza Joe's." Her negotiations finalized, she hopped down and squeezed his hand in hers. "Let's go."

CHAPTER 36

TOMMY NAVIGATED THE Pathfinder down the mountain switchbacks, fighting to steer through the rain and fog and wishing he'd never agreed to take Nellie to dinner. But if things went wrong and the police decided to arrest him, then this might be his last chance to have a father-daughter outing with her for a long, long time. Even if he wasn't arrested, the press would still be hounding him, and he needed Nellie safe from that.

"Shit," he muttered, ratcheting the SUV's headlights to high beams, trying to see through the rain and mist.

"Daddy, you said a bad word," Nellie sang out from the back seat.

It wasn't yet five o'clock, but the entire sky was a wash of black and gray, and even the high beams dimmed to a wavering silver. His stomach knotted as he made the next hairpin turn, water splashing up both sides of the SUV, high enough to spray against the windows.

"Daddy, I don't like this. I'm scared." Nellie's voice

sounded close to breaking.

"It's okay," Tommy told her, using the falsely bright tone he'd adopted all day. As if he were fooling anyone—least of all Nellie. "Pretend we're at the car wash. You like riding through the car wash."

She said nothing, and when he glanced in the rearview mirror her face was scrunched up into its "there's no such things as monsters under the bed" grimace. Before he could think of anything more consoling to say, a blinding light stabbed his eyes, reflected by the rearview mirror. He hit the mirror, deflecting the glare, but the light was still bright enough to flood the interior of the car.

Another SUV, right on their rear bumper. And it didn't seem to be slowing. Tommy gingerly sped up, but even the all-wheel drive lost control in the standing water. When the road opened up to allow a passing lane for a short distance, he steered to the right-hand lane and put on his four-ways, hoping the car would pass, but it stayed glued to the Pathfinder's back end.

Why'd Gloria and Peter have to live so far out of town anyway? He clamped down on the steering wheel and hunched forward to peer through the darkness. Anger surged through him as the car continued to tailgate. He debated pulling over, but the shoulder was too narrow and it was just as likely that if he braked suddenly the car behind him would hit them.

"Daddy?" Nellie's voice was tentative, as if she wasn't sure she really wanted to say anything.

"Hush, sweetie. Daddy needs to concentrate."

"That car behind us is really close."

"I know. Don't worry. Everything will be all right." Could he come up with words more absent of comfort? Reminded him of all the empty handshakes and hugs and advice he'd gotten after Charlotte. Don't worry, be happy. You'll get over this. As if losing the love of his life was something he wanted to "get over."

The Pathfinder skidded, hydroplaning as he braked for a curve. He steered furiously, trying to keep the car on the road and avoid the sheer drop to the right. The erratic movement must have surprised the driver behind him into braking. For a moment, as the headlights faded back to a safe distance, Tommy dared to wonder if maybe the driver was simply lost and following his taillights in the dark and fog.

They entered a short straightaway, and his hopes were instantly dashed. The car behind them didn't just speed back into position, it moved aggressively, giving their bumper a tap. Not enough to send Tommy out of control, but enough to knock his teeth together and force him to speed up. Rain slashed at them in a continuous drumbeat that drowned out the sound of his pulse pounding in his ears.

Another love tap. Tommy cursed, was half tempted to hit the brakes and let the driver behind him see what a real impact felt like. But not with Nellie in the car. "You okay, sweetie?"

"Yes, sir." Her voice barely quavered.

"Good girl." He gingerly pressed the accelerator as they came out of another curve. "We're almost there."

"Okay."

The driver behind them must have known the road as well as Tommy did, must have realized this was his last chance before they reached civilization. The car surged forward, its lights filling Tommy's vision from every mirror, and pulled alongside, crossing the center line, forcing Tommy to steer onto the narrow shoulder.

"Hang on!"

"Daddy!"

The Pathfinder somehow found traction on the mud-slicked gravel berm. Tommy braked hard, expecting the other car to whiz past, but instead the driver steered toward them once more. Tommy reflexively pulled the wheel to steer them farther off the road, even though there was nowhere left to go. Sparks flew and there was the sound of metal screeching as the guardrail and car met on Nellie's side.

The other SUV finally sped past, sending a wave of water crashing against Tommy's windshield. There was no hope of spotting a license plate—Tommy was too focused on steering the car away from the guardrail without skidding out of control. His breath caught and everything slowed to a crawl as he wrenched the steering wheel, and finally, blessedly, they came to a stop, half on the road and half on the shoulder.

"Nellie," he called out, yanking off his seat belt and twisting around in his seat. "Are you okay?"

He reached over the middle console, straining to get back to her. Her face was pale, ghostly. Even her lips had lost their color, and her breath was coming fast. Tears streaked her cheeks. But she met his eyes and nodded.

He grabbed her foot, the only part of her he could reach, and squeezed. "Good girl. You were great. It's okay. Everything is going to be all right. That car's gone. It's all right."

Was he talking to comfort himself, or her? He couldn't tell. But the color slowly returned to her face. The tears didn't stop though. Best thing was to get her out of here as soon as possible, get her back to the farm.

It was too dangerous to make a three-point turn on the mountain road, but the highway was just a half a mile ahead and he could turn around in the shopping center at the foot of the mountain. He climbed back into his seat and refastened his seat belt. "Okay, everything's going to be okay."

He pulled the car forward, testing the steering to make sure nothing had been damaged by going off the road. It handled okay, although the front end was definitely out of alignment. There was no sign of anyone else on the road, and soon he could just make out the traffic light up ahead, signaling Route 51, a busy four-lane highway.

"We'll do Pizza Joe's another night. Let's go back to the farm for dinner." Despite the sudden change of plans, Nellie didn't argue, merely nodded in the rearview—a sure sign of exactly how scared she was. He didn't blame her; his own hands were trembling and sweat had plastered his shirt against his skin.

The rain was slowing, thank goodness. As he approached the traffic light it turned red. He got into the left-hand turn lane and waited. There was a large mall across the street, with a cinema, and a crowd of people was gathered under the main entrance, watching the storm. Tommy began to relax. There were people all around; they were safe now.

A car pulled in behind him in the turn lane, but it seemed to be acting normal. Tommy couldn't tell if it was the crazy guy who'd almost killed them—the only thing he could say for certain was that they both had light-colored SUVs with tinted windows.

Then the SUV sped up to pull alongside him on the right, its driver's side window open despite the rain. Tommy glanced over. The other driver's face was obscured by a large shotgun, held high, aimed right at Tommy.

Chapter 37

BY THE TIME Lucy arrived back at Beacon Falls, the rain surged like waves around the Queen Anne. The beacon was obscured by mist and fog, and the house appeared to float on a black swirling cloud. She parked her Subaru and fought past the gusts of wind to the shelter of the front porch. Xander Chen had the door open for her before she could reach for the knob.

She stepped inside, the warmth of the house enveloping her as Xander shut the door on the storm. He took her sodden jacket, handed her a towel for her hair, and said, "The others are waiting upstairs. I'll be up with dinner shortly, as I suspect it will be a long night."

Lucy simply nodded as she toweled her damp hair and returned the towel. She still wasn't used to Xander and his all-knowing ways. TK thought he was "a hoot," while Wash considered him "spooky," and she suspected Tommy simply didn't care one way or the other.

She walked through the front parlor and up the steps. TK and Wash were in the group's workroom, along with Valencia.

"We have something here," TK said when Lucy entered.

"On Charlotte?"

"No. On Sarah."

Disappointment hit Lucy. She'd almost forgotten about Sarah. "Shouldn't we be concentrating on Charlotte? Burroughs is getting close to charging Tommy."

"I told them," Valencia said. "But we found a possible connection between the two. It's not much—not yet."

"But maybe," Wash said, always the optimist.

"Tell me," Lucy said, sinking into a chair and crossing her arms against the chill, wishing she'd kept the towel.

"I'm going to tell you the way we found it, not the way it happened," he cautioned.

"Just tell her," TK said, bouncing behind Wash's chair.

"First, I was running Sarah's name and social through neighboring states, since not everything will show up in the NCIC database the cops search."

Made sense. The National Criminal Information Center was designed to give police officers rapid access to information that would impact their immediate encounters with civilians. Did they have a criminal record? An order of protection? An open warrant? Were they a missing person? A registered gun owner? Had a history of violence?

"So I went looking in other databases, and I found this." Wash clicked, and a birth certificate appeared on the screen.

"Sarah has a son?"

"And the son has a father," TK put in. "So we searched for Walter T. Putnam, along with Sarah's name—"

"And we found this marriage certificate. The son was born in DC, but they were married here in Pittsburgh. Made me figure that at least one of the families lived here, so we kept focusing on Walter T."

"Got a picture?" Lucy asked. Valencia had moved behind her to open the door and help Xander distribute soup and sandwiches.

"Actually, we think you sent us one. Here's Walter's PA driver's license, and here's your surveillance shot of Sheetz from Friday." The screen split to reveal both photos. The man in the Jeep Sarah had gotten into on Friday looked a lot like this Walter T. Putnam.

"Why hasn't he come forward? Anything else on him?"

"He's a lobbyist, spends most of his time in DC," Wash answered.

"We're guessing Sarah kept her maiden name because of her photography business," TK added.

Lucy ignored her food, hard to do given the heavenly smell of the French onion soup, and leaned back, staring at the screen. She shook her head. "There's something not right. Did Sarah call in? Does she know about Walter? Have you talked to him?"

TK and Wash both looked to Valencia. "I told them to hold off," she said.

"Why?"

"Because when Tommy asked me to act as his attorney today, I ran his name through LexisNexis and Westlaw." The legal databases contained information on both criminal and civil cases as well as rulings nationwide. "I found summary judgment in his favor for a malpractice suit. It came down just a few days before Charlotte's disappearance. Depending on how efficient his malpractice insurance company was, he might not even have known that the case was closed. And of course, once Charlotte went missing—"

"Who cared about a malpractice case. What was the case about?" Lucy asked.

"The files are sealed, so all I have are the plaintiffs' names. Walter T. Putnam and Sarah Brown. Suing Dr. Thomas Worth for wrongful death of their son."

"Their son?" Lucy spun to face them. "Sarah thought Tommy killed her son?"

Wash shrugged. "No idea. Obviously the judge who dismissed the case didn't agree. And Tommy didn't recognize Sarah, so maybe it was dismissed because he didn't have anything to do with it."

"In a teaching hospital, that could easily have happened," Valencia agreed. "Doctors' names end up on all sorts of patient charts even if they're not involved in a case. Walter and Sarah may have sued the hospital and never have known that Tommy was also named as a defendant. And since the case was dismissed, they'd never have encountered him in person."

"Sarah obviously can't remember, so we need to find this Walter Putnam and talk to him," TK said. It sounded like it wasn't the first time she'd proposed the plan.

"And what?" Lucy challenged her. "Tell him his wife is missing and has amnesia, one of the people helping her is the doctor he accused of killing his son, and by the way, how did your son die?"

"We can ask Tommy," Valencia said.

Lucy thought about it. "He's got so much on his plate right now. But..." She jerked her chin. "Wash, give him a call. There's just too much coincidence here. Charlotte and Sarah's lives intersecting this way—"

"No answer on his cell," Wash reported. "Or at his home."

"Let me try his in-laws," Valencia said. She slipped out of the room, only to return a few moments later. "He's taking Nellie to dinner. But his mother-in-law will give him a message as soon as he's back."

"Wash, what more do you have on Walter T. Putnam and this malpractice case?" Lucy asked, settling back in her seat and tackling her soup. Xander was right, it was going to be a long night. "Find me someone we can talk to. Tonight."

ADRENALINE, ANGER, FEAR. Tommy didn't have time to catalog the emotions rocketing through him—all he knew was that suddenly the world grew both larger and smaller at once. He wrenched his gaze from the shotgun and glimpsed a minuscule opening in the traffic in the intersection ahead. The roaring in his ears was punctuated by honking, screeching brakes, and Nellie's scream as he yanked on the wheel and hit the gas, shooting the Pathfinder into the opening, running the red light.

Two cars that had been approaching from the left skidded

on the wet pavement, horns blaring, barely avoiding a collision with each other and him. He raced across the intersection into the entrance to the shopping plaza, but the SUV didn't follow.

Tommy's throat was tight. He had to force himself to stop holding his breath and inhale. He pulled up at the cinema's entrance, seeking the safety of the crowd. Nellie was bawling, "Daddy, Daddy, Daddy," and as he replayed the last few moments, he realized just how close she'd come to being hit. From her perspective in the rear seat it must have been terrifying.

Hell, it was pretty damn terrifying from his perspective in the driver's seat. He hunched over the steering wheel, palms sweaty, fingers and wrists aching from clenching, his breath coming in gasps.

"It's okay, Nellie," he said as soon as he could manage it. Her sobs had quieted. It took everything he had to squelch the nausea rising in his gorge, lift his head, and look back at her. "It's okay."

She didn't look like she believed him. Which only added to the pain. Not to mention the headache gathering at the base of his skull, preparing a rampage, complete with lights and sirens.

He blinked—and realized the lights and the sirens were for real. It was as if his hearing had been dampened by adrenaline, but now he heard the people talking outside the car, and they seemed to be everywhere, surrounding it. The windows were steamed by his and Nellie's breath, making the figures outside appear like monsters clawing their way through the mist.

"Turn the ignition off and put your hands on the wheel," came the blare of a man's voice amplified by a speaker.

Tommy glanced into the rearview mirror—not one cop car but two, with flashing amber lights. Two cop cars? Where had they been when a madman was trying to run him off the road, threatened to blow his brains out?

"Driver. Turn the ignition off. Hands on the wheel." The voice sounded testy, annoyed.

It took Tommy three tries—adrenaline had left his fingers numb and trembling, —put the car in park and shut off the ignition. He placed his hands on the wheel as directed. Through the fog obscuring the windshield he saw the crowd suddenly scatter, fleeing back inside the cinema.

A knocking came on the passenger side of the car. He looked over and was facing a gun held by a uniformed man.

Before he could react, the driver-side door was yanked open and another man reached in and yanked Tommy off balance, as far as he could with the seat belt on. Within seconds Tommy found himself face down on the asphalt, fighting to keep his face out of a mud puddle, arms wrenched behind him, strange hands patting him down, going in and out of his pockets, under his waistband, his wrists shackled.

"He's clean."

"The kid's back here."

"Nellie, are you okay?" he shouted.

"Daddy!" Her screech was more frightening than the guns. "Daddy! No, let me go! I want my daddy!"

“Don’t hurt her!”

“Hurt her? Buddy, we’re saving her. From you.”

CHAPTER 38

THE FIRST SET of "cops" turned out to be mall security, who turned him over to the township police, who only had two officers on duty—out of eight total, the officer told Tommy, so he should count himself lucky he hadn't gone off shift yet, because then he might have been sitting in the mall's security office for hours instead of here in the police station.

Tommy didn't feel so lucky as he sat on an unforgiving metal bench, soaking wet, mud and gravel staining the front of his shirt and pants, handcuffed to a railing running the length of the bench, shivering every time the door opened, trying to figure out how the hell he'd gotten here.

He'd tried in vain to explain to the mall cops and the uniformed officer who'd arrested him that he was the victim, that he'd done nothing wrong—certainly nothing to harm Nellie—but they'd ignored him. He'd answered their questions, had taken a breathalyzer test, even waived his Miranda rights, trying to barter it all for a chance to see Nellie, make certain she was okay.

All for nothing. Relegated to his seat on the bench while "we sort things out," he waited in misery. Where was Nellie? What did she think was happening?

Finally they gave him a phone call. An officer escorted him to a small cubicle with a sweat-stained telephone on a shelf. He should have called Valencia—it was pretty obvious that he might be needing her services as an attorney again—but instead he made the call he'd dreaded: Charlotte's mother, Gloria.

"It's a long story and I'll explain everything when you get here, but I need you to come get Nellie." He hoped by keeping the focus on Nellie he could avoid a long explanation. As soon as Gloria and Peter heard about the shotgun-wielding driver, they'd go ballistic themselves. Not that he blamed them. Most of the tremors that shook his body weren't from the cold but rather the thought of someone targeting his daughter.

"At a police station?" Gloria's voice heaved with resignation. "What happened? Is Nellie all right?"

"She's fine. But I don't want her here longer than necessary."

"Did they—are you—Tommy, what the police were saying, this morning—"

"I'm not under arrest for Charlotte's murder. We ran into some trouble on the way from your place. A man following us. Tried to run us off the road. I need you, I need Nellie..." He choked on the words, hating himself for thinking them, much less saying them out loud. What kind of father abandoned his daughter? Especially after everything Nellie had been through?

The kind who would give his life to keep her safe. The

kind who had finally awakened to the truth that Charlotte had been killed and that he and Nellie might now also be targets.

The kind of father who could not face life if anything happened to his daughter.

"I need you to take Nellie. Maybe go on a trip. Get her away from all this." Somehow he made the request sound perfectly sane despite the fact that his heart shattered as he uttered the words.

There was a long pause. "Is she in danger?"

"If she stays with me, I think so, yes."

"We're on our way."

"Gloria, thank you."

He hung up and considered his options. He needed someone who could access official footage, review all the evidence. As the officer returned to escort him back to his cold bench, Tommy said, "I need to speak to a Pittsburgh police detective. Don Burroughs."

The officer made note of his request and returned him to the bench, snapping the handcuffs shut once more. Tommy sat there, not sure what was happening, as most of the lights in the building were turned off, leaving his hallway and lonely bench in half-light. Not to worry, the woman manning the desk had told him in a cheerful voice, it was just how they saved money on energy costs after hours.

Finally the officer came back for Tommy. But instead of escorting him to the desk to collect his belongings and his daughter, he led Tommy to an interview room that, except for the fact that it boasted cinderblock walls, looked identical to its

Pittsburgh counterpart. Burroughs waited inside, huddled over his laptop at the table. He didn't even glance up when Tommy and the patrolman entered, just waved his hand. "We can lose the cuffs."

"Sure thing, Detective." The officer released Tommy from his metal bonds. "I'll be at the front desk, you need anything. If you could let me know when you're done—we'll be shutting down for the night and the chief doesn't like overtime." He closed the door behind him.

Tommy remained standing, trying to assess Burroughs' mood. The detective finally looked up, took in Tommy's bedraggled appearance, and leaned back. "Sit."

"Where's Nellie?" Tommy didn't sit. He'd been sitting around doing nothing for far too long. "I need to see her."

"In due time. Which is after you sit down." Burroughs snapped the last in the tone of a platoon sergeant.

Tommy hesitated, just long enough to make it clear he was taking a seat under protest.

Burroughs continued, "I went over the statement you gave the officer. Does this look familiar?"

He turned his laptop around so Tommy could see the screen. On it was a grainy black and white image of an SUV. The driver's face was obscured by the rain on the windshield and a ball cap pulled low, but there was no mistaking the shotgun in his hands pointed out the window.

"You got lucky. New red light camera at that intersection, installed last week."

"Did you find him? Is he under arrest?"

"No. The plate," he clicked a key and a shot of the SUV racing away filled the screen, "was covered with mud. We're working on other cameras in the area."

"So he's still out there." Tommy was glad he'd called Gloria. "Where's Nellie?"

"Down the hall in the break room with the secretary—whose shift is over, by the way. Gonna be up all night with the sugar rush."

"I called her grandparents to come take her. She's not safe staying with me."

"Not if someone is really trying to run you off the road and aiming shotguns at you. The charges against you are dropped."

"Charges?"

"Reckless endangerment of a minor, about a dozen moving violations."

Then the rest of Burroughs' statement kicked Tommy in the gut. "Wait. What do you mean, 'really' trying to run me off the road? You've seen my car—you can see the guy right there. Why don't you believe me?"

Burroughs met his gaze, his face expressionless. "I see a guy. I see a guy so desperate to clear his name and keep his daughter he would do anything."

"You think I *faked* all this? Hired some actor to terrorize my daughter? I would never—" He couldn't even find the words to finish his sentence.

"A man who killed his wife would." Burroughs appeared unmoved.

Tommy stood, his chest burning as he forced his fists to relax. "If I'm free to go, I'd like to be taken to my daughter, Detective. Now."

Chapter 39

THE BEST WASH could do was locate Walter and Sarah Putnam's address in Pittsburgh from two years ago when their baby died. To TK it didn't seem much to go on—the new owner was a leasing company, so was closed for the business day, even if they had any information about the former owners. But Lucy seemed determined to find someone to talk to tonight. So here they were on a fool's mission to knock on doors in the middle of a monsoon in the hopes that someone would remember neighbors from over two years ago.

TK had wanted to go alone, had argued that Lucy had a husband and daughter to go home to, but it was obvious that Lucy's battle instincts had been aroused and she wouldn't rest until they uncovered the truth. Didn't help that no one had been able to reach Tommy yet.

Lucy had driven them across the river to the Putnams' former duplex in Bloomfield. The rain hadn't slowed but Lucy had seemed impervious to it, driving more aggressively than TK had ever seen her.

First they tried the neighbor in the adjoining half of the divided Victorian. No one home. Next, they tried the townhouse on the other side. There they got lucky. An elderly African-American woman with high cheekbones and silver hair opened the door.

"We're trying to learn more about the owners who lived next door to you two years ago," Lucy said, pitching her voice over the sound of the rain drumming on the porch roof and sounding very much like the FBI agent she used to be. Someone not to be trifled with. "A Mr. and Mrs. Walter Putnam? Her name was Sarah?"

"Why?" the woman asked. The mailbox beside her read: Barnett. TK tried a personal appeal.

"They're not in trouble or anything, Mrs. Barnett," TK rushed to explain. "Sarah needs your help."

"We're from the Beacon Group," Lucy continued. "Sarah has had an accident, lost some of her memory."

"I saw it on the news this morning. Barely recognized her, she's changed so much. Different hair and all. I wasn't sure if I should call or not. They said her name was Brown, and I thought maybe—" Barnett's expression dimmed. "I thought with everything, she might have moved on, gotten remarried or the like..."

"So you remember them?" Lucy prompted. "Could you tell us what happened?"

"I guess. If you think it will help."

"Yes, ma'am. At this point anything will help. You'll have details that the police won't, little things that could help her remember."

"Are you sure she wants to? I mean, maybe it's a blessing—"

"I'm not sure that's for us to decide. Wouldn't you want to know?"

"No. I don't think I would. But, all right, then. Better you hear it from me than some lawyer or such. You'd best come in out of the rain." She ushered them inside and settled them on a couch in the front room. "Would you like some tea or cookies?"

"Thank you, no." Lucy sat still, arms open at her sides, palms up. TK realized that her body language was inviting the old lady to fill the silence, to trust her. She quickly uncrossed her own arms and tried to mirror Lucy's posture.

"It was a terrible tragedy." Barnett shook her head, looking puzzled, then smoothed her skirt across her knees. "Those two. Poor things. Absolutely devoted to each other. And to that baby."

"Can you tell us what happened?"

"Well now, they'd only just moved here from DC. He had a fancy consulting job, was commuting to the capital, talking to senators and congressmen and such. Handsome man, sharp dresser. And how she loved to fuss over him. Straightening his tie, smoothing his hair. You could just see how it pained either of them to be out of the other's sight. But he didn't want his boy to grow up in DC, so they moved here right after the baby was born—I mean, they bought the house before, actually planned to have the baby here, but the Good Lord brought him early, threw a wrench in their plans."

"A pretty stressful beginning, then?"

"Oh my, yes. That baby, so colicky—like so many of them born a bit early, you know. First three weeks he was home, I don't think either Walter or Sarah got a lick of sleep. Then Walter had to go back to work, and it was only Sarah." She folded her hands in her lap and sighed. "If they'd only let me help. But you know how it is, young, independent, new to an area, not sure who to trust. I offered, I did, but she insisted—"

"What happened, Mrs. Barnett?"

"Walter was due back that night, but his flight was canceled. Sarah had been up for days; the baby just wouldn't settle. And I guess, it all just crashed down on her."

"Did she do something to hurt the baby?"

"Lord, no. She fell asleep, that's all. Perfectly understandable—and perfectly forgivable. She was only human." Barnett paused. TK started to say something but heeded Lucy's example and instead waited. "Walter finally got home in the middle of the night. He found them. Sarah asleep on the couch. The baby must have been nursing, had fallen between the cushions. Oh, the screams when he woke her. I ran out in my nightdress, thought the building was on fire. But it was Sarah. Holding her dear little baby in her arms, begging for someone to do something, shrieking, crying. It broke my heart."

"Did an ambulance come?"

"I called 911, but they didn't wait. Jumped in Walter's car and drove to Three Rivers, carrying that poor baby. Sarah collapsed in the waiting room, I heard later. Burning up with fever—mastitis, infection from the baby not nursing. They rushed her up to OB—she was there for days getting antibiotics. I went to visit her. She kept asking about the baby, when were they going to let her see her baby." She looked away and patted her eyes.

Lucy gave the old lady time to compose herself again before asking, "So they blamed the doctor at the ER for not saving the baby?"

"Well, now, that's what I don't understand. I mean, I know Walter and Sarah sued over it, saying the baby was still breathing and the doctor should have saved him. After she came home, Sarah even told me she thought they, the doctor and some social worker, were covering things up. She had this idea that they killed him, that it was all a conspiracy." She shook her head. "Poor thing. That was before she went into the hospital the first time—not Three Rivers, Western Psych."

"She was delusional, is that it?" Lucy asked in a neutral tone. "Or was there something to her theory?"

"Oh, no. Poor, poor thing. And she had him convinced as well. No surprise there, I guess—those two were inseparable, like two pieces of the same person. And he was so obsessed with her, of course he'd believe her rather than the truth."

"What was the truth, Mrs. Barnett?"

"I thought you knew. Isn't that why you're here?"

"I'd like to hear it in your own words. What did you see that night?"

"What did I see? Well, now, I'm no doctor, but it was obvious that poor baby had been dead for a long, long time. Hours, maybe all day. It was black and purple and its head and belly were swollen. Anyone could see that poor thing was long past saving—no sense blaming any doctor. If Walter hadn't seen for himself that it was an accident, the way Sarah had fallen asleep, her body smothering the poor child, I think the cops might have thought she'd done it herself. Not that it was any consolation to either of them. Can you even imagine it? The pain? Knowing you'd killed your own baby?"

TK and Lucy exchanged glances and shook their heads.

Mrs. Barnett grasped one hand in the other as if washing them clean of the Putnams and their tragedy. "Something like that? It would drive anyone insane."

CHAPTER 40

BURROUGHS ESCORTED TOMMY down the hall to a small break room where a middle-aged woman sat with Nellie at a table surrounded by empty vending machine-size cereal bowls. Nellie looked up, her face smeared purple and lime green. "Daddy, we're having breakfast for dinner!"

"So I see. Guess you finally got your Sugar Loops."

The dispatcher stood up. "Thought it was better than candy bars or chips."

"Thank you. I very much appreciate you looking out for her."

She nodded and left. Burroughs watched from the doorway, but Tommy ignored him. He took the seat beside Nellie. She was kneeling, bouncing, as she scooped cereal into her mouth with a plastic spoon.

"So, I called your Gramma and Papa. They're coming to pick you up," Tommy began.

"No Pizza Joe's?"

He patted her belly. "Not tonight, sweetie. I don't think

you'd have room anyway."

"You're coming too, right? That way you can help me feed the horses and brush them in the morning and I'll teach you how to rake out the dirty straw and poop and then you can watch me ride my pony." Her words emerged in a rush. He wasn't sure if it was because of the sugar or her anxiety. Until she dropped her spoon to squeeze his fingers tight, and he had his answer.

"No, sweetie. I think it's best if you go with your grandparents alone. They're going to take you on a fun trip."

She shook her head, not releasing his finger. "Not without you, Daddy. The horses are okay without me. We can just go home."

"I'm not sure when we can go home."

"Because of the bad men?"

"Right. If you go with Papa and Gramma, then I won't have to worry about you because I know you'll be all right." A thought occurred to him. The man in the SUV had followed him down the mountain, so probably knew where Peter and Gloria lived. Hell, a two-second Internet search could give them a map leading right to their front door. He turned to Burroughs. "Can we have a police officer go with them? Make sure the house is safe?"

Burroughs nodded and stepped outside.

Nellie met Tommy's gaze, worry creasing her brow. "But what about you, Daddy? How will I know you'll be all right?"

Her earnest tone almost shattered his resolve. Thankfully, Gloria and Peter arrived just then, bustling into the room, their coats dripping with rain.

"There she is," Gloria exclaimed, crouching down beside Nellie to hug her tight. "I hear you had quite an adventure."

Peter stood silently beside Burroughs, mirroring the detective's scowl.

"I was just telling Nellie that she was going with you guys and that you'd be taking her on a trip," Tommy said.

"Right. We'll leave first thing in the morning. Hershey Park. They have rides, and you can see where the chocolate is made, won't that be fun?" Gloria gushed.

Nellie didn't seem so certain. "Where will you go, Daddy? Why can't you come with us?"

"I have some things to take care of here," Tommy said, standing up to give Gloria his chair. He turned to Peter. "Maybe you could leave tonight?"

"Tonight? I thought you said you were the target."

"I am. I just worry—"

"Don't. Nellie will be fine with us." He turned to Gloria. "Time to go."

Tommy moved back to Nellie. "Give me a hug before you go."

She bounced up in her chair, almost sending it toppling over as she hugged him fiercely. "Promise me you'll be okay," she whispered.

"I promise. You be a good girl. And remember, I love you." He kissed each cheek and her forehead.

"I love you too, Daddy." She wrapped her arms around his neck so tight that he couldn't breathe.

Then Peter joined them, gently lifting her away from Tommy and into his own arms. "We'll have tons of fun, won't we?"

Nellie nodded. "Did you know you could have breakfast for dinner?"

Gloria joined Peter and Nellie. Tommy followed them out to the corridor. "Call me before you leave?" Tommy said. "And I'll talk to you every day, Nellie."

She waved at him from Peter's arms, and then they vanished out the doors into the night. Tommy kept watching for a long moment, a weight dragging at him, pulling him down into a well of uncertainty.

Burroughs joined him in the hallway. Without looking at the detective, Tommy said, "Let's get started. How do I prove to you that I'm innocent?"

"HOW DID WE not know?" TK asked as Lucy steered through standing water that sluiced the car with mud and silt. Thankfully the rain had slowed to a drizzle and the sky was clearing. "I mean, seriously. How did we not see that she was crazy? No one. Not the doctors. Not Burroughs or your friend the marshal. None of us."

She flounced back in her seat, her knees drawn up to her chest, feet planted on the dash just like Megan did. "I've heard of shit like this. Guess I've even seen it. Guys wrapped up in these crazy conspiracy theories. Knew a Force Recon sniper who believed God spoke to him through his scope. Others like him.

Totally nuts, but they could do their jobs so no one cared. But this?"

Lucy ignored the tirade; she was busy doing some serious thinking of her own. When TK paused for a breath she said, "Call Wash, fill him in. Top priority is to find Tommy and warn him. Then we need to call Burroughs."

"Hell no. I'll call Wash and keep trying Tommy, but you need to break it to Burroughs. Did you see how possessive he was of Sarah? He's going to freak."

Lucy said nothing, listening as TK updated Wash and left another message for Tommy. Then she called Burroughs and filled him in.

"Are you certain?" he asked.

"As I can be—remember, I'm only a civilian. Limited resources and access to official information." It was petty to berate him for not discovering Sarah's background for himself, but it wasn't his team member caught in the crossfire of Sarah's delusions. "We haven't been able to find Tommy to warn him."

"I can help with that. He's at the Forward Township police station. And so am I."

"What happened? Is everyone all right?"

"Everyone's fine. But I pretty much just accused Worth of hiring a man to threaten him in public with a shotgun. Still not a hundred percent sure I'm wrong about that. Or that you're right about Sarah."

"We're on our way. Keep him there, will you?"

"Oh, believe me, he isn't going anywhere. Not until we get to the bottom of this."

"Think you can also put out a BOLO on Sarah and her husband?" Asking police to be on the lookout for a person or vehicle was one more ability Lucy had lost when she became a civilian. "And maybe run Walter Putnam through NCIC?"

"On it." He hung up.

"So, is Sarah crazy? Like post-partum psychosis or something?" TK asked as Lucy steered them toward Route 51.

"Her pregnancy might have triggered it, but it's more common than you think," Lucy answered. "Fixed delusions. It's what drives stalkers, assassins, even terrorists."

TK lowered her legs and sat up straight. "Obsession, is that what you're talking about?"

"More dangerous than that. People driven by obsession think they can change reality to fit their vision. People driven by delusion are in total denial of reality."

"They're living in their own fantasy world."

"Something like that. Nick could explain it better."

"And when reality and their fiction collide?"

"Utter devastation."

Chapter 41

GRAMMA RODE IN the back seat of the car, holding Nellie's hand while Papa drove through the storm, following a police car. At first Nellie was sad, worrying about leaving Daddy all alone, but the beat of the rain and the bounce of the car quickly had her nodding in her booster seat, chin drooping and eyes closed. Not asleep, but not really awake either. Her mind felt as foggy as the world revealed in the headlights each time she jerked up and opened her eyes before nodding off again.

Then the car came to a stop. Gramma squeezed her hand and Nellie slit her eyes open. They were sitting in the driveway, the police car beside them. Papa had the window halfway down, gave the policeman his keys, but kept it open even after the man left, vanishing into the fog. Papa's head was tilted as he listened for something. After a few minutes, the policeman appeared through the fog to hand Papa a set of keys and an umbrella he must have gotten from the coat stand.

"No signs of any disturbance, sir," he said. "You folks have a good night, now. Call if you need anything more."

"Thank you, Officer," Gramma said, leaning forward. Papa nodded his thanks as well. Then the policeman left, his car whooshing through the rain, spraying their car, before vanishing into the fog.

Papa got out with the umbrella while Gramma unbuckled Nellie, even though Nellie could have done it herself. Then Papa opened Gramma's door, walked her around to Nellie's side of the car, and handed Gramma the umbrella before opening Nellie's door. It was funny, Gramma stretching almost on her tiptoes to cover both Nellie and Papa after Papa scooped Nellie into his arms. The wind almost blew Gramma over and slammed the car door shut behind them. Nellie wrapped her arms around Papa, shivering as the rain rushed in beneath the umbrella.

They hurried around to the front of the house. A tiny light guided them to the front door. Gramma pushed it open and finally they were safe inside, the storm locked out behind the thick front door. The storm didn't like that, its wind and rain pounding against the wall of windows.

"Bedtime for you, young lady," Gramma said firmly.

Nellie was too tired to protest, her grip on Papa's neck slipping as he carried her up the steps. She didn't look down—the steps scared her because they only had the step part, their backs open, and she was always afraid she'd slip right through them. Papa huffed a little by the time they reached the loft that stretched out along the back wall of the foyer and living room, but he jiggled her on his hip, redistributing her weight, and they crossed down the hall to her room.

He set her down on her bed. Gramma came in behind

them with a towel to dry Nellie's hair, and before she knew it she was out of her wet clothes and in her warm PJs, tucked in with hugs and kisses, and the lights were out.

She fell asleep, the storm churning beyond her window, dreaming of Mommy caught in the rain, and Nellie was running with an umbrella trying to keep Mommy safe and dry, but she was too short and the wind kept pulling her off her feet until finally it flipped the umbrella inside out and sent Nellie tumbling, falling, falling, falling...

"Mommy!" She jerked awake, sitting up in bed, except it wasn't her bed. Where was she? "Daddy!" Her voice was croaky, barely made it to her own ears.

A shadow moved through the darkness, sinking onto her bed that wasn't her bed, not her real bed, as she tried to shake free of her dream. A woman's arms surrounded her, held her tight. "It's okay, Nellie. It was just a bad dream. Everything is going to be all right. I promise."

Not Gramma. Not Mommy—at least not how she remembered Mommy. But it felt so good, the lady's arms so warm, secure, her heart beating against Nellie's back. "You're safe now," the woman said.

Nellie blinked, finally realizing this wasn't part of her dream. "Sarah?"

"I came to take care of you. Was worried about you. You've had quite a day, haven't you? Here, drink this. You'll feel better." Sarah held a sippy cup up to Nellie's lips.

Nellie started to protest that she wasn't a baby, didn't need a sippy cup, that she wouldn't spill, but she was thirsty, so she drank the juice. It was her favorite—cherry—but sweeter than normal.

"Are you staying?" Her words were slurred, and her mouth and lips felt weird, like they weren't hers.

"I'm never leaving." Sarah set the empty cup down and hugged Nellie tight.

Nellie didn't want to go to sleep—she had so many questions she wanted to ask—but somehow her body got so heavy, her eyelids just wouldn't stay open. She fought and fought, managed to open them a slit, just in time to see the door to her room open and a man's shadow appear.

A man who wasn't Papa or Daddy. Fear surged through her, her heart racing, and she fought to form the words to warn Sarah, but she was powerless to move as her body surrendered and her eyes closed for good.

Chapter 42

AFTER THE PATROLMAN called Burroughs to let him know that Peter, Gloria, and Nellie had arrived safely at their home, Tommy and Burroughs sat down together in the interview room. Tommy wasn't sure if the detective's attitude toward him had truly shifted or if he was simply humoring Tommy in the hopes of getting a confession—more of those games cops played—but he didn't care.

"I'm serious. Lock me up if it will help. As long as Nellie's safe, I don't care."

"So you're saying that keeping you behind bars will keep Nellie safe?" Burroughs countered. He was typing at his laptop, Tommy wasn't sure why—it wasn't as if their conversation was leading to anything productive as far as the investigation went.

"If it keeps whoever that man was away from Nellie, yes."

Burroughs considered that. "Okay. Let's start from the beginning. The tire iron. The charm bracelet. Both tie you directly to Charlotte's grave."

Tommy noticed that Burroughs didn't offer any evidence

that the tire iron was the murder weapon or that forensics had confirmed that it was Tommy's. "Whoever took Charlotte had her keys. Including the key to the Volvo. I changed the locks on the house after, but not the cars."

He hadn't even thought of changing the locks on the cars—it had been hard enough to change the locks on the doors to his home. He had kept imagining Charlotte coming home, trying to get in, and finding herself locked out. But Peter had finally come over with his toolkit and together they'd gotten the job done.

"You're saying whoever took Charlotte came back to your house, took the tire iron, and planted her bracelet?"

It did sound pretty far-fetched when Burroughs said it like that. "Was the tire iron—" Tommy swallowed, unable to finish the thought. "I mean, was it up there the whole time?"

"Why? Do you think someone waited a year and then decided to frame you?"

"I guess not. Just that the charm we found yesterday—it didn't look like it'd been out in the woods for a year. So, I thought..." He shook his head. "You're right, it makes no sense."

"My working theory was that you dropped the charm when you went back to visit Charlotte's grave, but then when you saw Sarah taking pictures of it, that's when you chased her off the mountain." Burroughs looked up. "If that helps."

"It doesn't."

Burroughs heaved his shoulder—either a dismissive shrug or a sigh, it was hard to tell. But then he said, "The tire iron wasn't the murder weapon. It was planted there, wiped clean of any prints."

Tommy brightened. "See? Why would I do that? Frame myself? And why use the tire iron from my own car when there was Charlotte's car right there?"

"Yeah, we got that."

"Not to mention how did I get Charlotte's car there and back from Fiddler's Knob to the river where it was found, and also get my car? Or did I call a cab from the middle of nowhere? Hitch a ride? It all makes no sense."

"Maybe that's what we're meant to think," Burroughs countered.

"Come on. You have to know I'm telling the truth. What are you looking up on your computer anyway?"

Burroughs scowled, but for once it wasn't aimed at Tommy. "Another piece of the puzzle that doesn't fit."

The desk clerk knocked at the door. Behind her stood Lucy and TK. "These folks said you were expecting them?"

"Yes, thanks."

TK bounded past Lucy and Burroughs to hug Tommy. "You look terrible. What happened?"

"Guy tried to run Nellie and me off the road, then threatened us with a shotgun."

Lucy moved to stand behind Burroughs and looked over his shoulder at his laptop. "What did you find on Putnam?"

Tommy looked up at that. "Who's Putnam?"

Burroughs made an unhappy noise at the back of his throat. He turned his laptop around. "Ever see this guy?"

"I told you, with the rain, I couldn't see—" He stared at the photo. It was a driver's license belonging to a Walter Putnam. "Yes. He was at my house. This morning, taking pictures through the window. And I know that name." He sank back in his chair. "No. I actually met him once. A few years ago. I had to tell him his baby had died." He glanced at them in confusion. "What the hell is going on here?"

"Sarah is his wife," TK said, practically bouncing with excitement.

"I never met the mother," Tommy said, still lost in a fog. "I remember the baby. Such a tragedy. Parents brought him in themselves, didn't wait for the paramedics. He'd been gone for a while—a long while. But the dad kept screaming at us to keep trying, wouldn't let go. The mom…I never saw her, they took her up to OB, she was pretty sick herself."

Then he jerked his head up. "Charlotte. Charlotte worked with her. At least that first day. Then she refused to talk to Charlotte, accused her of covering up my mistake, that I'd killed her baby. She had a raging infection, was feverish, out of her mind with grief. It wasn't until months later when the insurance company told me about the lawsuit. It was dismissed almost immediately. That case, it was so sad. I always wondered, never knew what had happened to them."

Burroughs pushed his chair back, gestured for Lucy to sit. It didn't seem to be from any sense of chivalry, more like he just couldn't sit still any longer. "Putnam is the witness who came forward, placed you with Sarah at Fiddler's Knob right before her accident on Saturday."

"If there was an accident," Lucy said.

Burroughs nodded, his gaze aimed out the door. "I can't believe..." He cut himself off. "Putnam also has a silver Jeep Cherokee registered to him. No wants or warrants, record's clean."

"Are we really thinking he and Sarah killed Charlotte?" TK said. "Why? To frame Tommy? Then why hide the body? Why all this charade a year later?"

Tommy couldn't stop staring at Walter's photo. It had been taken before his son's death. In it, despite the harsh lighting of the DMV, the man looked happy, hopeful. One of those confident, got-the-world-in-my-pocket type of guys with everything to live for. Exactly the way Tommy had lived his life before Charlotte... "What do they want?"

"You," Lucy answered. "They want you to suffer just as much as they have."

A rush of cold flooded over Tommy as he shoved his chair back and reached for his phone. "Nellie."

He stabbed the screen, dialing Peter's cell then Gloria's, then their landline. No answer.

CHAPTER 43

THE RAIN HAD slowed the tiniest bit, just enough to allow a dense fog to form on the mountain. Lucy drove with Tommy beside her, still trying to reach his in-laws. Poor guy was shivering despite her turning the heat to high. He didn't even have a coat.

TK sat in the back seat, hunched forward, watching Burroughs' taillights as they vanished then reappeared in the fog. The township only had one officer on patrol this time of night, but he was also heading this way, although it would take him twenty minutes or more.

"I've got a Remington 870 in the back," Lucy told TK. "Fold the seat down beside you and you can reach it. Grab the flashlight from the pack as well."

"Guns?" Tommy asked. "No. What if she has Nellie?"

"Exactly." Lucy focused on the road ahead. There were no guardrails and the fog hid the steep drop-off down the side of the mountain, making each curve treacherous.

"I kinda understand Sarah," TK said as she pulled the pump-action shotgun from the rear compartment and checked its chambers. "Post-partum psychosis combined with severe grief, I'd guess that could make anyone delusional. But her husband? Him I don't get. How could he buy into her fantasy? Enough to kill?"

"I saw it once before," Lucy answered. "A shared delusion. In a cult. They stole children from parents they considered unfit, raised them as their own. Really believed they were the children God meant them to have."

"*Folie à deux,*" Tommy muttered. "That's the clinical term."

"Leave it to the French to have a name for it." TK grabbed the Maglite from Lucy's knapsack and slipped it into her pocket. "What's the plan?"

"We'll let Burroughs and the patrol officer clear the premises while we wait." Lucy glanced at Tommy. His gaze was focused on his phone, tapping in a text. "Did you hear me, Tommy? We can't go in right away. Not until the police are sure it's safe."

He said nothing, just shook his head.

She tried a different tactic. "How far to the turnoff?"

That got his attention. He looked up, eyes narrowed as he squinted through the fog, trying to get his bearings. "Just around the curve ahead."

"And then how long is their drive? Before we get to the house?"

"Maybe half a mile."

"TK, can you call Burroughs, let him know?"

TK nodded and pulled out her phone. Burroughs' brake lights lit up as he slowed for the final hairpin turn. "He says the patrol car is behind us, just turned off 51. Wants us to hold off at the end of the drive."

Before Lucy could reply, bright lights swung around the curve ahead, slashing through the fog, aiming right for Burroughs' Impala. Instinctively she braked to give Burroughs more room to maneuver. Good thing, because a muzzle flash flared from the oncoming vehicle.

Even without TK's phone being on speaker, Burroughs' shout of "Shots fired!" echoed through the Subaru. Lucy braked even more. Burroughs steered the Impala away from the oncoming SUV and dangerously close to the drop-off. "It's Putnam."

"Does he have Nellie?" Tommy asked, craning his head to shout toward the phone TK held.

Burroughs didn't answer right away. The SUV came close to hitting him and another flash from Putnam's shotgun sparked off the rain. The fog closed in, giving the drama unfolding before them an intimate, almost claustrophobic surrealism.

Putnam's SUV hurtled past the Impala and was now headed toward Lucy. Caught at the sharpest angle of the curve, there was nowhere for her to steer without risking the steep drop to her right. Ahead of her, Burroughs was able to regain control of his vehicle, spinning into a U-turn that almost rammed him into the mountain.

Lucy focused on the bright headlights aiming toward her.

Instead of braking, giving Putnam longer to steer toward her, she hit the accelerator.

Gravel flew as her two outside tires went off the pavement and onto the narrow berm, but the all-wheel drive kept the Subaru steady. She yanked the wheel, steering directly at Putnam, counting on Putnam's survival instincts to make him reflexively turn away.

The maneuver worked—almost too well. Putnam's SUV screeched past them, swerving erratically as he fought to regain control, but now Lucy was across the centerline and headed straight into Burroughs' path. She yanked the wheel back to the right, gave the accelerator another nudge as they came out of the curve, and breathed again once Burroughs flew by, the Impala so close that if her window had been open she could have reached out and touched it.

"Where's Nellie?" Tommy asked again, apparently unaware of the drama unfolding around him.

TK had one hand gripping the back of Tommy's headrest, the other holding the phone. "You okay, Burroughs?"

"Yeah. Couldn't see who was in the vehicle with Putnam, damn fog. I'm hanging up to call the patrolman. We'll pursue Putnam."

"Okay," Lucy said into TK's phone. "We'll wait for you at the farm."

Now that the danger was past, she slowed the car and squinted through the fog, searching for the turnoff to the drive leading to the farm.

"There." Tommy pointed to a faint blip of red that caught

her headlights. Reflector lights marking a mailbox and the end of the drive.

As she turned down the drive, the fog enveloped them in an impenetrable cloud of white. More reflectors marked the curves of the drive, but otherwise she was driving blind. Suddenly the house loomed up before them and she hit her brakes, coming to a stop much closer to the house than she'd intended.

TK's seat belt clicked as she released it. Lucy undid her own and reached across Tommy to take a second flashlight from the glove compartment. "Tommy, you wait here. Do you understand?"

"No. What if Nellie's in there, hurt?" He fumbled with his own seat belt. Lucy closed her hand over his and squeezed until he raised his gaze to meet hers.

"You will wait. Do you understand?"

He stared at her blankly.

"It won't do Nellie any good if you get hurt—and you might endanger her." Lucy kept her tone calm and steady, hoping to break through his panic. Finally he took a breath and nodded. "Wait here."

"Okay." He undid his seat belt. "Do you have a first aid kit?"

"In the back. You can access it from TK's seat. Do not leave the car."

"Right."

TK hopped out, wielding the shotgun. Lucy followed her, closing the door carefully—not that anyone could hear it over the sound of the rain. She watched Tommy climb between the front seats to the rear.

"Visibility sucks," TK said, stating the obvious. "How do you want to do this?"

"We stay together."

"Good idea. I'd prefer not to risk friendly fire."

Lucy drew her Beretta and studied the house. It sat at an angle, probably to take advantage of views that were invisible in the fog. The garage in front of them was to the left-hand side of what appeared to be the front. She could make out the faint waver of light—windows.

"Let's check out the front, see if we have a line of sight inside. No lights, not yet." Lucy didn't want to make them an easy target for anyone on the other side of those windows.

TK took lead, Lucy placed one palm on her shoulder, and together they marched toward the front of the house, staying close to the ground, using the shrubs as cover. They both left their hoods down—better to maintain a wide field of vision for what little they could see between the dark, the rain, and the fog. Water sluiced down Lucy's collar and matted her hair to the back of her neck, but she ignored everything except the area surrounding them, scanning the dark for danger.

The wind picked up, swirling the fog into thick tendrils that almost appeared as human figures racing through the night. TK startled at something, and Lucy spun with her to take aim. Silhouetted against the fog was a horse. Lucy felt TK release her breath as they returned to their slow advance.

They reached the corner of the house—not a ninety-degree angle, but wider, almost curving—and a wall of floor-to-roof windows appeared. There were a few shimmers of light inside, small circles braving the storm. Interior lamps. Another step and they could see a living room, with a fireplace along one wall, an armoire, sofa, and chairs. A loft area ran along the back wall, extending past an arch into a darkened foyer.

Another step closer and she felt TK jerk to a halt. Lucy looked past TK's shoulder and spotted two bodies lying on the floor, partially hidden by the two club chairs. One, a woman, was moving, trying to help the motionless form of a man, but her hands were bound behind her and her mouth was duct-taped.

TK's gait remained steady as they finished passing the window, staying low and out of sight of anyone on the inside by pushing against the shrubs.

"No sign of anyone else," TK whispered. "But I don't like that loft above the inside wall. Good sniper perch with the front door right there."

"Once we're in, I'll go right into the dining room, you take the stairs and second floor." Usually Lucy would prefer to stick together, but with at least one injured man, they needed to quickly secure the premises and sweep it for any obvious danger.

"Roger that."

They reached the front door. It stood ajar. TK waited, listening, then raised her shotgun. Lucy tapped her shoulder to indicate that she was ready. TK pushed through the door into the dark interior and silently jogged toward the staircase while Lucy hugged the wall to the right, crossing into the black void of the dining room.

She found the light switch, stretched out as far away from it as possible, then flicked it on as she continued moving. The room held a large table, chairs for eight, a china cabinet, and a buffet. She scanned the area under the table and behind the china cabinet, the only places large enough for someone to hide, and continued back into the kitchen. Another table, this one more rustic, and a pantry that she quickly checked with her flashlight. She flipped open the lower cabinet doors too. No one.

As she circled through the passage at the rear of the foyer, behind the stairs TK had gone up, she was in time to see TK jogging down the steps. "Clear upstairs."

"Clear down here."

Together they moved into the living room. The woman had managed to get the man's head propped up against an ottoman. He was bleeding from a deep cut to his scalp.

"Go get Tommy," Lucy ordered as she pulled her folding knife and began slicing Gloria and Peter Callabrese free of the duct tape that restrained them.

Gloria gasped as the tape pulled at the skin around her mouth. "There were two of them. A man and a woman. They took Nellie."

Chapter 44

TOMMY WAS USED to waiting. Myriad lab tests and X-rays. The anticipation of a trauma rolling in. But in the ER, he was in control. If the labs were late, he'd use his diagnostic skills to reassess the patient and decide on a course of action. When he and his team waited for a trauma, they prepared, rehearsed, and examined all scenarios, leaving them ready to jump into action.

But this. This was pure torture. Not knowing what was happening in the house. Were they alive or dead? Injured? Was Nellie there? Was she okay? What would he do if she wasn't?

He busied himself inventorying Lucy's emergency supplies. She had a nice stash in her go-bag including tourniquets, chest seals, trauma shears, several knives, duct tape, hemostatic agents to stop bleeding from open wounds, pressure wraps, even large-bore needles that could be used to create an airway or decompress a pneumothorax. The FBI must have sent her through a Basic Trauma Life Support course, which meant he'd have an extra pair of hands. And TK was also a certified trauma medic, so personnel wouldn't be an issue—once he got inside and saw what he was dealing with.

The windows had fogged over. He wiped the nearest one clean with his palm, and the lights at the front of the house made the fog glow eerily. He'd just about decided to disobey Lucy and join them in the house when he spotted movement. TK was running around the corner and beckoning for him to join them.

As soon as he leapt from the car, clutching Lucy's knapsack to his chest, the rain slapped him, cold and stinging. He raced to TK. "Is Nellie all right?"

"She's not in there."

He faltered, his feet slipping on the wet flagstones. For a moment his vision blanked, erasing TK, the house, this moment from eternity. But then he regained control and continued forward.

"There's no sign that they hurt her," TK continued as they reached the front door. "But your father-in-law is pretty bad off."

She led him inside to the living room. Both Peter and Gloria appeared bruised. Gloria was favoring her left arm—he wasn't sure if it was dislocated or maybe a broken clavicle—while Peter was ashen, his skin pale against the dark blood matted at his scalp. His breathing was rapid and jugular veins distended.

"It's not the scalp wound," Tommy told them as he knelt beside Peter and took his pulse both at his neck and wrist. "It's his heart. Gloria, is he on any medication?"

She didn't answer; her gaze was bouncing around the room. TK said, "I'll go check the medicine cabinets."

"Gloria, did you hit your head? Or anywhere besides your shoulder?" Lucy asked, crouching in front of the older woman. She turned to Tommy. "I think she's in shock."

"No," Gloria said slowly. "They didn't hit me. But when he pulled my arms behind me I felt something pop. But Peter, they hit Peter. They didn't have to, he wasn't fighting back. Why did they do that?" She jerked and glanced behind her as if startled. "Where's Nellie?"

"You said they took her," Lucy said gently.

Gloria frowned. Then her tears began to flow. "I'm sorry, Tommy. We couldn't—"

"We'll find her," Tommy said with determination. He hoped Burroughs and the other police officer were careful when they stopped Putnam. Thought about calling Burroughs to tell him Nellie was in the SUV, but decided the detective was already factoring that into things. "What medicine is Peter on?"

"Nothing. Oh, aspirin. Just one a day. And his machine at night."

TK appeared at the top of the steps. "Nothing prescription in the medicine cabinets."

"There should be a CPAP machine and mask beside his bed," Tommy called up. "Can you get it?"

He didn't have a stethoscope or blood pressure cuff, but he was fairly certain his father-in-law was in the midst of a coronary event, probably with congestive heart failure. It had been a few years since he'd recertified his adult cardiac life support—not that it mattered since he had no meds to work with. But the CPAP machine, which kept lungs inflated to combat sleep apnea, should help. Certainly wouldn't hurt.

TK came galloping down the steps carrying the machine. Lucy handed Tommy her cell. "I called 911 for an ambulance—want to tell them what to expect? They said it'll be about fifteen to twenty minutes."

Not bad for an all-volunteer ambulance squad. Tommy gave the dispatcher a quick rundown while Lucy and TK placed the CPAP mask on Peter. He was taking Peter's pulse again when his phone rang. Hoping it was Burroughs, he answered without looking. "Did you find her?"

"Yes."

It was Sarah. Her voice was a menacing, throaty whisper that made Tommy's skin ripple with fear. He scooted back, the phone pressed to his ear, ignoring the look Lucy gave him. She came close, obviously listening. "Where is she? Is Nellie okay?"

"You'll need to come to look for yourself. Come alone. We'll be waiting in the barn, the stall at the far end, the one that's empty. Hurry, Tommy. You have no idea how long I've waited for a sweet, sweet baby like Nellie to take care of."

Somehow he ended up on his feet, headed toward the door. "Don't you dare hurt her!"

"Come quickly. Alone. Now."

She hung up.

CHAPTER 45

LUCY LUNGED TO stop Tommy before he reached the door. "You can't go. It's a trap."

He whirled on her. "Of course it's a trap. I don't care. Not if it gets Nellie back safe. And don't tell me to wait for Burroughs and the cops. We don't have time for that."

TK joined them in the cavernous foyer, keeping her voice pitched low so Gloria and Peter wouldn't hear. "We don't know what she wants. She might just want to kill you, or she might want you to watch Nellie die. Either way, the best way to buy time for both of you is for you not to go."

"Tell us about the barn. What's the layout?" Lucy asked as TK grabbed her raincoat and the Remington.

"It's just a barn. There's a tack room in the front, then..." Tommy paused, frowning as he concentrated. Lucy was asking a lot, she knew from personal experience. It was the equivalent of asking a drowning man to do calculus, but she hoped her diversion helped him to focus, see the facts beyond his emotions. "Four, no, six horse stalls lined up."

"Are the horses in? Where's the lighting?"

"They should be in for the night—but I saw one outside when I was waiting in the car, so maybe not. The lights? Uh, overhead. Along the center aisle, hanging from the rafters. There's a switch at each end of the barn."

"Junction box? That controls the electricity in the barn?"

He frowned and thought. "In the front, right beside the tack room door."

"Entrances?" This from TK, who handed Lucy her still sodden jacket.

"One at each end—both big sliding doors, but also smaller, regular type doors. The stalls on the right-hand side also open out into the paddock. And the hayloft, there are doors up there, but you need to climb a ladder."

Lucy placed a hand on Tommy's elbow, drawing his attention. "Here's the plan. You're going to wait here, take care of Gloria and Peter. TK and I are going to take care of Sarah and save Nellie."

"But she'll know it's not me."

"Not in the dark she won't." TK reached for a dark-colored ball cap hanging on a wrought iron coat stand near the door. She tucked her blond hair inside and wore it backwards. Drew her Beretta and nodded to Lucy. "Ready?"

Lucy drew her own weapon. "Ready."

"I should go," Tommy protested once more.

"No," Lucy said firmly. "You can't. If we lose you, we have no one to bargain with to save Nellie." It was a cruel thing, making a parent wait, helpless, but she'd rather be cruel than see both him and Nellie die.

He nodded slowly and opened the door for them. "Be careful."

Lucy and TK moved back into the rain. It had slowed to a clammy mist that danced along the wind, coming at you in all directions. With it, the fog had thickened, so much so that as soon as the door shut behind them, Lucy lost sight of TK. She stepped forward, almost running into TK, and placed a hand on the other woman's shoulder.

"We'll divide when we get there," TK said. "You go in front, hit the lights. I'll come in from the hayloft. If that fails, I'll use the rear entrance or come in through one of the horse stalls."

"Got it."

Lucy stumbled on the slick, uneven ground as they left the flagstone path for the grass. The small patch of maintained lawn quickly gave way to the high grass of a meadow. To their right, strange images blurred the fog, and she felt a rumbling through the ground. The horses. Uneasy with the storm.

Thunder rumbled and lightning shot down, hitting a short distance up the mountain, its flash shredding the fog into nightmarish specters of light. More thunder, louder, closer, as the fog closed in once more.

A horse cried out. It seemed close, somewhere behind Lucy's right shoulder, though in the fog, sound was hard to track. But the rumbling grew stronger, and then came the sound of hoofbeats—and a large, dark form escaped the fog's clutching fingers. The horse pulled up, pivoted, and charged directly at

Lucy and TK.

Lucy pushed TK out of the way and tried to run. Her bad foot slipped against the mud and wet grass, and she skidded, falling, her free hand reaching out, flailing. TK whirled and tried to catch her, but it was too late. Lucy fell directly into the wire fence surrounding the paddock.

A jolt of electricity spiked through her left hand and forearm, pain like a thousand needles dancing along her nerves. She flew back, landing in the grass and mud, gasping.

"Shit," TK said, kneeling beside her and helping her sit up. "Are you okay?"

Somehow, Lucy had retained her grip on her weapon, but her left hand hung useless. Numb unless she tried to move it, and then the pins and needles pain cascaded down each digit. "I'm fine. Just give me a minute."

"No." TK looked past Lucy to the house behind them, a warm glow taunting the storm, then over her shoulder to where the barn sat invisible in the dark and fog. "Look, you know me. I work better alone. It's just one woman. She has no military training. Hell, we don't even know if she has a weapon." She tugged Lucy to her feet. "Go back to Tommy."

"I can do it," Lucy protested. Although she realized it was her pride, not her logic, doing the talking. "I don't need my left hand to shoot."

"But you do to open doors and manage the circuit breakers. Not unless you want to holster your weapon every time. Plus, you're already down a leg—maneuvering in this terrain, your ankle just isn't cut out for it. I'm sorry, Lucy, but

I'm better off on my own."

Translation: Lucy had become a liability. Painful as it was, she had to accept that fact. A girl's life was at stake.

"All right. Go. Be careful. If there's a way to stall, wait for Burroughs and the police—"

"Don't worry, I'm no glory hound. All I want is to get Nellie home safe."

CHAPTER 46

TOMMY SHUT THE door behind Lucy and TK. He leaned against it for a long moment, feeling the storm's wrath pushing against him.

"No!" Gloria called from the living room. Her tone was panicked. Peter—had his condition deteriorated?

Tommy pivoted and crossed through the archway into the living room. He stopped short when he saw the large armoire in the far corner with its doors hanging open. Sarah stood in front of it, a pistol in one hand, her other arm wrapped around Gloria's chest.

"Poleaxed." A wide grin slashed across her face. "That's the word you're looking for."

Tommy raised his arms in the universal sign of surrender. He took two cautious steps farther into the room, just far enough so that he could see Peter. The CPAP seemed to be helping: his color was marginally better, his breathing slower. Peter met his gaze and flopped one hand against his lap. Definitely no help coming from that quarter.

Returning his focus to Sarah, Tommy met her gaze. "Where's Nellie?"

Her eyes tightened and her lips curled into a sneer. "You were a lousy father. You admitted that yourself. She's better off with me."

His nod was forced. His face felt like a mask as he fought to keep his emotions in check. Just like the ER, he told himself. Stay calm, ignore their outbursts, try to understand what they really want.

"Maybe she is," he admitted. Gloria made a noise at that, but Sarah tightened her grip, cutting it short. "Is she okay?" Then he answered his own question, trying to find a way into her delusion, the upside-down world she'd built around her life to block out reality. "No. Of course she's okay. You're a good mother. You'd never hurt her."

He kept nodding, slowly, slowly. Holding her gaze as gently as he would a wounded bird. She began to nod as well, matching his cadence. "I'd never hurt a child."

"I know that. Where is she? Can I see her?" Her posture tightened. He softened his tone. "Say goodbye?"

"Do you think you deserve that? After the terrible things you've done? You're a monster, and it's time you admitted it. Go on, tell these people. Tell Nellie's grandparents how you killed my beautiful baby."

"I'm a monster." The words caught in his throat. "I'll confess everything. After I see Nellie."

"She's better off without you. Would be better off dead than living with you."

Her change in tone spun him off balance. "You said you wouldn't hurt her."

"Ending someone's misery isn't hurting them," she countered, with her own twisted brand of logic. "That's why Charlotte died. She was in so much pain. Walter couldn't bear it."

"Walter? He killed Charlotte?"

She jabbed the pistol into Gloria's cheek. Gloria cried out in pain, her hands flailing against Sarah's grip. "He shouldn't have. I had so much more I wanted to do to her. Bitch deserved it, helping you cover up Brian's murder."

"Brian, he was your son? Tell me about him."

"No!" She shoved Gloria aside and aimed the pistol at Tommy. "No. You don't get to say his name. Not ever."

Gloria scrambled to Peter's side near the back wall. Tommy felt a sudden draft at his back and edged in the same direction as Gloria, taking Sarah's attention with him. If she was looking toward the rear of the room, she wouldn't have a direct view through the arch leading into the foyer. He strained, but didn't hear anything from behind him. Maybe he'd imagined the draft?

"What do you want?" he asked, risking her wrath, but hoping to keep her focus on him and him alone.

She held the pistol with both hands now, her aim disturbingly steady. "I want you to pay for what you've done. I want you to suffer the way we have. To admit that you're a killer."

She licked her lips, her grin vanishing as her mouth

settled into a thin line of determination. "And then I want you dead. You'll die never knowing if Nellie is dead or alive. You'll die knowing that whatever happens to her, what happened to your wife, it's all your fault. Yours and yours alone."

He sidled closer to the rear wall where Gloria covered Peter with her body. Sarah pivoted with him, keeping her aim trained on him. A rush of air and a loud crack startled him. It was quickly followed by two more as Lucy moved forward and pushed him to the ground.

It all happened so fast that he had to replay the events in his mind before he could absorb them. Had that rush really been a bullet speeding past him? He looked up from where he lay on the ground to see Sarah's body slumped back against the armoire—no, the chifferobe. A hysterical giggle flooded his mind; thankfully he was too stunned to utter it out loud.

Only a second had passed, just long enough for Lucy to cross the room to Sarah and kick Sarah's gun away. When had she dropped it? He hadn't even heard it fall. He pushed up to his feet and rushed to join Lucy.

"What did you do?" he shouted at Lucy, his own voice echoing in his head. "She didn't tell me where Nellie was." He turned to Sarah, who lay face up below him. "Sarah, please. Tell me. Where's Nellie?"

Sarah tried to push him away, her expression livid with hatred. "Monster."

Her breath came in fast little gasps, one hand fluttering between a small wound on her belly and another on the right side of her chest. The other arm lay limp—a third wound there.

Tommy shook the fear and anger from his brain, focusing on what needed to be done. Nellie. If he was going to save Nellie, he had to save Sarah.

"Help me with her," he told Lucy as he regained control. "Get me that first aid kit."

"Where's Nellie?" he asked again as he applied pressure to the belly wound.

Sarah shook her head and smiled. "Never going to tell."

Lucy joined him, unrolling the first aid kit between them. Without his asking, she opened a roll of hemostatic gauze and handed it to him. Too late for gloves; they were both covered in her blood.

He pulled Sarah's shirt up. The entrance wound wasn't very big, only a centimeter, maybe two. But there was no exit wound. That was bad.

"This is going to hurt." He packed the gauze in as tight as he could, hoping it would reach whatever was bleeding internally.

"It's hot," Sarah muttered, trying and failing to push his hands away.

"That's the medicine. It's going to help stop the bleeding."

Lucy took over holding pressure on the wound, and Tommy turned his attention to Sarah's chest. This wound did have an exit, leaving blood puddling on the floor beneath her. No signs of a tension pneumo; her breathing was steady, only slightly labored. He used Lucy's chest seal to prevent air from being trapped inside the lung cavity.

The door crashed open. Burroughs, accompanied by a

uniformed cop, barreled inside.

"We're clear!" Lucy shouted as they came around the foyer wall, weapons sighted. "Send in the medics."

Burroughs nodded at the cop, who left to get them.

"What the hell happened here?" Burroughs asked.

"Nellie." Tommy craned his neck to look at the detective. "Was she with Sarah's husband?"

"We got Putnam. Crying like a baby, saying it was all his fault, to let Sarah go. But the girl wasn't with him."

Sarah's laughter filled the room. Her eyes were wide open, staring into space, her mouth twisted in a grimace of hate. She began coughing, choking, her laughter dying. Blood seeping from the corner of her mouth.

"Damn it." Tommy pressed harder on the wound, ignoring the blood seeping through the dressing. "The gut shot hit her stomach, maybe even penetrated her diaphragm."

Her eyes rolled back, then her muscles relaxed. He felt for her pulse. There was none.

CHAPTER 47

NOW THAT SHE was alone, TK decided to change tactics. Instead of taking the time to climb up to the hayloft, where she might have the element of surprise but would lose the advantage of being able to clear the entire structure, she skirted the front of the barn to where the fence started. She'd been prepared to go over the fence, but luckily there was a small gap between the barn's wall and the first fencepost, enough for her to slide through sideways.

The ground on the other side of the fence was sloppy with mud. There was little grass, not here where it was most easily accessible to the horses. Probably a ton of horse shit as well, but she didn't think about that. She kept her shotgun at the ready as she sidled around the corner of the barn to the first horse stall.

The door to the paddock stood open. The stall inside was empty and dark. Straw was matted in puddles on the concrete floor nearest the open door, but farther inside it was dry. TK kept the wall to her back, inhaling the odor of wet hay, horse shit, ozone from the storm, and a sweet cedar scent. At the front of the stall was an open railed gate.

There was a horse in the stall across from her. It made a sniffling noise and shuffled its hooves against the concrete floor, arousing similar responses from its neighbors, invisible in the dark. TK listened. No human sounds. Could an amateur like Sarah, already amped on adrenaline and fear, really stay that quiet as she waited for what she had to know would be an ambush?

She silently eased the latch on the stall's gate open and crept into the hall that ran the length of the barn, between the two walls of stalls. Now that she was away from the rain and fog, her night vision sharpened. What she wouldn't give for a thermal or infrared sight. Still, every sense told her she was alone except for the horses.

She turned her Maglite on, risking exposure. Nothing. More certain than ever that this was a diversion, she quickly ran the length of the building then back again, ensuring that no one was hiding, waiting to attack.

Finally, she reached the front of the barn. The tack room was the last place to clear, except the hayloft overhead, but given the plank flooring above the rafters, she'd decided that if anyone was hiding up there, they would have exposed themselves with stray bits of straw floating down.

Taking up a position to the side of the tack room's door, she yanked it open and waited a breath. Nothing. She held the light out and flicked it to slice the pie, covering all angles from floor to ceiling except the blind corner on the same side of the door as she stood. Then she moved into the room, flat against the opposite wall, and scanned that blind spot.

Nothing. Just tools, hanging bits of tack, and bags of food. The far wall was lined with special hooks that held saddles. Below them was a mound of quilted blankets. The last wall had stacks of carefully folded blankets, woven rugs, saddle pads, and wraps.

Damn. If Sarah wasn't here, that meant she'd either escaped with Nellie or...the house. Anyone as obsessed as Sarah wouldn't leave without finishing what she came for—killing Tommy.

She pivoted, ready to leave, when the faint sound of gunfire reached her.

But then she heard another sound. Rustling. Coming from the blankets on the floor below the saddles. She raised her weapon. Every muscle tensed, battle ready.

"I'M LOSING HER." Tommy began chest compressions. The medics swarmed into the room, dropping their gear and taking over. He quickly told them what was going on—not just with Sarah but also with Peter. "I suspect an acute MI."

One of the medics broke off, taking a monitor over to where Gloria huddled with Peter. His two partners bagged air into Sarah and tried without success to start an IV. Tommy tried as well, although as her belly grew more and more distended, he realized how futile their efforts were.

"What do you think, doc?" the senior medic said, sitting back on his haunches. "We could try cracking her chest, but I have to tell you we don't have the gear."

"And it's an hour to the nearest trauma center," his partner added. "No way the choppers are flying tonight, not in this weather."

Tommy stared down at Sarah's pale body. "Cracking her chest won't help. The bleed is in her belly. Even if I was able to cross-clamp her aorta, no way could we get her to a surgeon in time."

The medics nodded their agreement. "Honestly, doc, she was a goner from the start. You did all you could."

He grimaced and nodded. Then he turned to Peter, trying with everything he had to shut out the realization that with Sarah's death, his last chance to find Nellie had also died.

"You're right," the medic monitoring Peter said. "Elevated ST. Good idea starting the CPAP. We need to load and go, get him to a coronary unit." His partners joined him, moving into high gear—time was heart muscle, went the adage. And this was a patient they had a good chance at saving.

They packaged Peter for transport and within minutes were steering the ambulance away, Gloria with them. Tommy watched them from the front door, torn between the desire to help and his need to search for Nellie.

As he turned away to ask Lucy where to start, he heard a woman calling his name, her words shredded by the wind. He stepped out into the fog. It swirled around him, taking the form of humans, caressing and reaching out to him as if they wanted him to join them in the darkness, to leave the light behind.

Again a woman called his name. It sounded so much like Charlotte—or maybe he just wanted it to—that he was half tempted. He'd failed. Failed her, failed Nellie. He took another step, the tendrils of fog swathing him like a cocoon of gray and cold.

"Tommy!"

He whirled. TK stumbled through the fog.

Carrying Nellie.

"Nellie!" Tommy rushed to them, steered them back inside the house. Lucy and Burroughs guided TK to the couch, where she gently positioned Nellie.

"She was in the barn. I can't wake her up."

Tommy knelt beside the couch and listened to Nellie's breathing, felt her pulse. Both steady, a comfort. "She's been drugged."

Lucy searched Sarah's pockets and pulled out a bottle. She tossed it to Tommy. "What about these?"

He scanned the label. "Versed. We use it in the ER."

"So she'll be okay?"

"Yes. She'll be just fine." He glanced heavenward and couldn't restrain his laughter. He pulled Nellie into his arms.

"What's so funny?" TK asked.

Tommy hugged Nellie tighter. Her eyelids fluttered open then shut again while she wrapped her arms around him. "The main side effect of Versed is amnesia."

CHAPTER 48

THE NEXT DAY, Tommy gave his statement to Burroughs, Corporal Harding from the state police, and the Forward Township chief of police. They met at Burroughs' office at the major crimes squad on Western Avenue since that was central for everyone and he had proper recording equipment. The building itself was pretty depressing and without character, with its beige brick walls and steel bars over the tiny windows. He'd have much preferred the worn but solid comfort of the Zone 3 station house.

This room did not resemble any of the interview rooms he'd been in before. It was modern, utilitarian, with glass walls that didn't block the noise of the men and women working at their cubicles beyond. There was a rectangular conference table and upholstered but uncomfortable chairs. About the only thing the room had going for it was a lack of graffiti—and the absence of a restraining bar designed for handcuffs.

Tommy was just finishing his statement when Oshiro

and Lucy appeared outside the glass door. Burroughs looked up. "I think we're done here. Thank you, Dr. Worth." His tone was formal for the video recording. Then he nodded to the videographer to turn it off. "Thank you all for coming."

The videographer left, along with the chief. Oshiro held the door for them before bounding inside, followed by Lucy.

Liz Harding gathered her folders and bag, hesitated, then extended her hand to Tommy. "Thank you for your patience, Dr. Worth. I'm sorry for all you've been through. Rest assured that we'll have your wife's remains released to you for burial just as soon as we can. You and your family are in our thoughts and prayers."

Tommy was startled by her kind words. Usually the state police trooper was a tough read—much harder than Burroughs, that was certain. But she seemed genuine and sincere, so he shook her hand. "Thank you, Corporal Harding."

"You can call me Liz. I'll let you know as soon as I hear anything." She nodded to Burroughs and left.

Lucy sat beside Tommy and stared at Burroughs across the table. Burroughs cleared his throat. "Yeah, doc. Guess I should apologize as well."

Not quite as sincere, but it was better than Tommy had expected.

Oshiro didn't even try to apologize. He just clapped his massive hand on Tommy's shoulder and said, "You're okay, doc. You did a good job, helping Sarah when we thought she was a Jane Doe, and you kept your head after we figured out what was really going on." He handed Tommy a card. "You ever need anything, call me. I owe you one."

Tommy wasn't sure what to say, but Lucy smiled. "Don't lose that card," she said. "He means what he said." Then she turned to Oshiro. "What's this 'we' who figured out what was really going on?"

Oshiro laughed and threw his bulk into one of the empty chairs. "Okay, when Lucy really figured out what was going on."

"Not just me, my entire team. Not bad for a group of amateurs, right, Burroughs?"

The detective scowled, but it wasn't directed at Lucy or Tommy. "Still can't figure out how the hell I fell for her act."

"That's the problem," Tommy said. He felt the detective's pain. He'd totally believed Sarah as well, let her into his home, into his life. The thought still made him angry. "It wasn't all an act. She truly, utterly, and completely, until her last dying breath, believed I killed her baby and that Charlotte helped cover it up. She'd do anything to find justice for her baby."

"Including turning in an Oscar caliber performance," Lucy added.

"That's what I mean," Tommy said. "When you're that delusional, you fit reality to suit the world you've created in your mind. She believed every word she told us—at the time."

Burroughs frowned. "I still don't get it. She didn't really have amnesia, but because acting that way fit her delusion, it felt real to her?"

"Something like that," Tommy answered. He slumped in his chair, really not wanting to put himself in Sarah's mind ever again. True, she was sick. But what she'd done...

"What about her husband?" Oshiro asked. "Is he delusional? Or just trying to protect his wife?"

"Verdict's still out on that," Burroughs answered. "My guess is we'll never really know, not once the lawyers and shrinks get involved. But after we caught him, all he talked about was that Worth got what was coming to him and that Sarah was innocent. He also told us what happened to Charlotte, but he seemed to think it was totally justified."

Lucy touched Tommy's arm. "You ready to hear this?"

"I need to know how she died."

"Better than hearing it from the press," Oshiro added.

Burroughs sighed, then hauled in a breath. "From what Putnam told us before his lawyer gagged him, and from the forensic findings, this is what we pieced together. First of all, they chose today—well, last year today—because it was their baby's birthday. In the year after the baby died, Sarah was in and out of hospitals, mostly in the DC area, until her husband lost his job and health insurance and brought her home to live with him."

"That's why we had no recent address for her driver's license," Oshiro put in. "And criminal checks through the NCIC wouldn't register anything like a hospital admission. So, with her keeping her maiden name and most of her information from other states—"

"Three other states," Burroughs interrupted. "DC, Virginia, and Maryland. We didn't have a chance of unraveling this in just a day or two. A fact that she and Putnam bargained on. All they needed was a few days."

"Go back to Charlotte," Tommy said. "Tell me what happened. Was she at my ball game? Is that where they took her?"

Burroughs shook his head. "No. It was earlier. Sarah was supposed to meet Charlotte at the convenience store. Told her she was being stalked by an ex who was an IRS agent and that he was getting violent."

"That's why Charlotte didn't take someone with her," Lucy said. "The shelter director told me an IRS agent was their worst nightmare because they have access to almost every database imaginable."

"Exactly. Sarah got Charlotte to come pick her up down the road from the store, away from any cameras. Still not sure how, but Sarah definitely wasn't on any of the store's surveillance footage. Although Putnam was. He must have been watching in case anything went wrong." Burroughs leaned forward. "Anyway, they took Charlotte up to Fiddler's Knob. It's where Putnam proposed to Sarah, so I guess in her own warped way, it meant something to her. He also rambled something about a witch's trial. Not sure about that, something called burking?"

Tommy startled. "Burking? It was a test for witchcraft. You'd pin someone to the ground and place rocks on them, heavier and heavier until their chest caved in and they couldn't breathe. If they lived, they were a witch, and if they died..." He looked away, wished there were real windows instead of being forced to face the strangers in the room beyond. "It's a horrible way to die. Is that how..." He couldn't finish the question.

"Yes and no. They did bury Charlotte in rocks—used the old iron furnace on the mountain. Putnam made it sound like some kind of ritual—again, who knows what's real and what's delusion. They thought Charlotte was dead and knew they had to ditch her car before you notified the police and anyone started looking for her. And that would take both him and Sarah to drive. But while they were hiking down the mountain, they heard Charlotte and realized she wasn't dead and had gotten free. It was a foggy night and they couldn't find her easily, so Putnam went to use her car to block the road while Sarah hunted her on the mountain and herded her down to the road."

Tommy's mouth went dry as he visualized what Charlotte had gone through. "She was alive? She escaped?"

Burroughs shook his head. "Not for long. Putnam found her on the road. She was hysterical, begging to go home, thought he was you, that she was saved. I guess that infuriated Sarah because she made Putnam drag her back up the mountain." Burroughs paused. Tommy braced himself. "She collapsed near where they ended up burying her, but she was still alive, so Sarah finished her off with a rock."

Tommy bit his lip, trying to hold back tears. "I saw her skull. It took time to do that."

"I know. I'm sorry." For the first time, real emotion colored Burroughs' voice. "When they were done, they buried her, then drove her car to the overlook on the river. Sometime after that they used her keys to take your tire iron and plant the charm bracelet. Except for the broken charm that Sarah kept as a trophy. She had another breakdown after everything, but without a job or insurance, Putnam nursed her through it—hell, he was so wrapped up in her delusion, he believed that what they'd done was the right thing. Justice for their son. Said the only thing that snapped Sarah out of her depression was planning what they'd do to you next."

"So everything—they planned it all?" Lucy asked. "The wedding dress? The bones in the photo?"

"If your team hadn't spotted them, you can bet Sarah would have. They'd been watching Tommy for almost two years. They knew exactly how to manipulate him."

"And we played right into their hands," Oshiro said. "Have to say, I was totally blindsided."

"We all were." Burroughs closed his file. "Even though we're trained to assume the worse and trust no one—"

"Who could resist a chance to play hero to Sarah's damsel in distress?" Lucy finished for him.

Tommy said nothing. There was nothing left to say. He pushed back his chair and stood. "I'm going home."

Epilogue

THREE WEEKS LATER...

"IT WAS A nice wake," Lucy told Tommy as he shoved the final covered casserole dish into his refrigerator. "Are you going to be okay?"

Tommy stifled his sigh. Everyone had asked him that, and no one believed his answer. But he knew what Charlotte would have wanted: for him to go on, not just sleepwalk through life, but to really live. For both of them. "Thanks for bringing Megan to watch Nellie for me. With Peter just out of the hospital, Gloria has her hands full."

"No problem. She loved it." Lucy closed the refrigerator door, leaning her weight against it to prevent it from popping back open. She waited a beat, holding his gaze as if deciding if he was ready for something. "So. Are you going to stay with us at Beacon Falls or go back to the ER? Not that I need an answer right away," she hastened to add.

"I love the ER. And I miss it." He shook his head. "But Nellie needs me. And I need to know I can be here for her."

She smiled. "Our gain, then. We'll have to find some good

cases involving medical conundrums, keep you sharp."

Megan and Nellie raced into the kitchen, hands joined, arms swinging, and plopped down at the table, propping their chins on their hands in mirror images of each other.

"I'm hungry," Nellie proclaimed, even though she'd been eating all day. "Can we have breakfast for dinner? Special treat for being a good girl alllll day?"

"I don't know. Were you a good girl?" Tommy asked even as he reached for the cereal bowls.

She flounced in her chair. "Megan, tell him."

"Nellie was a very good girl."

When Tommy glanced their way, they began to giggle as only girls can, heads together. He poured Sugar Loops into four bowls while Lucy opened the fridge once more and grabbed the milk.

"Nellie," Megan said, giving Tommy and Lucy a wink as he slid the bowls in front of them, "why don't you tell your dad how much you love his chicken salad."

Nellie ladled a spoonful of neon cereal and milk into her mouth before answering. "I don't like chicken salad. I never liked chicken salad."

Tommy stared at her, his spoon halfway to his mouth, the milk turning a disquieting purple color. "You don't have to say that to make me feel better, Nellie. I know you loved your mom's chicken salad."

Nellie shook her head, slurping some rainbow-colored milk from her bowl. "Nope. Yours is better than mom's. At least you don't put pickles on yours. But I still don't like it."

Megan sipped at her cereal from her spoon daintily, one pinky extended, a Cheshire grin on her face. Tommy frowned at her, wondering if she had coached Nellie into lying just to make him feel better. "You always asked for chicken salad last year."

"Uh-huh," Nellie said, nodding. "That's because you and mom never packed cookies. Stephen's mom always packed cookies. Lots of cookies."

Tommy was getting whiplash trying to keep up. "Who's Stephen?"

"The boy in my preschool who loved chicken salad sandwiches, Daddy," she said in a tone that implied an eye roll. "But his mom always packed peanut butter and jelly."

"Your favorite." Comprehension dawned. "So you'd ask Mom for chicken salad, make the trade, and get extra cookies on top of the PB and J you wanted in the first place."

"Too bad Stephen doesn't go to my school this year." Nellie sighed, upended her bowl, and slurped the last of the Sugar Loops. Her milk mustache was a blend of green and orange, and Tommy didn't even want to think about the spike in her blood sugar. He stared at his daughter, as much an enigma as her mother, and felt lighter. As if he could dare to hope that he might actually be able to give Nellie everything she needed from both a mother and a father—even if it was only PB and J.

"Can I go watch cartoons now?" She jumped down from her stool.

Tommy watched in amazement as she grabbed her bowl and, without prompting, put it in the dishwasher. Wow. Catch 'em being good, he thought. And by the expectant look on

Nellie's face, she'd already figured that out. "Sure, half an hour, then it's bed."

Nellie skipped from the room, Megan in tow.

Tommy looked over at Lucy, who was concentrating on her Sugar Loops as if they held the key to the Rosetta Stone in their strange shapes. "You don't have to eat those, you know."

She looked up. "Actually, they're not bad. Better than my usual dinner, and the box says they supply a complete and nutritious breakfast." She dangled her spoon in front of the colorful cereal box. "I'll bet you two things."

"What?"

"One, that you're going to start packing cookies in her lunch. And two, that Nellie's going to grow up to be a lawyer."

He groaned—on both counts. "Really? I'm thinking with her negotiation skills she could be a CEO of a Fortune 500 company."

"Why not President?"

He smiled. The first, genuine, deep down to his toes smile he'd had since Charlotte died. He could make it past this pain, he could start to enjoy life—starting with his daughter—again. "Why not? I have a feeling she's destined for great things."

"Her mother would be proud."

He thought about that. "Yes. Yes, she would."

About CJ:

New York Times and *USA Today* bestselling author of twenty-nine novels, former pediatric ER doctor CJ Lyons has lived the life she writes about in her cutting edge Thrillers with Heart.

CJ has been called a "master within the genre" (Pittsburgh Magazine) and her work has been praised as "breathtakingly fast-paced" and "riveting" (Publishers Weekly) with "characters with beating hearts and three dimensions" (Newsday).

Her novels have won the International Thriller Writers' prestigious Thriller Award, the RT Reviewers' Choice Award, the Readers' Choice Award, the RT Seal of Excellence, and the Daphne du Maurier Award for Excellence in Mystery and Suspense.

Learn more about CJ's Thrillers with Heart at www.CJLyons.net

CPSIA information can be obtained
at www.ICGtesting.com
Printed in the USA
LVOW08s1723270417
532419LV00003B/744/P